GREATER

THINGS

A Novel

Book 3 of the

Anyone Who Believes Series

Jeffrey McClain Jones

Greater Things

John 14:12 Publications

www.jeffreymcclainjones.com

Cover photo from Shutterstock

For Gabe, who courageously pushes past old boundaries to the Kingdom's impact on the earth.

A Life That Demands an Explanation

Anna Conyers knew who to ask about finding Bobby Nightingale. She knew to talk to Jack Williams at his big Northern California church. She knew to check for an update at the Dupere house in Malibu. She knew to consult Willow Pierce in Colorado. That other reporters didn't recognize those touch points probably had to do with the broad lack of understanding of Beau Dupere among the press. Dazzled by his star power, they failed to perceive the mesh of deep relationships that were the context of his miraculous life. If anything, Anna was paying too much attention to all of that. Still obsessed by all things related to Beau Dupere even after his death.

Was she looking for someone to take Beau's place in her life? A powerful miracle man? A guru of sorts? Or was it just plain curiosity? She couldn't stir up enough curiosity in her editor to get him to agree to running a story, but that had seldom stopped her before. It didn't stop her from finally connecting with Bobby Nightingale in a northern suburb of Chicago less than an hour drive from her downtown office.

They met in a mall. It was Bobby's idea. Anna wasn't sure why. But she didn't waste her time with him on questions about odd logistical requirements. That the rumpled older man in front of her didn't seem to fit into the brightly lit mall wasn't important. That he had a scarred and wrinkled face like a relief map of a desert wilderness barely distracted her. She mostly wanted to know one thing—if it was true what Beau Dupere said.

"Are you the greatest miracle worker in America, like Beau said?" She crossed her legs, her new navy slacks making a slipping sound she could hear even in the wide mall.

Bobby frowned as if he were working on an answer, not as if confused by why she asked the question. He bowed his head, giving her a better look at his thinning hair swept in stripes of brown and white. His contemplation of how to answer seemed a promising sign. "I git questions like that once in a while. It's impossible to really answer it, o' course. But it don't really bother me that folks ask. It's better than livin' a life that don't require any explainin'." He grinned impishly at her.

"Okay." Anna checked her digital recorder. "How do you explain your life? How did you get to where you are, however you evaluate that destination?"

Bobby leaned back, cast a glance at an invisible horizon, and started at the start. He told her about being born in Topeka, Kansas, and spending his first ten years there with his mother, Adeline, and his father, Peter. The wistful look in Bobby's eyes hinted at blue skies, dewy grass, and flirting butterflies. He didn't claim it was idyllic, not one who seemed likely to use that word about anything. But when his eyes glistened in that reminiscent way, Anna could see beyond his words.

The cloud in those blue skies, for Bobby, was school. He admitted to being a boy who couldn't sit still for long. Luckily for him, he attended school after corporal punishment had dropped out of the arsenal of most teachers and principals. He joked that he did tempt a few educators to reconsider the good old days of broken rulers and broken spirits.

Bobby got his bruises in school anyway—from kids on the playground. Those fights tended to look very one-sided. That was because Bobby's side of the altercation consisted of smart remarks. He wasn't the brightest student, but he excelled at making other students look dull. The bigger boys didn't settle for that, of course. And thus began the sculpting of a scarred and bent face that only a mother could love, as he said with a shy chuckle.

Besides his mother and father, Bobby was also dearly loved by his grandmother on his mother's side, Grandma Casey. Instead of dewy reminiscence, recalling Grandma Casey's house elicited laughter that squinted Bobby's eyes nearly shut, as if he might just close those eyes and go right back to that cabin along the Big Blue River just over the Nebraska border.

Bobby's affection for Grandma Casey's house was about more than the bullfrogs and bluegills he caught there, or about the fireflies and cicadas he collected in glass jars that smelled of dill pickles. The thing about Grandma Casey was that she loved Bobby no matter what he did, no matter what mood he was in, and no matter whether he knew how to love her back. While his father called him a "smart aleck," Grandma Casey never said anything like that to him. With her, he always felt he was at home and safe.

"She was the closest thing to God in my life back then." He grinned and winked at Anna.

While his parents took him to the Baptist church every week, it was at Grandma Casey's little country church that Bobby first met God. "He showed up there with an old woman named Iris and a preacher named Brother Joe—God, that is."

The little country church was subdued and proper, though not formal, on most Sundays. Once a year, however, they held revival meetings. Generally, the old creaky wooden building, mostly painted white, looked like a variety of churches—Baptist, Methodist, Nazarene, or Wesleyan. But during revival week, the members rolled in the aisles and wept about their sins at the altar rail like a house full of Pentecostals.

Bobby loved revival week, and made sure Grandma invited him to stay with her for that part of the year, no matter the season. Whether they stoked the wood-burning stove in January or opened all the windows, allowing the bugs and hungry birds through in July, Bobby wanted to see the faithful reeling and squealing their repentance.

He was, however, not merely a spectator. Once Gladys Raider got the Spirit in her and began to dance and sing gibberish, Bobby would feel his soul rise like he was on a Ferris wheel. When Dick Johnson howled for mercy from the Lord Almighty, Bobby would shake, his little teeth chattering together, even if it was ninety degrees in the shade.

Grandma Casey called Bobby her "partner in revival." Reviewing the extraordinary events of revival week filled many conversations at the dinner table while Bobby emptied plates of ham and cornbread, lima beans and scalloped potatoes. Grandma kept it fun for Bobby, not inclined to get very religious, even about the Holy Spirit convicting people of their sins. The two of them would laugh and tease each other, and even make a little fun of some of the odd behaviors of their fellow churchgoers.

It all got serious, however, when Bobby was eight, and Brother Joe pointed his wrinkly index finger in his direction. "God has a *mission* for you in this world, boy. And you better get down here right now to get filled with the Holy Ghost so's you can *do* it."

Bobby staggered to the railing and fell to his knees, just grabbing the old oak rail in time to keep from concussing himself. And that was where Iris Planter met him, with her fiery hands and quavering prayers. Her words rose and fell like a stormy wind among the trees along the river. And her prayers that day left Bobby prone on the floor with moisture pouring from every orifice in his head. According to Bobby, oil had even poured out of his ears as he lay facedown on the iced-tea colored wood.

As dramatic as that conversion experience was, not much changed about him for the next two years, and what changed after that wasn't about revival. It was about loss and sadness.

A story Anna found in the local newspaper filled in some of the details. Bobby's father was driving the family's 1963 Impala on their way home from Grandma Casey's house. When a fuel tanker swerved to avoid a boy on a bicycle along highway 75, the huge rig clipped the Impala. The fact that Peter Nightingale was going 85 miles per hour at the time contributed to the spin and roll, a career that included one cartwheel before the vehicle landed against a cottonwood tree forty feet from the highway.

No one wore seatbelts in those days. "In most cars, ya couldn't even *find* the seatbelts." But Bobby was in the habit of strapping himself in, especially when his father drove fast. This was not out of fear or caution, but a game of astronaut or fighter pilot. Bobby rode his imagination right out of that car on many a drive over the narrow rural highways of Kansas and Nebraska.

Both his mother and father died at the scene of that accident. Bobby was unconscious when the local sheriff arrived. He survived with several broken bones and cuts that required fifty stitches. His body would recover in a few months.

"But my soul would stay in intensive care for a few decades." He sucked a long breath and sent his eyes well past Anna.

I Don't Talk to Strangers

That evening, Bobby was still thinking about what he had told the young reporter, Anna, when the sun reached the top of the trees just below the level of the church steeples and McDonald's signs along the edge of downtown. He squinted against the fiery orb that still heated the summer day even after suppertime. He scratched behind his left ear, glad at not having cut his nails for a couple weeks. Something had bit him up the night before, and those bites needed scratching. He put little thought into what had bit him, or whether scratching those bites was a good idea.

Right now he was following a prompt to watch a spindly woman walking past the YMCA. Her frame leaned to the right,

starting at her scarecrow waist. Her right shoulder hung a foot
lower than her left. He had seen this woman with her raggedy
gray hair before, as he came and went from his current lodgings
at the Y. An urgency seized his spirit as he watched now. That
urgency turned into a sort of indignation that someone would
bend that poor woman like that, twisted to the right, as if the
cruel hand of a child had tried to break a doll in two. Bobby recognized that indignation as confirmation that he was to speak
with her.

Praying for an opening to address her, Bobby slowed when
the woman stopped to look at the leaves on a lilac bush, an odd
thing to do under most circumstances. That the woman probably
lived in one of the mental health facilities in the area, where
most of the patients were emotionally impaired, was no reason
to expect her to stop and examine those leaves. Bobby took her
inexplicable pause as the answer to his prayer for a chance to
talk to her.

He sauntered past her and then stopped, turning back to
look at the leaf she held between her thumb and middle finger.
"Hello." He scratched his chin—nothing to do with bug bites,
just the usual itch of growing out his beard.

Without lifting her head entirely from the bush, the woman
turned one eye on Bobby. "I know not to talk to strangers." And
she returned to her horticultural preoccupation. This late in the
year, the lilac blossoms were long gone, and the leaves seemed
particularly uninteresting. Her response, on the other hand, was
fascinating.

"Seems pretty smart to me. I was just wantin' to fix yer back
for ya, is all."

The skeletal woman looked up at him with both eyes now,
pale gray under black eyebrows. She had said what she needed
about talking to strangers, apparently, and let that stand as her
response.

Bobby had more to say. "Okay, well, I tell that back to
straighten up right now." Then he turned and continued down

the sidewalk, honoring the woman's choice of discretion regarding strange men.

Ten steps later, Bobby heard a yelp behind him. Stopping, he pivoted slowly with his hands in the pockets of his baggy corduroy pants, his head tipped slightly to the left.

The thin woman stood looking at him, her arms raised at her sides, and her back only half as bent as it had been a minute before.

Bobby saw the gap, and slowly raised his head to fully upright. In sync with straightening his head, the woman's back straightened the rest of the way.

When she stood at full height, she shook in a way that could only be described as a shimmy, her hips shaking back and forth like a flapper dancing in the 1920s. It seemed an involuntary movement.

Bobby shifted his weight in preparation to walk back toward her.

But she spoke up. "I still don't talk to strangers." Her tone remained flat and insistent.

Bobby nodded slowly and kept his feet planted right where they were amidst the tar-like spots of chewing gum and scattered breadcrumbs. A small flock of sparrows chirped and flitted impatiently. Bobby stepped away from their dinner and nodded to the woman. As he turned to walk away, he called over his shoulder. "God is not a stranger." His shout came out tight and rough.

As he paced slowly toward the next corner, he listened for some cry of repentance, or perhaps a note of thanks. But none came. When he reached the turn, he glanced back to see the woman walking gingerly in the opposite direction, as if she had a crown perched precariously atop her kinky gray hair. Apparently she needed some practice with her new back.

A Fatherless Child

Clearly uncomfortable with sitting in one place for very long, Bobby led Anna on a stroll around the mall after about a half hour of narrating. But he agreed to keep talking. He told her about how, at the age of ten, he moved to Grandma Casey's house by the river. He explained that, even though they had been the best of friends before his parents died, that transfer of responsibility had involved more than the double loss of his parents. He found that Grandma Casey could no longer be his friend as in the good old days. She had to be his mother and father from then on. Add to this that Bobby had to leave his school in Topeka—"a case of leaving the devil ya know in exchange for one ya have not met"—and the devastation of his life was total.

One way Bobby compensated for his losses was to eat, and eat some more. As robust as was the food Grandma Casey served, he supplemented it with candy bars, bought or stolen, from the drugstore in town. He often skipped his last class to visit that little five-and-dime, careful to eat all his sugary windfall before he got to the bus. One armed robbery at the hands of a giant sixth grader had been enough to teach him that precaution.

Until puberty, Bobby grew to rotund proportions, his body "stretching like a Thanksgiving Day parade balloon." Grandma Casey, who had raised two girls, had not been fully equipped to deal with a troubled boy. She was nearing her seventies. It might have been better for her to stay Bobby's best friend, for her sake, instead of that stressful attempt to replace two parents.

During those years of soothing his pain with food and adding to his grandma's gray hair, Bobby had learned to appreciate what he lost. Tossing a softball with his father on the sidewalk in front of their house in Topeka had seemed boring at the time. But, in retrospect, Bobby could feel the way those face-to-face games with his dad provided a framework for his young life. He began, at age eleven, to crave a father in his life. And at the age of twelve, the annual revival stoked that craving even more.

Wilhelm Rothenberg had been the speaker that year, a thirty-something Lutheran who had strayed from the stolid faith of his youth. He had ended his stint as a seminary professor to pursue a closer walk with God and itinerant ministry. When Bobby first saw him, Wilhelm was five years into his new calling, and his seminary-professor suits were somewhat frayed at the edges. Like Bobby, Wilhelm had lost both his parents before he reached adulthood. And Wilhelm's faith that God was the only father he had ever needed infected young Bobby.

Though he returned to the little country church four more times, and sent Bobby an occasional letter, Wilhelm passed out of the boy's life. The notion, however, that the father Bobby needed was the great King of the Universe, stayed with him the rest of his days. It was the foundation of his faith—along with those lightning moments under the hand of Sister Iris, of course.

Parenthood Surprise

On his final night at the YMCA, a two-week stint being the maximum allowed, Bobby received his first visitor. He was sitting on his bed in his semi-private room. He was reading a book by Katherine Kuhlman he'd found in the library downstairs, wedged between *Pilgrim's Progress* and *Angels* by Billy Graham. Together they constituted the spirituality section of the meager library, unless he counted *Tarantula*, by Bob Dylan, as a text on religion.

The desk manager called Bobby over the intercom. "You got a guest, Bobby."

That phrase seemed to have no place in the lexicon of his present life. But having God active in his life necessitated a peace treaty with the unforeseen. The unexpected visitor felt instantly like one of those life-altering surprise moments. He held down the talk button on the intercom and hoped it worked. "Send 'im up."

The speaker cracked and squawked. "... a her." Only that fragment came back over the ancient intercom.

If the guest was a woman, Bobby had to meet her downstairs. It occurred to him that it might be Anna, but why would she track him down here? They were scheduled to meet again the next day. Perhaps it was the scrawny woman with the healed back. But he suspected she hadn't yet given up her resolve about talking to strangers. After that he stopped guessing, left his room, and spun around the end of the banister on the way down the stairs. The elevator took too long.

When he arrived at the lobby, the late sun was stretching a leg through the front door as another resident stepped in from the heat. He looked around for a woman who seemed a likely guest, but the only woman he could see seemed very unlikely.

Looking out at the street, only a quarter of her face visible from where Bobby stood, a woman who must have been in her thirties gripped a newish black leather purse. The purse hung over her shoulder so that its strap cut diagonally across her back. A light suit jacket hung bunched up at the conjunction of the bag and its strap. Revealed by that peeled-off jacket was a sweat-stained blouse that might have been made of silk. It was cream colored and sleeveless, much cooler than the linen jacket. She wore sharp heels and a pale tan skirt, slightly darker than the jacket. Her hair, a bit disturbed, otherwise looked stylish and shiny in the angling sunlight. She was better put together than most of the women Bobby knew at this stage in his life. Maybe even better than Anna Conyers.

16

The woman turned and looked at him as he crossed the lobby on tiptoes. She looked familiar. And, for a moment, the world skipped backward.

That skip reminded him of a vision that once flipped him onto the streets of heaven. The déjà vu feeling from seeing this woman also recalled his reminiscences with Anna Conyers.

"Lori?" His voice faltered at the impossibility of what he was saying. Lori had been his wife thirty years ago. Two things made meeting her now seem impossible. The first was that his ex-wife hated him more than she hated the devil, last he knew. And she had genuinely hated the devil. The second problem was that this woman was much too young to have traversed the same thirty years Bobby had crossed since his last glimpse of Lori, the year of their divorce.

"No." The woman stood up a bit straighter. "Lori was my mother. I'm Tracy." She stopped there.

Bobby paused to sort the implications of those few words.

"I'm your daughter." She apparently didn't want to wait for his slow sorting.

The Price of Freedom

When he agreed to the interview, Bobby told Anna that his part in her article wouldn't ever be published. He said it with a grin. Anna half believed him, but she sat and talked with him anyway. Maybe he was wrong about the article. Or maybe it didn't matter if he was right. She was *that* curious about how he got to be who he was reputed to be.

Bobby told her that by the time he was fourteen, he had decided being fat and miserable was much worse than simply being miserable, so he stopped stealing candy—and sneaking leftovers when Grandma was asleep. The usual sprouting growth of a

17

teenage boy solved the rest of his weight issues. He didn't lose weight in his fourteenth year. Rather, he grew to a height that matched his weight.

He also found first love to be a strong diet pill. Bobby knew Grace Carstens wouldn't look at him seriously until he trimmed down and got fit like Roy Shelton, the best athlete in the class. Grace was the daughter of the United Methodist minister in town, a sort of social and spiritual royalty, though not spiritual in the sense of conforming to anyone's religious rules. Bobby liked her iconoclastic style, not very discerning about the value of her rebellion at the time. Grace was infamous for snubbing her father's religion in favor of a bottle of cheap wine and a tussle in the back of various boys' cars. She was a bad girl, but the most beautiful bad girl Bobby had ever seen. So he set to toning his muscles and learned a thing or two about hygiene and style.

Grandma Casey lived off her late husband's railroad pension as well as Social Security, which she referred to as her welfare check. That combination left little for such niceties as new clothes with which a teenage boy could fetch the hottest girl in school. Once again, Bobby resorted to shoplifting, augmenting his dowdy wardrobe by petty crime.

"Where'd you get them pants?" Grandma said once when she saw him heading out the door on a Friday evening.

At age fifteen, he could drive the car in those rural parts, and would head into town for whatever party the kids at school could assemble. "These pants? Oh, Joe gave me these. They don't fit him no more." Bobby guessed Grandma knew it was a lie, but they seemed to have agreed that she wouldn't challenge him directly on such things. She was wearing out as the years passed. Standing up to her stubborn grandson was probably more than she had wind in her lungs to sustain.

"Mm-hmm," she would say to his lies.

"Where were you so late?" She confronted him one Saturday night, standing in the kitchen in her nightgown and robe, leaning on the back of one of the metal kitchen chairs with its puffy fake-leather covering.

Bobby tried to keep his face turned enough to hide the black eye he got that evening. "Just hangin' out with some o' the kids from school. Mostly at Kristen Thompson's house."

Kristen's father was a trustee at the Baptist church, so Bobby hoped that slice of information vouched for the holiness of his nighttime endeavors. That Kristen's parents weren't home, and that the kids had spent very little time there, didn't factor into his testimony.

Grandma was not inclined to cross examine. She seemed to ask just enough for Bobby to perjure himself, gathering further evidence that he didn't trust her anymore and that she could not trust him either. But he always knew she still loved him. Perhaps she figured it was too late to start punishing him for a lifestyle born from the loss of his parents. Instead, she would address those issues on her knees.

Many nights, Bobby passed her bedroom door to hear her muttering to her divine confidant, punctuated by an occasional sob or sniffle. Bobby assumed he was the cause of that grief, but didn't see how he could change it.

"What do you think you wanna be when you finish growin' up?" Grandma asked him that when he was fifteen, helping her shell peas in the kitchen.

"Me? I don't know. I been thinkin' about travelin'—seein' the country and seein' what's out there." He had read a book by Jack Kerouac that stirred his curiosity and opened an account filled with irrational optimism.

"How ya' gonna feed yerself while you're wanderin' around like that?" She sounded no more concerned about his plan than when he told her he needed five dollars to pay some activity fee at school.

"I can do this and that. I been helpin' Denny and his dad at the store, openin' boxes and throwin' stuff away to make extra money. I can do stuff like that easy."

"That don't pay much."

"I don't need much."

After the failed attempt to hitch himself to Grace by means of upgrading his wardrobe, Bobby had decided to abandon the fantasy and just be himself. At fifteen, he was a boy with longish dark hair like Jack Nicholson's. He knew he would never be Robert Redford. Between the scars from the car accident and his repeatedly broken nose, as well as his head shaped like a football, he had little hope of winning anything by his looks. So he turned his aspirations toward character and uniqueness. With the 1960s nearly over, he found a hobo style expressed all he wanted about who he was in the world.

Bobby told Anna that the first seed of his real destiny showed up on a hot summer day after his sixteenth birthday. He was with Joe Gregg, Pete Wasser, and Kevin Ericson on a train trestle over the river, drinking beers Kevin had stolen from his father's fridge. Kevin was even shorter than Bobby, a sly boy with the look of a criminal across his glassy dark eyes and expressive brows. Kevin had been Bobby's lighthouse, warning Bobby where the rocks were, rocks that would crash his life and maybe even end it. Bobby planned to stay clear of where Kevin often stood, on the edge of disaster.

Pete and Gregg, as they all called him, were church kids like Bobby, but not very different from Kevin. They did manage to stay with Bobby on the side of the law that generally looked *into* and not *out of* a small room with metal bars on the windows. Pete was over six feet tall at sixteen, a good enough athlete to star in their small high school. Gregg was the class clown who constantly tested his physical limits, goaded by Kevin's deviance and challenged by Pete's greater size and strength.

So, after two beers, Gregg was standing on the rusty railing that sagged away from the abandoned tracks.

The other boys howled and backed away nervously.

Gregg just inhaled their fear as fuel for more foolishness. "You boys ain't afraid, are ya?" He hooted this question with a beer bottle in one hand and a rusty support in the other.

Whether already drunk or simply lacking common sense, he danced on that railing like a trained monkey. That dance ended abruptly with a wild, flailing fall that broke the beer bottle and pulled loose the rusted metal rod he held in his other hand.

Bobby reached impotently toward his friend as Gregg flipped forward and banged his head on a splintery railroad tie before plummeting twenty feet to the greenish-brown water. If the clumsy fall against the bridge didn't kill him, whatever rusting metal lay beneath the surface of the river might finish the job.

Without thinking, Bobby ducked under the twisted railing.

Kevin stayed frozen in place, swearing at the top of his lungs.

Pete hesitated, then followed Bobby over the edge after uttering an inarticulate prayer.

Kevin apparently recovered his senses enough to figure out where they were likely to come ashore, and crossed the bridge to scramble through the thistles and tall grass down the dusty riverbank.

Bobby's was the first head to come up from the water, which resembled chocolate milk. He waited for Pete to come up, to see if he knew where Gregg was, but Gregg was the next one up. He was, however, floating facedown. Pete came up half a second later, pushing Gregg toward Bobby. The two of them managed to turn Gregg faceup as they maneuvered toward the shore.

Gregg was unconscious. His head was bleeding from a two-inch horizontal cut on his forehead, but a heavier stream of blood seemed to be coming from his neck.

Bobby pushed Gregg with a hand under one armpit while Pete dragged at the other arm. They covered the few yards of relatively calm water in less than a minute. Neither of them had passed lifeguard training yet. Pete was working on it for his job at a church camp near town. Saving Gregg from drowning was, however, not the real rescue.

Kevin helped drag Gregg up onto the bank, his feet slipping once, landing him on his backside while still gripping handfuls of Gregg's T-shirt. Now all three boys could see the huge, jagged cut on his neck where he must have jammed the jagged end of that broken beer bottle. The trickle of blood from his forehead was trivial compared to the flood from his neck.

Seeing that flood, Bobby did the only thing he could think to do—an irrational act. He yelled at the blood to stop. "You stop bleedin' right now! I forbid you to kill him. Stop bleedin'!"

Pete and Kevin just stared, certainly assuming Bobby was losing his mind. But they offered no better solutions.

And then Gregg opened his eyes. He looked surprised and then confused. "What happened?" His voice seemed far too calm for a boy with an open vein in his neck.

None of the other boys answered. They just gaped. Kevin looked like he was about to flee a zombie from outer space. Pete looked like he was about to curse Gregg for his stupid stunt. And Bobby just shook his head in disbelief—disbelief at his own outburst against the gruesome injury. And that it apparently worked.

The cut on Gregg's forehead had slowed to an ooze, blood tracing down each side of his face, just missing his eyes. But the flow from his neck had stopped. Looking down at his formerly gray Nebraska football T-shirt, Gregg swore and then looked like he might pass out, his face going doubly pale, and his eyes rolling back in his head.

"Hey, don't do that." Pete grabbed Gregg and shook him back to alertness. "Stay awake."

They carried Gregg to the car, though he insisted repeatedly that he could walk. None of them ventured to look more closely at his neck, focusing instead on getting to the emergency room of the little hospital in town.

The emergency room doctor and nurses were surprised at the quantity of blood soaking his shirt, given the tentative flow from Gregg's head wound, which required six stitches. But there was no cut at all on his neck to account for the massive hemorrhaging the boys had seen, and to which the shirt bore witness.

"You saved his life." Pete was looking at Bobby as they sat on Naugahyde waiting room chairs, smelling of catfish and beer.

Bobby shook his head. "I don't know what happened. I think I went crazy for a second."

Kevin looked more grown up than Bobby would have ever imagined. He spoke solemnly. "You saved his life as sure as anything, ever. It was real. I saw it."

Bobby stopped fighting it. Absorbed the truth and then sank back into being a teenage boy, self-consciously avoiding eye contact.

Over the next year, they didn't discuss what happened that day in the river unless they were half drunk or seriously tired.

For Bobby, it became a smooth stone he carried in his pocket—something to rub when he had a moment to think. It had weight and solidity, like so little of his religious life. Looking back over nearly five decades, he told Anna with confidence that his first healing miracle also shaped the rest of his life.

Meeting Tracy

Bobby sat with his elbows on a marble tabletop outside the café on the corner of Maple Avenue and Davis Street. He looked at Tracy, who was looking everywhere but at him. This gave him the chance to study her. That he hadn't seen his former wife for decades made the likeness more present, more haunting—the upturned nose, the high-arching eyebrows. The pronounced widow's peak to her hair gave her face a slender valentine shape. He cleared his throat. "Sorry about yer mom. I really didn't know. And I woulda contacted you if I'd 'a known ... you were ... you."

Tracy was looking at him now. "It was hard to find you to let you know about her passing, just like it was hard to find you here." She nodded toward the street sign as if Bobby simply existed in this neighborhood or lived nowhere in particular.

"How long was she sick?"

"About two years." Tracy fiddled with a paper napkin weighted by a bundle of silverware wrapped in another napkin. She folded one corner of the white paper distraction, then unfolded it and tried to make it flat again. "She thought she just had allergies or a cold that was hanging on too long. She didn't go to doctors much, so no one told her anything about smoking all those years."

Bobby decided not to point out that people generally know about the hazards of smoking without going to a doctor. "She still smokin' at the end?" Bobby wasn't really curious, just making conversation, treading on the path Tracy had laid out for him.

Tracy looked at his hands. She probably noticed the yellow stains on his right middle finger and index finger, his nails slightly brown. He bore the signs of a smoker himself, though he hadn't taken the opportunity of the open-air café to light up. "Yeah, she smoked right up until she was on oxygen."

Again, Bobby spoke only to carry his end of the conversation, not the most important conversation. "Nasty habit. I decided to keep it up though, to give me chances to talk to folks. Smokers standin' outside a building make an instant community."

Bobby noted a change to Tracy's face, a brief flush. The shift was so subtle that a passing stranger wouldn't have noticed. Was that fear? The fear of a child who had just lost her mother, now fearing another loss?

He tried to assure her. "I haven't had any symptoms at all. I think I'm protected because of what I do."

"What ... is it ... you ... do?" The stop-and-start pace of that question implied she knew something, but wasn't willing to believe what she had heard.

The waitress interrupted at that strategic moment. Bobby ordered coffee and a Reuben sandwich. Tracy ordered a caesar salad and water. They hadn't discussed who was buying, but the woman who had found her father living in a YMCA was probably making some assumptions.

"What is it I do?" Bobby picked up the question when the waitress turned to walk back into the café. "I'm an itinerant missionary. I go where God sends me to bring people good news and a bit of the Father's love."

"I heard you were traveling around a lot."

"Yep, which is why I'm hard to find."

"Do you have a home base or something?"

"Well, you could find a pile of my stuff in a closet in a big house in Malibu, California, but that ain't my house, and it ain't what you'd call a home base. There's some books in a basement in No Cal—a pastor friend of mine looks after 'em."

"No cal?"

"Northern California." He grinned the slightest apology. "When I was young, livin' in Kansas and Nebraska, I thought California was the Promised Land. I did find some promise out there, but didn't ever really settle down."

"That was after you left Mom?"

Bobby nodded slowly for several seconds. The divorce happened so long ago that he had to scrounge for the answer to who was to blame—who left whom. "Your mom and I were livin' in Nevada when we broke up, and I did go to the West Coast from there. Yep." He let go of that strand and grabbed another. "How old are you?"

"Thirty-one next month."

Bobby had to take a few deep breaths to clear out the best mathematical parts of his brain. But he decided to ask for some help. "So what year was it you were born?" It wasn't just that he couldn't do the math off the top of his head. He genuinely doubted he knew exactly what year it was.

"Eighty-eight. 1988. I was born in September. September ninth."

That gradually deepening specificity fulfilled the purpose of the question. Bobby paused to replay the events of 1988. His divorce that year was one way of anchoring his recollection. They had been married in Illinois, where Bobby met Lori. The divorce was relatively easy, given the laws of that state, but it did take most of 1988. Lori had not been in court the day it was all finalized. She was still in Nevada. Bobby recalled that when he did see her that summer, she was sitting in a car. He could only see her from the shoulders up. He had not known she was pregnant. If he had known, he would have assumed another father—unless the child was to be born in early September. "You were a full nine months when you were born?" Bobby wanted to clean up the last of the alternate possibilities.

"A full nine months." Tracy sighed briefly.

He shook his head. "She never told me."

"I know."

On His Own

In 1971, at the age of sixteen, Bobby lost his remaining parental support. Grandma Casey died of a heart attack.

On one of the days that Bobby had actually gone to school, he barged in the front door of the little cabin on the river full of annoyance at being scolded by the principal for his poor attendance record, and even more annoyed at being rejected by Connie Tenopir, who had a reputation for not rejecting any of the boys. But Bobby stopped mid-sentence when he saw his grandma lying on the kitchen floor, a dish towel still clutched in one hand, pressed to her face as if it might staunch the pain of a heart attack.

Moving in slow motion, Bobby sank to his knees like at one of those revival meetings. But there was no sound of weeping in the air, no organ music to stir the soul. And there was no doubt in Bobby's mind that his grandmother was dead. Her skin was gray and her body perfectly still, like a stone carving of his grandmother, a sad likeness of the woman who had kept him alive, who was normally warm and joyful. Her chuckle had always lifted Bobby's spirits like a favorite song—the sound of hope, the sound of comfort and belonging. He had never considered what he would do when that hope was gone, when that chuckle fell silent once and for all.

Briefly, he considered whether he could do something like what he had done for Joe Gregg. Gregg had been as good as dead when Bobby told death to leave him alone. But his grandma was dead and long gone by then, not pulsing blood out of an open wound. Her blood was still. Besides that, Bobby was pretty sure God was mad at him. He couldn't count on any special favors. The breaking of at least seven of the ten commandments was good enough reason to not even try.

Essentially, he felt that he deserved to lose the only person in the world who he knew truly loved him. He had earned that much. The snarling warnings from the principal that day rewound and played back to accompany those feelings. "You'll never amount to anything. You don't take anything seriously. You have no prospects, Nightingale."

He told Anna that it was "sheer stubbornness and a need to show other people how wrong they were" that kept him from loading his grandpa's old shotgun and ending his life there beside his grandma. He didn't cry. He was certainly in shock. But he found a kind of survival mode.

What would happen to him now? He wasn't yet seventeen. It would be an institution or foster home for him. That would add the loss of his freedom to the loss of his grandma. All he could think to do was escape before anyone found out Grandma was dead.

He pulled together all the cash in the house—about sixty-five dollars, counting change from the cookie jar on top of the fridge. Then he packed a canvas duffle bag with some essentials. Not being a traveler, he wasn't sure what *was* essential, but he made his best guess. He added his grandpa's World War II surplus sleeping bag, plastic on one side, moldy fabric on the other. And he changed to his best work boots.

Bobby could have taken his grandmother's car, but it occurred to him that could be construed as theft, and he didn't want the authorities to have added motivation to hunt him down. He would hop on a freight train over by Barneston, a smaller town than where he went to school, and one where no one would recognize him.

As it turned out, those work boots that had been fine for chores around the cabin or the back room of the store were not ready for a brisk ten-mile walk. Stopping to put Band-Aids on his blisters—one necessity he had thought to include among his supplies—and slowing to a determined limp put him on the edge of Barneston at ten that night. He had eaten all the leftover fried chicken during a brief stop under the thin shade of poplar trees beside the gravel road. He finished the biscuits while he waited for the train, washed down by the last of the grape juice he had pulled from the fridge.

The first train that passed didn't slow down enough for him to jump it, but the next one halted to drop off fuel oil cars in the small train yard where Bobby crouched in the shadows. He was beginning to shiver, though the temperature was not yet below sixty on that calm night in May. His arms and legs shook, his joints strangely weak, nearly preventing him from climbing aboard a freight car rolling at less than two miles an hour. He was relieved to find the car unoccupied—for safety's sake, but also because of what followed the shaking and shivering.

As the train gained speed on its way to Beatrice, Bobby could feel a ripping in his heart. The separation from his home had cut to a deeper level, like the difference between a bruised muscle and one that's been torn entirely through. His heart muscle was the one torn. He sobbed violently for miles and miles, sadness swirling into despair, despair to depression, and then all of it vanishing down the drain to leave a sediment of numbness.

As if remembering his lost parents would inoculate him from the pain of losing Grandma, he sat silently thinking of his mother and father. To keep their little ranch-style house in Topeka, they had both worked. His father was a department store manager near downtown in the time before malls sprouted like mushrooms around the edges of cities and towns. His mother, Adeline, worked as a secretary in a small insurance company back when there *were* small insurance companies.

Adeline, known to everyone as Addy, waded into the business world each day after dropping Bobby off at school—or at a neighbor's house during the summer. And she never seemed to bring any of that world back with her. It was as if she were a scuba diver in one of those spy movies who could magically rise from the water and remove that skin-tight rubber suit to reveal perfectly pressed and dry clothes underneath. The working world seemed not to soak into her. Bobby only saw her as his mother, not as someone's employee, someone's assistant or secretary.

His favorite time of day during the work week was when his mother came to his bedroom to read him a story and say goodnight. *Curious George, Ramona the Pest*, and a long string of Dr. Seuss books punctuated his day with humor and a bit of excitement. But most of all, he enjoyed the gentle touches from his mother's hands. Her fingers were somewhat short and stout without being fat or childlike. Her skin was soft even after all the housework she did, the ever-present yellow rubber gloves protecting her well.

When he thought about those touches, while riding the northbound train away from life as he knew it, he could recall the mechanical way she stroked his cheeks or smoothed his hair. But even those habitual touches formed an emotional foundation for his soul. They were the tactile experience of home, a home without fear or worry, a home where he was free to be a boy.

The sort of freedom he sought on that northbound train at age sixteen was completely different. From here on, all the worries would be his alone. He could not afford to be a boy anymore.

But, in the early morning darkness of that freight car somewhere north of Wilber, Nebraska, he thought he heard a voice. *"You are* my *boy. You always will be. Just stick with me, and I'll show you what my boy can do."*

To Bobby, that reminded him of something Pastor Rothenberg might have believed. But he couldn't recall the itinerant revivalist saying those words or teaching Bobby to actually hear the voice of God saying anything at all.

Bobby worried that his escape from his civilized life had led him into insanity. But maybe he was entering some mystical realm away from church and religion and even away from God as he knew him. It was as if he were finding God outside the boundaries, outside of church, like the stray corn seed that sprouts in the farmyard ten feet from the fence that protects the field.

There on that bench in the mall, he grinned at Anna. "I think I'm still livin' off that discovery of the God who's outside the fence."

Who's Paying for This?

When they finished their dinner that night, Tracy and Bobby looked at each other. Though she was the well-dressed one with the expensive hair style, he knew that Tracy carried inside her a deep need to be taken care of. It was one of those secrets his heavenly Father shared about someone he wanted Bobby to bless.

Bobby assumed blessing Tracy that night meant picking up the check. That assumption might have been challenged by what Bobby knew about the contents of his pockets. But, by this stage in his life, he had become accustomed to God's quantum accounting. Bobby had read an article about quantum physics once. He even heard a pastor using the newfound scientific notion as an analogy. He didn't entirely understand any kind of physics, but this reminded Bobby of a long string of monetary experiences during his life. One and one did not always add up to two.

When Tracy reached toward the check, hesitating with no convincing intent, Bobby intervened. "I'll get this." He didn't have time to wait until he knew exactly *how* he was going to do that, but he reached into his pants pocket like a miner panning for gold. Next to the pack of Marlboros and the disposable lighter, stiffer and fresher than the crumpled dollar or two in the corner of that pocket, Bobby found a folded bill. He extracted it and snapped it on top of the check like a dealer at a casino. That was, in fact, one of the dozens of jobs he could list on his résumé—if he had a résumé.

Bobby paid with a smile. Only after that smile did he glance down to see that the bill was a fifty. He assumed then that he was leaving a big tip, not that God had slipped that bill into his pocket to pay for dinner and a bit of walking around money. That's not how Bobby and his Papa did things.

Tracy stared at the crisp fifty-dollar bill as Bobby removed his thumb and set the saltshaker on it. He had seen this kind of instant miraculous provision so many times that he wasn't even tempted to laugh—or to share how the money just appeared in his pocket. There would be time for stories later. And he had better stories.

One of his favorite stories happened ten years before that night. He had been working as a dishwasher in a diner in Bozeman, Montana. He had managed to save up a few hundred dollars, because he thought his Papa was saying he would need some cash soon. When it was time to move on, he wasn't following a travel directive from his heavenly guide, just responding to the usual wandering impulse.

In his hotel room, he packed his big canvas backpack. He had accumulated some new clothes and a few keepsakes from the mountains and towns around Bozeman, and was disturbed to see how tightly it all fit. He packed on a Friday night, woke up on that Saturday morning, and walked to breakfast at his former employer's, where he would pick up his last check. Entering the front door of the restaurant for a change, he wondered exactly how he had accumulated enough goods to make his pack so tight. But he had to turn his attention to saying his goodbyes and catching a bus instead of solving a mystery that seemed to be creeping along behind him like a shadow on that sunny September day.

After eating a large breakfast in the warm and savory air of the dining room, he got his paycheck from the assistant manager, shook his hand, and bid him farewell.

Bobby hugged Joaquin in the dish room and then stopped to say goodbye to Francine. He could see rings under her eyes that lied about her age in the opposite direction from which she often fudged the numbers.

"What's eatin' ya?" With Francine, he used a brotherly and tender tone.

She shook her head and pursed her lips. "You don't wanna know. Just money troubles, as usual."

Francine had been taking care of her sickly old dad for all the months Bobby lived in Bozeman, and he imagined the old man might be the cause of some financial strain. "What is it, exactly?" He sounded as if he intended to do something about it before being aware of that intention.

Francine looked a little surprised. Bobby had always been friendly, but not nosy. "Well, if you must know, the bank is threatenin' to dump Daddy out on the side o' the road if they don't get sixteen thousand dollars from us." She sighed. "I can make the payments month-to-month, but he got behind before I moved back out there. And Roger, at the bank, ain't willing to wait any longer for me to win the lottery."

Bobby and Francine were standing in the space between the last table for four and the last booth, the only two empty tables in the place. Bobby took her by the arm and led her through the door marked Employees Only, next to the restrooms.

Francine allowed herself to be towed with no resistance. "What are you up to?"

"I think I can help ya out." Bobby settled his backpack on the floor. He had suddenly realized why the backpack felt so full.

"What ...?"

Unzipping the main section of the pack, Bobby reached in and found an unfamiliar parcel. It was a bank bag, bulging with something he assumed was not dirty underwear. "This should cover it." He handed the bag to Francine and took a few seconds to resettle the contents of his pack before zipping it shut again. Zipping was easier this time.

Francine stood staring at the bank bag, which probably bore the name of the very bank to which she owed all that money.

When Bobby stood up, he saw her stalled there. He laughed at how he had finally discovered a way to get Francine to stand still and be quiet.

"What did you do?" Her voice was conspiratorial.

Bobby knew that his lack of a high income and no evidence of rich relatives might lead Francine to assume he had done something illegal to get a bag full of money. In Bozeman, he had mostly kept a low profile. He had stayed away from the churches, knowing he would have to explain some very unusual events if he got too close to a building full of people worshipping God. He was in hiding for those few months.

He blew his cover just as he was headed out of town. "Sometimes God just tells me to do somethin' sorta crazy." Bobby tried a reassuring grin. "I believe he gave me that money to give to you."

"But where did you *get* it?" she persisted, certainly knowing too-good-to-be-true when she saw it.

"You wouldn't believe me if I told ya. It's clean. No crimes were committed." Then he knew how to convince her. "Go ahead and count it."

Francine hesitated. Perhaps she didn't want to get her fingerprints on dirty money. But she finally unzipped that bank bag and pulled out a bundle of hundreds—a whole bundle. Ten thousand dollars. Then she found three full stacks of twenties. That was six thousand. What remained were several one hundred dollar bills—seven, to be exact. Then four twenties and a single. Sixteen thousand seven hundred and eighty-one dollars. There were a few coins clanking in the corners of the dark bag. Francine left them where they were. "How did you know? This is exactly ... How did you know how much? I didn't tell no one about this. Did Roger at the bank talk to you? But why would he ...?"

"I tell ya, Francine, God gave me that money to give to you. That's all ya need to know. That's why it's the exact amount ya need. I didn't know that amount, but God did."

Francine started to cry, her makeup drawing a map of a meandering river down her cheek.

Sitting at that sidewalk café with Tracy ten years later, Bobby did pause to offer silent thanks to his Papa for providing just what was needed for the hundredth time. As he maintained his smile for a few seconds, eyes exploring Tracy's face again, he detected another one of those shifts in her demeanor. It was sort of like someone relaxing after forcing a smile for forty-five minutes of wedding photos.

It was a start.

Free to Roam and Destined to Be Alone

Bobby described to Anna how he'd wandered around the western half of the United States in search of his identity, though mostly he was just searching for survival. At first, he'd managed to pass for eighteen years old, keeping the authorities uninterested. He used his Social Security card as ID, and took jobs wherever those hiring didn't ask too many questions and didn't demand a driver's license. He managed to procure one of those in Cheyenne, Wyoming, when he was seventeen—with some help from a sympathetic employer and some bendable laws.

The stock boy, delivery van, and landscaping work he snagged during those years hardened new layers of muscle onto his maturing physique. By the time he actually *was* eighteen, he could pass for twenty-five. But he had no interest in anymore fraudulent aging by that point, not being an avid drinker, and cigarettes requiring no more than eighteen years.

Bobby learned to sleep in freight cars, on park benches, and in the back seat of abandoned autos. He learned to enjoy a soft bed when he found one, and to walk away when it was time. He learned to enjoy what he had by evading the fear that the hard times would become worse, and by not anticipating whether the good times would become better. Such a nomadic existence forced him to find a unique source of companionship, some consolation that would travel with him.

"That's when I started really talkin' to God." Bobby nodded to Anna and stood from the bench.

She assumed they would be walking again with him talking to *her*.

He admitted that part of his conversation with God might have just been talking to himself. Part of it may have just expressed the insanity of his loneliness. But Bobby believed he often heard responses to his questions, answers to his pleas, and even chuckles to his jokes. That was when he began to think of God as his Papa. No one he knew had referred to God that way—

not even Wilhelm Rothenberg. Bobby's faith didn't fit into the catalog of Christian institutions whose numbers multiplied year by year. What he had with his Papa was not an institution, it was a relationship.

But Bobby didn't stay away from church. He merely got in the habit of transitioning from one building to another—from one with a steeple to one without, from one with incense and bells to one with no music at all, to one with a massive choir swaying to the glowing music that filled their spirits and rocked their souls.

It was in an African Methodist Episcopal church named Zion where Bobby met Cecil Tomlins. Cecil was a deacon in the biggest predominantly African American church in a small Midwestern city. To many in that church, Cecil was something of a prophet, perhaps more in the Old Testament tradition than the New.

Cecil kept his eye on Bobby—often the lone white man on a Sunday morning—as Bobby arrived, worshipped, and quietly departed. Cecil told him later that he was waiting for a signal from the Spirit of God inside him, a sign that it was time to talk to the serious young man.

"You have to let that angry bear out of your soul and learn to be a playful cub again." Cecil finally heard the prompt to talk to Bobby. They were standing outside the black-painted wrought-iron fence between the church and the brick street where people parked when the church lot was full. Bobby was on foot, and Cecil had hooked his arm and pulled him aside on his way out of the late service that Sunday. Cicadas whined all around them as the shadows of maple trees danced over the brazen bricks on one of the oldest roads in town.

"A bear?" Bobby looked hard at the old man, a bit shorter than him, certainly in his seventies, with salt-and-pepper hair and a wiry beard. "Angry about what?"

Cecil smiled slyly, laughing in a way that sounded a bit like a cough. "You have to figure that part out for you'self."

"So this is somethin' God told ya to say to me?"

Cecil nodded in threes, pauses in between, and then more nodding.

That began a weekly conversation between the seventy-five-year-old black man and the twenty-five-year-old white man. Bobby knew from the start that Cecil was an answer to a need, if not an answer to a precise prayer. A father figure of sorts. The prophetic sort.

"Your grandma didn't leave you, Bobby. She didn't go anywhere. It was you who left her, before she died *and after*." Cecil spoke through the salty smell of fried chicken and gravy, heavy in a little restaurant near the church. "But you got to also know fer sure that fo'giveness is real. It's real for you personally."

Bobby sucked in a breath meant to open more space for his swelling heart. "She was good to me." That was all he could say before the tears took over.

In their frequent meetings, Cecil seemed to make yards of progress in healing Bobby's soul, yet he demanded nothing of Bobby. He didn't demand that Bobby settle down, that he become a church member, or that he do or say anything in particular. Bobby marked that experience, in his interview with Anna, as another fatherly grace that had stayed with him since.

He noted that Cecil's and his grandma's influence in his life might have been proportional to their contrast with his earthly father.

Peter Nightingale missed his chance to play football when he couldn't afford college and wasn't good enough to win a scholarship. When Bobby was a year old, his father pursued his dream of playing football one last time. He later spoke to Bobby about this with pain obvious even to a child. Early in the second half of his first game on a local semi-pro team, Peter broke a tackle only to tear his hamstring in the process, a tear that would take the entire season to heal only enough for him to walk normally.

That shattered dream was replayed for Bobby throughout his first ten years via his father's reminiscences and regrets. And their game of catch with a softball on the front sidewalk was not just father-son bonding, it was a warm-up for the company soft-ball team. It was his dad limbering his arm for that throw from shortstop to first. He spared Bobby the rocket throws, but always pushed Bobby to throw harder, to step into a catch and not cringe back. Bobby learned what he needed, not to win at base-ball or any other sport, but he did learn to please his dad.

Grandma Casey didn't push Bobby. Cecil Tomlins prompted and boosted but did not push. His insightful advice and tree-like patience kept Bobby coming back to that church long after he normally would have been boarding a Greyhound for a warmer climate.

In November of his twenty-fifth year, Bobby made his first visit to Cecil's house, having found that the old man wasn't at church, reported to be ill. After knocking at the front door and thinking he might have heard a beckoning voice croaked from deep in the old house, Bobby stepped inside, the door unlocked and the house dark.

"Cecil? You here?"

"Bobby? 'Zat you, boy?"

Bobby stepped around piles of old newspapers, *Reader's Digest* magazines, a folded TV tray, and a box of canned goods in the dark foyer of the house. Cecil seemed to be upstairs. "Can I come up, Cecil?"

"You better. I'm not comin' down." That reply ended in a humorous wheeze.

Bobby had heard Cecil was ill, but this seemed more serious than a mere cold. A packet of feelings strongly reminiscent of that last day at Grandma Casey's house popped open inside him as if the packing tape had grown old and brittle and couldn't hold the bulging parcel together anymore. For some reason, Bobby also recalled Joe Gregg with a jagged gash in his neck. Those seemed a random pair of recollections at the moment.

"All right, I'm comin' up." His words were meant to coax himself as much as to warn Cecil, the coaxing necessary under the shadow of those two traumatic memories.

At the top of the stairs, a few more piles of paper and cardboard, nondescript in the dark interior, loomed before him. The yellowed shades were drawn in every window Bobby could see.

"In here." Cecil's voice sounded weaker, though Bobby was nearer.

Bobby followed that hollow voice to a doorway framed in dark-chocolate colored wood. The door stood half open, another pile of magazines preventing it from opening any farther, and a dog lay next to it. The dog looked up at Bobby and whined a plea. It was a shaggy gray dog, part sheepdog, part Scottish terrier, perhaps. "Mutt" might not have been an insult where that old dog was concerned.

He stepped over the dog even as it rose to its feet, half tripping him. As he regained his balance, he focused on Cecil's face, framed by a white pillow. Having never seen Cecil lying down—and without his glasses—the old man looked like a stranger. But Bobby thought he could detect more than an unfamiliar context. Something was wrong with Cecil's face. His right eyebrow sagged, as did the right side of his mouth.

Cecil seemed to reply to Bobby's startled observation. "I had some brain thing happen to me. Maybe a stroke, or maybe something else I can't remember just now."

Even as the old man spoke, Bobby could tell that the stroke was preventing Cecil from pronouncing his words as carefully as he was accustomed.

"Ya see a doctor?"

"Oh yeah. And he saw me." Cecil sighed conclusively.

"You dyin'?" Bobby's reply surprised himself, as if he were accompanied by an undisciplined child who didn't know how impolite that question would be.

Cecil tried to nod, then resorted to moaning the answer. "Mm-hmm. Think so."

Bobby swore. That rude little boy with him was not behaving himself.

"You got that right."

"You ready to die?" As soon as he asked, Bobby knew he had to say something else. "I don't think y'er ready to die. I don't think this is yer time."

Cecil licked his lips noisily, as if he hadn't practiced that since his face became half helpless. "Do what you know you should do." Then he gurgled what might have been left of his laughter.

Bobby thought for a second. He even looked at the dog as if he needed an assistant and was considering the mutt's qualifications. Then he stepped over to the side of the bed and felt an urgency grab him, just like back on the bank of the Big Blue River.

"Ya gotta live!" And then, feeling it wasn't Cecil he was supposed to be addressing, he spoke to an invisible presence in the room. "Death, you get outta here right now!"

The two men would tell it differently later, but both sensed something rise and stare down Bobby. Then it jumped from the bed and flew through the ceiling. To Bobby, it looked like a dark creature, black as coal, rising and glaring at him with red eyes before choking and heading for the sky. Cecil said it was an old fat lady that left his bed, a lady that had been smothering him with her lazy girth. Bobby was glad he saw it the way he did. Cecil's version sounded less heroic.

Just like in the Bible, when death left Cecil's room, he said he was hungry. "I gotta cook us up a proper breakfast." And he threw off the covers and rolled toward the side of the bed.

Despite looking a devil in the eyes and telling him to get lost a second before, Bobby feared that Cecil was being rash with his offer to cook. Nothing had been said about healing the stroke, restoring Cecil's energy, and recovering the full use of his body. But Cecil was clearly assuming all that had been taken care of.

When he stood up and picked his glasses off the nightstand, Cecil laughed his full-throated laugh at Bobby's saucer eyes. "I knew you had it in you, Bobby. I knew all along."

How Do You Start This Thing?

Bobby looked at the sharp-dressed woman standing on the gritty urban pavement and wondered briefly whether a paternity test was in order. Tracy looked just like Lori, that was certain. The math worked out for the last time he was intimate with his former wife. But Tracy didn't look like she belonged to someone like him. This was only a brief lapse. He knew in his heart that she was his girl. He did note the need for some quiet time to talk with his Papa about why he hadn't told him about this before, but he stayed focused on that moment on that street corner.

"Where ya stayin?" He stood with his hands in his pockets, as was his habit. His arms were relatively short, and the front pockets on a pair of baggy pants seemed to catch his hands whenever they fell to his sides.

Before answering, Tracy regarded Bobby as if he might magically produce a guest room out of those baggy pockets. "I'm at the Sheraton near the airport."

"Nice place?" Bobby was just asking, not really curious about that hotel or any hotel, really. He had stayed at The Ritz in Chicago for one week and at the Beverley Hilton, in Beverley Hills, for nearly a month. He was content at the Y for tonight.

"It's nice." She didn't sound very interested in the hotel either.

Bobby cleared his throat, wanting a strong voice for what he said next. "I wanna get to know ya. I'd like to spend some time together. It probably ain't too late for us, right?"

A rainbow of emotions seemed to pass over her face in a few seconds. But Tracy avoided his direct question. "How long are you staying here?" She looked up the street toward the Y.

"I need to move on. They have a limit to how long a guy can put up. I've done my time. I'm on my way tomorrow."

"Where to?"

"Have a meetin' in the mornin'. Then I don't know. I expect I'll find out tomorrow."

Then that sharp-dressed woman he had never seen before, except in the face of his ex-wife, said the most surprising thing. "You could come stay with me for a bit." Her head twitched to the right as if she had surprised herself.

Bobby checked to see if his Papa had any messages for him. A sudden urge to see Minneapolis in early fall arose. "I'd be glad to come up yer way for a while."

Tracy gestured up the street. "I have a rental car." She was looking at a late model Ford sedan. "Should I pick you up tomorrow? We could drive back. That would be cheaper than getting you a late plane ticket."

Bobby was calculating the possibility that he was still on the TSA's no-fly list, but it didn't seem important to say anything about that just then. He nodded. "That sounds like a good plan to me. You can pick me up at the mall west o' town. That's where my meetin' is." He reached out his hand, and Tracy took it.

Not raised in a hugging family, Bobby didn't seriously consider that option for saying good night to his newly-discovered daughter. That hand-to-hand contact, however, offered opportunity for him to sense something about her that was beyond the physical eye. In his spirit, he was seeing a starving little girl hanging around Tracy's neck, clinging, crying, and hopeless.

Tracy shook his offered hand probably more gently than she would to close a real estate deal for her agency back home. And she allowed Bobby to hang on for an extra two seconds. He knew that was all she could allow just then.

When they parted, Bobby couldn't help thinking about Lori. Tracy's well-styled hair and makeup made her look as young as her mother had when he'd first met her.

Lori Raymond had been a runaway, leaving her home in Scottsbluff, Nebraska at the age of fifteen. She never articulated what her father had done to make her want to leave home so early, but Bobby had a pretty good idea what it was. He had learned enough about people in general to not always wish he had all the details about a person, even about a pretty girl with whom he was deeply infatuated.

When he first saw her, Lori was working as a stylist in a beauty salon in Moline, Illinois. As a teen, she had run away to Chicago, but had gradually backed off the big city—first to Cicero, then Joliet, and finally Moline. That river city was still far from home, and her father was unlikely to find her there. Though she was eighteen by the time she landed in Moline, she still feared her old man when Bobby met her at age twenty.

Bobby had walked past her salon at the end of a day of mowing lawns at office buildings around the edge of town. He smelled like grass. So, when he saw the pretty girl cutting hair, he ran to his hotel and showered before coming back to get a haircut. That he was the only man in the place didn't slow him down. That he didn't have an appointment didn't deter the pretty little stylist either.

"I can take him, Maggie." Lori had interrupted her boss, who was trying to acquaint Bobby with their policy on walk-ins and dropping heavy hints about the impropriety of a man barging into their feminine sanctuary.

Lori was sassy and fearless, aside from her fear of her father. She was also the best young stylist in the place and seemed to know that her job was safe. As Bobby soon found out, she had also just broken up with her latest boyfriend.

"Where ya from?" she said, after establishing directions for Bobby's haircut.

"All over." Then he backed off the braggadocio. "Originally from Nebraska."

"Really? Whereabouts?"

"Southeast, near the Kansas border. You heard of Beatrice?" Bobby pronounced the name of the biggest town near Grandma's cabin the way only Nebraskans would pronounce it. "*Be-AT-riss.*"

Lori stopped combing and clipping to stare at the man in her chair, perhaps studying the scar on his forehead. "Dang! I haven't heard anyone say 'Be-AT-riss' for I don't know how long."

Bobby laughed. "A real Nebraskan." He aimed his sideways smile in her direction as she resumed the haircut with a few chuckles.

Lori told him she believed in "fate."

Bobby was beginning to believe in his Papa in heaven taking care of him and directing his path. Those directions often sounded muddled, however, when strong emotions got involved. Bobby didn't see any warning signs about a relationship with Lori.

They were married less than a year later, after breaking up three times along the way. Bobby felt that the guy who said, "Can't live with her, can't live without her," must have known his Lori. Her dimply smile, long lashes, and baby-doll blue eyes left him powerless to resist. Her temper and her tendency to flirt with any guy within reach infuriated and baffled him a hundred times each.

Because she could find work anywhere, and Moline was just a temporary stopping place, Bobby easily talked Lori into moving to Las Vegas with him just two months into their marriage. He had heard about abundant construction work in that growing little city, and he longed for a warmer climate. The bright lights and party atmosphere enticed Lori to head to the desert paradise.

But paradise proved to be as hard for Bobby and Lori to hang onto as it had been for Adam and Eve.

A Visit Up North

The ride toward Minneapolis was congenial enough. Bobby had learned how to get along with anyone, and Tracy seemed to fall back on her professional persona. She clearly struggled to maintain that pasted smile, however, as the car filled with odors Bobby didn't notice in open spaces. He had conscientiously showered, washing his hair and beard thoroughly. But his clothes were old, and the laundry at the Y was industrial and perfunctory when it came to preventing his shirts and pants from resembling those of a homeless man. Bobby and Tracy rode with the windows open much of the way, giving up on the air-conditioning for want of greater air flow.

"I'll get some new clothes when we get up by yer place."

She looked at him for as long as she dared while driving on the interstate at seventy miles an hour. But she didn't ask him where he would get the money.

Bobby answered the implied question without meeting her eyes on that prolonged assessment. "Don't worry, I have re-sources. I don't have to wear Salvation Army hand-me-downs if I don't want to."

Tracy pursed her lips and hummed a noncommittal answer.

Bobby could see how his daughter fit in with the tight-lipped Midwesterners, reserving their judgements for later conversations and a different audience.

"So, how's business?" Bobby asked that to break the uncomfortable silence over his odoriferous clothing.

"I'm making a good enough living without having to work all night and day. The housing market was hard the last few years. Just settling down now."

"Good. That's good to hear." Bobby could think of other safe topics, but wanted to ask more personal questions. "You have a boyfriend or somethin'?" He kept his eyes on the road to minimize the imposition of that question.

"Still recovering from my divorce. It takes time."

"It does."

During the silence that followed, he realized he had asked that question as an echo of his experience with Tracy's mother. Lori found a boyfriend *before* the divorce was even started, back in their Las Vegas days.

After a big fight, which included Bobby disparaging some minor flaw in her figure and Lori claiming his parentage was in question—namely not human—Bobby had stormed out. For lack of a better place to go, he sat in a bar for two hours, making a single beer last longer than was polite or thirst-quenching. That time, he didn't go back and apologize to her. Instead, he cleaned out the old camper parked on their driveway, a payment for work he did earlier that year, in lieu of cash from a failing contractor.

They had dreamed of pleasant trips to the desert, even to the Pacific Coast. But Bobby had never spent the time to get the camper into habitable condition. Over the next three weeks, he gradually turned that little metal box into a home.

"Bobby," Lori called from the driveway one evening on the third week of his stay in the camper, "I'm goin' on a date, and I don't want no guff from you about it, ya hear?"

Lori had stopped by the camper a few times to check if he needed anything. She had once stopped by to finish part of the argument that ended his stay in the house. And she stopped by another time to try to discuss the options for their future as a couple. "So what's it gonna be, Bobby? You in, or you out?" That was how the latter discussion began. It didn't end well.

The words "I'm goin' on a date" hung in the air like the smoke from a pistol shot. Bobby shook physically with the impact of that shot aimed at his heart. He hadn't even realized his marriage was over. To find out on the evening of Lori's first date was brutal. He didn't know what to say. If Lori had only agreed to go out with some other guy to see what Bobby's reaction would be, to see if he would fight for her, he failed the test.

In the face of his silence, she huffed and walked away, her bouncy bleached-blonde hair waving him goodbye and taunting him at the same time.

Bobby just sat down on the steps of the camper and cried. Later, he would consider those tears an improvement over the silent shock of his previous life losses, as if he had matured to the place where he could fall apart when his world did the same.

Bobby returned to the present and the anonymous miles of the interstate highway. "I've been to St. Paul a couple o' times."

"Oh, how long ago was that?"

"Maybe ten years or so, the last time." He slid into some of those memories, much less painful ones than those final days with Lori.

"Mom stayed with me for her last few months."

"You took care of her?"

"As much as anyone could. She knew she was dying, and she knew how painful it was to hear her cough, and to watch her wasting away. She didn't let me get close most of the time, even though we lived in the same house."

"So, she was able to stay at yer place to the end?"

"Almost. Right up till the last month. She had to be in the hospital then. I couldn't handle giving her all those drugs and doing all the nursing stuff. I still had to work to pay the bills."

"You didn't used to have to apologize for that sorta thing." He was intentionally not looking at that woeful little girl still hanging around Tracy's neck. "You can let that go. Ya did what ya could."

He could see her shoulders relax, and the slow shake of her head didn't seem like denial.

Bobby reached over and gently patted her twice on the shoulder. She was driving, so he was careful not to stir more emotion with further words.

Bobby knew that a father's blessing could make a big impact on a person. And he knew his broader spiritual authority in the invisible world—invisible to almost everyone else. He saw one of those annoying little hangers-on leave the vehicle when he encouraged her to forgive herself. He couldn't tell how much Tracy would know about that.

The Hardest Day

"So what happened with your wife's first date with some other guy?" Anna stopped biting the end of the ballpoint pen and cocked her head, wondering if she dared ask. But the appearance of a daughter Bobby hadn't known about seemed to demand deeper digging.

"Well, I woke up in the middle of the night to see the house lights were all off, and my wife's date had not gone home."

There in the dark, staring at the torn and patched ceiling of the camper, Bobby had lain paralyzed. His stomach churned, and his mind ground large stones into gravel, and gravel into sand. And from somewhere, more stones arrived. When he shoveled away some of his shock, he began to think of reasonable explanations for the date's car still being there at two thirty in the morning. Perhaps it failed to start and the guy had to walk home or had to get a reluctant ride home from Lori. There were possible explanations. But none seemed likely.

Though it was a warm seventy degrees outside, Bobby shivered. Then he felt like throwing up. He sat up to make a break for the chemical toilet, but the nausea passed. Sitting up, visions of entering the house and confronting the man in bed with his wife began to come together like the parts of an impromptu stage play. It seemed a familiar drama. It included lots of shouting, threats, and eventual violence of one kind or another. Bobby didn't own a gun. Everyone on the property that night would be glad of that. Large kitchen knives and a couple of softball bats constituted the arsenal at Bobby's disposal. Those would be messy. He had worked for a butcher once, but had to quit. Too much blood. Though there was certainly no humor about the situation at the time, for Anna, Bobby seasoned his telling with irony.

But that had been the hardest night of his life—harder than riding on the freight train away from the dead body of his grandmother, harder than waking up in the hospital with broken bones and fifty stitches to find out that his parents were both dead. The night in the camper was harder, perhaps, because there had been nothing Bobby could do about those other tragic events. With his wife in bed with another man, in Bobby's house just twenty feet away, he had options.

Setting the guy's car on fire had been the leading possibility around five in the morning, but Bobby didn't want to go to jail, and he figured the police would know who started the fire. His anger was sufficiently muted by shock that he remained paralyzed for most of the night—physically at first, and emotionally throughout.

His solution, arrived upon at sunrise, was to do what he had been doing all his adult life. Bobby hit the road. He didn't look back. He didn't leave any bloodshed or fires to look back on. He just walked. He did empty their joint bank accounts before leaving town. That was the closest thing to revenge. He wouldn't have done that, however, if he had known Lori was pregnant with their daughter.

If he had known that, everything would have been different.

As it happened in reality, not in perfect retrospect, Bobby disappeared from Lori's life, only connecting again after she filed for divorce back in Moline. They were not required to confront each other, and he felt no need to shout his indignation at her, nor to hire a lawyer to explain it. No-fault divorce was the way in the Illinois courts, but not in the hearts of living and breathing people.

Though Bobby was certain that their marriage ended because of Lori's infidelity, he also knew he had set himself up for that fall. Sitting in a bar in Spokane, Washington, a few months after his departure from the camper and the night of murderous thoughts, Bobby talked to the wisest man he had met since Cecil Tomlins.

Jonny Bernal explained that he was not the regular bartender. He had merely fallen into the position when someone else called in sick. Jonny didn't even drink, sober for twenty years by the time he met Bobby. And Bobby didn't ever drink enough to disqualify him from legally driving home. All of this, of course, made a bar a very unlikely place for Bobby and Jonny to meet.

"So, what was her name?"

Bobby had been hinting around about a deep wound he had just suffered, but he had kept the specifics to himself. "You assume it was a woman?"

"You gay?"

"No."

"It was a woman."

Bobby sipped his ginger ale, forgoing even his usual beer that particular night. "Yes, it was a woman—my wife, in fact."

"Didn't know you were married."

"*Was* married."

"Ex-wife, then?"

Bobby nodded. "You married?"

Jonny lifted his left hand from behind the bar and thumbed his wedding ring, which hung a bit loosely on his fourth finger. "Happily."

Bobby looked down at the bar, briefly distracted by the handful of Spanish peanuts in the cut glass dish just to his left. He crunched through half a dozen more. He always left a big tip, so he expected Jonny wouldn't mind the excessive protein consumption. "Good." Bobby was sincerely glad about Jonny's satisfaction in his marriage.

"I have a great wife. Clearly do not deserve the woman. She's as true as any person could ever be—except Jesus, I guess."

Bobby looked up from the last of the peanuts, but he didn't say anything. He didn't feel that he had anything to say.

"But the thing that makes it so happy isn't just how great Amanda is. The thing is that God is the one who makes me happy. I learned even before I met Amanda that there's no happy life if you don't have a speaking relationship with your Father in heaven."

"My Papa." Bobby said it without thinking how it would sound.

Jonny smiled his Henry Fonda smile, movie-star big and full of pure joy. "I see you know him."

Bobby looked at Jonny, making sure they were understanding each other. "I decided to call him Papa 'cause it just felt like what I needed a few years back, alone on the road."

"The Bible says we can call God 'Abba,' which is exactly the same thing."

That sounded familiar, but Bobby was confused about the pop music icons with a similar name. He set that aside and pursed his lips. "I thought I was inventin' my own religion."

"Well, I don't know about that, but traveling through life with your Papa is pretty righteous as far as I can tell."

That looped Bobby back to Jonny's comments about a happy marriage. "I guess I can't say my life is happy, given the way she betrayed me. But it's at least sane, which is likely a lot better than it would have been without my Papa."

"Amen to that, brother."

"That wasn't what I expected to hear at a bar, but it sounded like the word o' God to me at the time." Bobby squinted at Anna as if assessing whether she understood what he was saying.

She nodded. "I hear it's a good psychological practice, counting your blessings."

Bobby nodded back, apparently satisfied she was tracking with him.

Late Summer in Minneapolis

Accustomed to waking up in a new place, Bobby only paused to appreciate that *this* place had a painted ceiling and a firm bed as he turned his head toward the window in Tracy's guest room. Against the clean canvas of the quiet morning, he took a moment to contemplate how their relationship had started like a dance among lighted torches. Bobby's clothes were made of asbestos, and Tracy's woven from firecracker fuses. He was determined to do what he could to keep her from those flames. It was a fatherly task.

Climbing out of bed in the first light of an amber sun, Bobby paused to assess the sunrise out of his second-story window. Clouds the color of glowing coals showed golden edges as the day opened with an artistic flourish. "That's a good one, Papa." And he paused to talk about his day, his hopes, and his concerns. He also listened for some advice on how to do that dance among the torches.

"*She's waiting for you to hurt her.*"

Bobby knew that meant Tracy would be looking for pain and would misinterpret his actions to fit her expectations. To some extent, there was nothing he could do about that besides be prepared to apologize. He had learned to discount the value of being right or of declaring his rights. Those had never brought him the same joy as being together with people he loved.

"*You do love her, then?*"

He heard the question the same way he heard the earlier warning. Even if this was just his own mind focusing on something that was true, something that he could know without divine revelation, he believed it was God who opened the doors in his mind.

Bobby ruminated on the rich gift he had received—a daughter. That was a pretty grand gift.

"*You're welcome,*" said that inner voice.

When Tracy came downstairs in her fleece robe and slippers, Bobby was sitting in the tall chair by the sliding glass door to the patio. The morning light shone on the book he was reading. He looked up and smiled at her, still basking in his welcomed gift.

Tracy smiled back, a smile that implied some effort. She shuffled through the dining room to the kitchen, keeping their reunion short and sweet.

When Tracy entered the kitchen, Bobby heard her exclaim, "Wow, this is nice. How did you get this so early in the day?"

Bobby let his book rest in his lap. He didn't know what Tracy was referring to. He had stayed out of the kitchen. But he had a feeling his Papa had played a trick on him. Instead of committing to his innocence or guilt, Bobby stood up to see the cause of her exclamation.

On the small island in the middle of her kitchen sat a large basket of fruit, the kind you get at Christmas from your office, or that you might send to an ailing relative if you have plenty of money. It was a large and elegant arrangement of at least five different fruits that Bobby could see.

It prompted a quick recollection while Tracy stared at him with her question still in the queue between them. "I was sittin' there thinkin' that I would really like some fruit this morning." It was the first thing that came to mind.

"Well, it's a good thing you found this," said Tracy. "I don't think I had a single bite of fresh fruit in here."

Bobby guessed he was benefiting from Tracy not being fully awake. She hadn't noticed how he avoided her question. Nor had she followed up on her assumption that it would have been very difficult for him to buy such an arrangement so early in the morning ... in a strange neighborhood ... without taking her car. That was a lot to ignore. He assumed she would sharpen her scrutiny as she opened her eyes and smelled the first pot of coffee.

Tracy filled a Pyrex pot with water, poured the water into the reservoir of the coffee maker, and slipped the pot into place. As Bobby predicted, she revisited her surprise. "So, how did you get this so early? I can't think of anywhere around here that sells such nice fruit. And you didn't borrow my car, did you?"

Bobby shook his head, a chuckle at God's little joke suppressed by guilt at being a party to it. "Well, it's like I said. I was wishin' we could have some fruit for breakfast, but that was all. I didn't *do* anythin' about it. I just wished. And I sat down to read my book." His voice sounded weak and doubtful even to himself. The real doubt was that Tracy would believe him. "I haven't been out o' the house, and I ain't been in the kitchen till just now."

Tracy set the bag of ground coffee on the counter and walked over to the edifice of fruit on her counter, watching Bobby as if he might make a break for the front door. She foraged for a few seconds, as if in search of a note. She found none.

"I wonder who would have sent it, and how they got it into my kitchen." Tracy shivered visibly. "Kinda creepy to think of someone getting in here while I was gone." Then she stopped again. "But I was in here last night. I got a glass of milk. How did I miss this big thing sitting here?"

This wasn't the first time Bobby had to decide how hard to try to get someone to believe something that had little chance of a credulous reception. Just two months ago, a friend of his had received a new car from an anonymous giver. Bobby knew who that giver was, but allowed the source to remain anonymous in light of his confidence that his friend wouldn't believe him. This, however, was just a basket of fruit, and this was his newly found daughter.

He wanted her to know him. And to trust him. "This happens sometimes with me." Bobby sighed. "I know it's unusual, and maybe hard to believe." He stopped and checked for signs that Tracy wanted to hear what followed his introduction. Her eyes were wide and her lips parted slightly, an expression that could only be described as blank. That look reminded him of Lori. But he decided to dodge that distraction and push on. "It's almost like a practical joke, in a way. This is the sort of thing God's done with me lots o' times."

Tracy shook her head in short, vigorous pulses. "Wait. You didn't go out and buy this?"

Bobby shook his head slowly, still restraining the guffawing grin that would have been his natural response to such a gift.

"And it wasn't here last night when I was in the kitchen, 'cause I would have seen it."

Bobby nodded, even though that wasn't really a question.

"God?" Tracy sounded as if she had just discovered that three-letter word buried in Bobby's explanation.

He grinned slightly, apologetically. He wasn't sorry that his Papa loved to give him things, and often in surprising ways. He was sorry for the discomfort this was likely to introduce between him and Tracy.

"God sent this basket of fruit?"

"I'm thinkin' that's what happened. He hasn't denied it."

She was still standing next to the island counter, her hands hanging in the air above the fruit basket as if she might catch something from touching it again. "I'm trying to think of why you would say something like that."

"I'm wishin' I hadn't said it now. And I'm wishin' I hadn't started all of it by thinkin' I would like some fruit. But, if he decided it was a good thing to give us, then I gotta say what I think is goin' on, just so ya don't drive yerself nuts trying to figure out who burgled yer house while we were sleepin'." He thought about it for a second. "Is it burglary if someone sneaks in and leaves you a gift?"

Tracy went to the sliding glass door to the patio and pulled at it. Locked. Walking briskly through the living room, she rattled the front door. Then she disappeared while she checked the garage door. She cast a glance at the windows, perhaps restraining herself from checking all those. "I don't know what to say." She propped her hands on her hips and arched her carefully shaped eyebrows as high as they would go.

Bobby knew what to say. "Let's have some fruit." Feeling a proprietary interest in this one thing in the kitchen, he eased out of his comfort zone to step toward the knives. "It looks darn good."

Tracy lurched into action and picked up where she had left off with the coffee. Her zealous attention to measuring grounds, starting the coffee maker, pulling out cream and sugar, spoons and cups, would have embarrassed a hard-working waiter in a busy restaurant. Finally, she stared out the window as the coffee began to drip.

Bobby imagined she was checking her brain for other possible explanations, like maybe an old boyfriend with a key to the house. But why the guy didn't leave a note had to be part of what crunched her skeptical brow.

Bobby enthusiastically devoured half an apple, half a pear, and half a banana. It seemed the polite way to help himself and answer his craving for fruit at the same time. What others considered the polite thing in most situations required a wild guess for Bobby. But that suited him, because he found that when he didn't know what to do, his Papa would help him out.

Tracy prepared toast and coffee for herself, then broke her silence. "Can I get you anything? Help yourself to the coffee. I made plenty."

Pulling a jar of preserves from one corner of the fruit basket, Bobby said, "How 'bout a couple o' pieces o' that toast. We can try this stuff on it." He read the label on the three-ounce jar. "Mmm, strawberry. My favorite."

Tracy turned to shelter herself in the business of food preparation again.

Suddenly Bobby knew that Tracy had watched jealously in years past as others received grand fruit baskets like this one, and she had never been the lucky recipient. She loved fresh fruit and would have been prolifically grateful if Bobby had simply said he was the source of this cornucopian blessing. As it stood, she felt trapped in her own kitchen with this invasive gift and her oddball father, but also with her fruitful fantasy being fulfilled.

As soon as the toast finished browning in the toaster, Tracy retreated from the scene. She did eat some of the sliced fruit Bobby left on the island, but didn't say anything more about its origins.

Bobby had no specific plans for how long he would stay with Tracy, but he felt some pressure to recover from the mixed blessing of the fruit basket. He settled into the idea of staying in the area, at least, for a few weeks. He would stay in Tracy's house for the time being and listen for other instructions from his Divine Provider, as always.

A Vision of Papa's House

As Bobby had explained to Anna at that last meeting at the mall, he had grown into the practice of calling God his Papa, expanding on some of what he was taught in Grandma Casey's country church, and pioneering the degree to which he took it seriously. This notion of God as a loving and present Father was carved more deeply into Bobby a couple years after he left Lori.

He discovered that he loved classical music, and especially Tchaikovsky. He discovered the Russian composer's music in a library in Salt Lake City. He went to the library to find air-conditioning during a hot spell and discovered their multimedia resources. As far as he could recall, he chose the Tchaikovsky piano concerto recording at random, perhaps for the artwork on the LP cover. But, through those old public-library headphones, he discovered a gateway to heaven.

It didn't matter to Bobby whether Tchaikovsky was a sinner or a saint. All that mattered was the elevating music. He couldn't tell the difference between a concerto and a symphony, but learned that, where Tchaikovsky was concerned, he loved them all. His first investment in quality electronics came from his desire to listen to this music in his little downtown apartment on cooler days.

One evening at home, Bobby was praying while he listened to a piano concerto, playfully raising and lowering the tone of his prayer to go with the music. When he stopped to listen for God's voice, a new experiment at that point, his mind began to wander. But that wandering seemed to have momentum, a sort of downhill gravity.

That was the night Bobby went to see his Father's house.

At first, it seemed only that he had found a source of light that was more clearly visible with his eyes closed. Then he could feel a sense of a place, and sounds filled in around the light.

He didn't see the face of his Papa during that tour, only his back and his hands as he pointed out the various rooms in the house. But Bobby knew who was leading him through that magnificent place. The one leading him through the halls and rooms of his house was a warm and welcoming Papa with an infinite invitation.

Bobby told Anna he didn't feel like he could accurately describe that experience or interpret all that it meant. It was primarily just that—an experience. Something to be felt and received and enjoyed more than understood.

In that house, he saw a room filled with music. There were saints and angels dancing wildly, laughing and singing with music that seemed to come out of the walls. He stepped into another room filled with small children each meeting with Papa as if Papa had been cloned so there were hundreds of him available to devote attention to the heart of every child.

In yet another room, people were leaping and laughing and showing off some part of their body that had been healed. Bobby couldn't tell who was healing them, but assumed later that they were healing each other.

Before entering one room, his Papa gave him a hard hat made of gold. It was glossy and heavy. When he stepped through the door, Bobby understood the purpose of the helmet. Small gold coins were raining down from the ceiling. He didn't look up to see how, or where they came from, not interested in getting his face pelted with the shiny money.

Toward the end of the tour, his Father paused before a huge set of double doors. Though Bobby maintained that he didn't see his Papa's face on that tour, he knew Papa was smiling extra big before opening those doors. When his Papa turned and swung those doors wide, Bobby saw what he understood to be a scenic overview of the expanse of heaven, a magnificent sight that Bobby refused to even try to describe to Anna. In the middle of that experience of beauty and wonder, Bobby became aware of someone flying toward him, up out of the divine city.

Then Bobby understood that Papa's excitement had not been about showing him the scenic overlook of heaven. Papa was excited about showing him his Son.

Jesus arrived on the sort of balcony on which they stood. Jesus's face, the laughing eyes and engulfing smile, Bobby saw quite clearly, leaving a tattoo on his brain—one that would never fade. Then Jesus wrapped him in a big hug.

The Father joined that embrace, but then pulled Bobby's attention to something he wanted to tell him. It seemed like this was the central message he wanted Bobby to take out of this experience.

Bobby held his breath in anticipation. He looked at Jesus and realized that he, too, was waiting expectantly.

Then Papa said, "Bobby, I want you to take this back with you. I want you to take all that you saw here back to your life on earth. It is not just for you to *tell*, but for you to *do*. You can take anything you saw in heaven back to earth. That's what I want you to do for the rest of your life."

The next morning, Bobby had recognized a new feeling, the feeling that he belonged somewhere else, and not somewhere he could reach on a Greyhound bus or Amtrak train. And this place in which he belonged, his true home, was something he could bring with him on his travels. Though it was difficult to see how it would impact stocking shelves in a grocery store or hammering shingles on a roof, Bobby began to understand that the things he witnessed in his Papa's house would be useful in the relationships he formed wherever he went.

Two weeks after his vision of heaven, Bobby was on a roofing crew, finishing up after a hot day on a high, steep roof atop some townhouses. Bobby was drinking the last of his water, tepid and tasting like his plastic thermos.

Miguel, one of the roofers, began shouting at his brother-in-law, Gerardo, who was also part of the crew. Though Bobby spoke little Spanish, he could tell that Miguel was cursing Gerardo.

Bobby allowed himself to notice the presence of one of those dark strangers that hung around people. The one standing on Miguel's shoulder, like a pet vulture glaring down at Gerardo, gave Bobby a shiver.

Miguel noticed Bobby watching them. He stopped, his head bowed in embarrassment at first, but then he glared at Bobby, someone for whom he had never had a harsh word. "What are *you* lookin' at?"

Without thinking it through, Bobby just said what he was seeing. "I'm lookin' at you curse yer brother-in-law with words ya don't really mean. And I'm seein' this sort o' devil hangin' over yer back, pushin' ya to do it, just like he's pushin' ya to yell at me." Though he couldn't have predicted the result of saying all that, right there on the front lawn of those townhouses, Bobby felt a surrounding peace as everyone sat speechless for a few seconds.

Then Miguel responded in a squeezed little voice. "I can feel what you're talkin' about. Can you get it off me?"

Since he hadn't formulated any expectations of a response from Miguel, Bobby didn't suffer the complication of surprise at that request. He simply complied. Looking at the gruesome demon, Bobby commanded it to leave in a stern and steady voice. "Get off o' him, you nasty demon. Let him go right now."

The first effect of that command was the dark creature wrapping one arm tightly around Miguel's neck as if he were getting a good grip for a fight. From Miguel, this resulted in a choking sound and his face turning deeper red.

Groaning at the change in Miguel's face, Gerardo jumped up from his seat on the grass and said something in Spanish that Bobby assumed was part prayer and part profanity.

"Let him go, and get outta here now." Bobby leaned toward the creature.

The demon cowered and scrambled to maintain his hold on Miguel.

"Go." Bobby said it more quietly the next time.

The creature turned and flew away, much like that spirit of death had left Cecil years before.

Gerardo was hopping around like his feet were on fire.

When the demon left, Miguel gasped for air and clung to his throat. "*Aaaiiiiiaahh!*" He flopped backward onto the grass, panting.

Bobby stood up with his hands still fisted at his sides.

When the three men all stopped to look at each other, they joined in a small chorus of uncomfortable laughter.

That event caused his coworkers to look differently at Bobby, of course, but he was still working out for himself the meaning of that visit to heaven, and he wasn't ready to be venerated as a saint. He moved on to another town soon after that incident.

But he continued to wake up each day with a growing sense of his Father's house surrounding him, even if he slept in an abandoned car or in a single-room-occupancy hotel. And, most of all, Bobby was beginning to feel that he *belonged* to that house, and it belonged to him. It wasn't just his Father's house, it was *his* house too.

What Is There to Do in Minneapolis?

Bobby's decision to stay in Tracy's house didn't mean he was resigned to being caged there. It wasn't a bad house, and there was nothing wrong with staying with Tracy ... for a little while. But Bobby was a wanderer. It was still early on that first Saturday when he began to consider finding a place of his own. That way he could stay in the area long enough to get to know Tracy without that confined feeling.

He forgot all about that when Tracy reappeared in the living room, all moist and fresh from her morning shower and makeup. "You wanna do some shopping?"

Bobby set his book on the dining room table. He didn't expect she intended to buy him things. He had already decided to get some new clothes, so the answer to her offer was an instant yes.

Tracy took Bobby to a nearby men's clothing store. After he picked up a pair of button-up shirts and a package of white T-shirts, Tracy followed him to the cash register. "In case yer wonderin'"—which he knew she was—"I'm payin' fer this stuff. I can take care o' myself." He smiled freely at her, detecting some relief reflected back at him.

Tracy nodded and watched as Bobby slipped a plastic card from his wallet. He handed it to the cashier along with the clothes, and she rang up the small order. Bobby had to enter his pin number since it was a debit card.

Having met him in a YMCA, from which he had been asked to leave at the end of the maximum-length stay, and seeing his homeless-man outfit, Tracy was surely curious how he supported himself. That he was her father would intensify that curiosity. But she seemed shy about asking him what she wanted to know. Perhaps his answers so far had been too disturbing.

When they walked out of the store, Bobby tipped his head toward Tracy. "I think I need some more stuff. How about we go to the Mall of America?"

"Uh, yeah. We could do that if you want. It's kind of crowded and noisy on a Saturday."

Bobby sensed she was trying to protect him, and didn't mind going there herself. "Sounds good to me. I feel like being around people."

Tracy stumbled slightly down the curb next to her car. Apparently he had surprised her. Again.

From the parking garage at the mall to the clothing stores, Tracy followed Bobby, though it was *her* city. He knew where he wanted to go, even zeroing in on the part of each store that he needed to visit. He was following his divine GPS.

By noon, he had accumulated a considerable pile of bags with large-lettered logos of various stores.

Tracy was helping him carry his loot, along with a couple bags of her own.

"How about I buy you lunch?" He noted weariness dragging at Tracy's face.

She followed him out of Macy's toward a Mexican place on that level. On the way, they passed the movie theaters. One of the movies playing there, among the huge assortment of pictures, was about Jesus—or at least a Hollywood rendition of Jesus. Bobby stopped next to the poster and looked at it for a minute.

Tracy stood next to him, alternating between looking at the poster and at her father.

He reached up and touched the glass display case. He muttered a blessing under his breath and turned back to their quest for lunch.

The cantina was bright and lively. The food was creative and not very expensive. Bobby had only been to Mexico once, but the restaurant reminded him of a touristy area south of the border. Tracy had recommended the place hesitantly, perhaps still trying to guess what sort of restaurant her father would favor.

"This is a lot of fun." Bobby chomped on a fish taco to punctuate the sentiment.

"You like the fish tacos?"

He chewed and swallowed. "I like shoppin' and' havin' lunch with you."

The lift of Tracy's eyebrows and tilt of her head didn't tell him much, but she did seem more relaxed.

Bobby leveled a friendly smile her way and watched her face go first blank and then contort in an apparent effort to stop an outburst of tears.

She grabbed her iced tea as if it might douse that urge.

He pretended not to notice, just praying for her silently.

Picking up the check, Bobby included his usual large tip. He ignored Tracy's truncated objection, part of a word that he didn't recognize. He wondered if he should apologize for surprising her so many times. He was thinking especially of what they were about to witness.

He led the way back in the direction they had come. He could feel Tracy's hesitation a half step behind his right shoulder. At the sight of a small pile of people lying on the floor near the movie theater, he reached back and took her arm. He was a little worried she might fall down as well.

"What ...?" Another truncated response.

"Oh. Well, the Holy Spirt does that to folks now and again." He knew his explanation was little help to Tracy, but he was hearing instructions about praying for some of those people, and had to postpone his duties to his daughter for a bit.

As they drew closer, Bobby could hear some of the strangers laughing drunkenly. He looked one more apology toward Tracy before stopping in front of the Jesus poster. He could sense Tracy doing that same turn from the poster to looking at him and back, probably making the reasonable connection.

Bobby squatted, placing his packages on the floor just behind him. He reached for a man with curly red hair whose glasses had worked their way up to his eyebrows. The man was weeping as hard as the others were laughing.

He spoke to the man on whose shoulder he had rested his hand, knowing his words also applied to others strewn around him. "This is what God feels like if you let him get close to ya. He met ya here, next to that picture o' Jesus, 'cause yer defenses were down. Ya didn't expect he'd find ya here, but he's always with you. I just set the door open a bit here, and you walked in. Just wanted ya to know that this is God."

Bobby stood up, gathered his bags, and looked at Tracy. He raised his eyebrows to say, "Ready?" and he set off toward the parking garage.

It was nearly a minute into that little march when Tracy finally closed her mouth.

Bobby checked on her again, being careful not to walk too fast, and waited for her to ask a question or two. Her rapid blinking seemed to imply she wasn't close enough to a question to get her hands on it, let alone to pass it to him.

Less than two minutes away from that pile by the theater, a woman caught up with them, breathing hard, as if her pursuit had started way back by that party at the picture of Jesus.

"You're him," she said. "You're the miracle man." She swallowed hard and struggled to catch her breath.

The woman was probably about Bobby's age, with a uniformly plump figure from her eyebrows to her feet, which were swollen out of her low-heeled shoes. Bobby didn't think she had been part of that pile of people, but she seemed somehow linked with that little scene by the theater.

"I saw you at that church in St. Paul four or five years ago. Or maybe it was longer. Anyway, it's good to have you back. Are you doing meetings somewhere?" She seemed to say all that with one breath.

The three of them now stood on the ramp to the west parking garage, people strolling and scooting past in both directions. Bobby focused on the red-face woman with the short gray hair. "No meetin's planned. Just visitin' my daughter."

"Oh, really?" The woman turned toward Tracy, maybe a bit suspiciously. "Can I get him to pray for me?"

Tracy did another of those hard blinks. "Uh, sure. I guess so. But ..."

Bobby didn't know what had fallen off the end of that reply, but he took up the initiative. "It's good to see ya. What was yer name?" He shifted a few bags to his left hand and offered his right.

"Mary." She glanced at Tracy before asking Bobby more directly, "Could you just pray for me real quick?"

Bobby smiled and kept hold of her hand. "Okay, Mary. Just take the power o' God. He wants to rearrange yer heart and mind the way you like to rearrange yer livin' room furniture."

Mary made a little descending "*Ooooo*" and then pitched backward onto the floor.

Tracy dropped her bags and tried to catch the older woman halfway down. She managed to deflect Mary away from her own feet.

Bobby hung on with that one hand and helped lower Mary to the tiles. He stood over her for a few seconds, redistributed his bags, and listened if there was more for him to say or do. Then he motioned for Tracy to follow him toward the car.

Tracy gathered her share of the luggage and clip-clopped after him. "Wait—you're just gonna leave her there?"

Bobby glanced back toward Mary and then locked eyes with Tracy. "Not me. It wasn't my idea. She wanted it right there, so that's where Papa put her. Not what I woulda recommended, but I think she was pretty hungry for it."

"Hungry for what? What did you just do to her? And those people by the movie theater? You did that too, didn't you? I mean, you did something when we went past that poster. What was that?"

Bobby kept walking at the same pace, but he looked squarely at Tracy again with an easy grin. He was glad to see she had broken free from her shock. Now they could get to know each other.

Stuff Just Started Happening

Anna leaned back in the medium-blue upholstered chair at the mall where she interviewed Bobby the second time. "So, after that visit to heaven when you were in your early thirties, your life was turned upside down?"

He nodded and proceeded to narrate his next major move. When he left Salt Lake City, he eventually landed in Oakland, California. During the three months in between, he had a dozen strange encounters like the one with Miguel and Gerardo. In a way, he knew why it was happening. But he wasn't sure exactly *what* it was, and what he was supposed to *do* about it.

Wandering on the west side of Oakland one Wednesday night, Bobby prayed as he walked, his hands dug into his jacket pockets. An unusually cool day in October made that posture more a necessity than mere habit. He turned up the collar of his Mackinac jacket and found his pockets again. Rounding a corner, he stepped right into a current of fervent singing. The sound emanated from a green and brown building with a stoop painted red and a hand-lettered sign next to the door—Blood of Jesus Holiness Church.

Bobby had been entering all kinds of churches since he left home, many of them the wrong kind of church if you asked the people at the previous church he had visited. This predominantly African American Holiness church would certainly have been offended by some of the places Bobby had worshipped recently, but he didn't let that stop him from enjoying their hospitality.

The building into which Bobby ventured had a small lobby like a butcher's counter area. There was no counter, of course, and no dispenser of numbers for those awaiting their meat orders. Where the back of the butcher's store would have been—or baker's or tailor's—a forest of arms and legs greeted the visitor. It was at least eighty degrees in that room, mostly accumulated body heat, judging from the aroma. But Bobby wasn't easily offended, including on an olfactory level. A few heads turned toward him. He was not the only white person in the room, so his presence probably didn't cause much distraction for that reason. He did, however, catch someone's sustained attention.

When he saw the gnarled old woman leave her pew to home in on him, Bobby's heart stopped. For two seconds he was certain it was Sister Iris, the woman who had brought revival fire to his grandma's country church when he was a boy. But that illusion passed, and his heart restarted. Then he thought he understood something about that heart-stopping moment. The woman approaching him—now with her hands raised above her head as if she were prepared to catch something before it dented her church hat—did not really *look* like Sister Iris. But something more profound connected her to Sister Iris. What Bobby saw in the little woman that stood in front of him, clicking away in an unfamiliar language, was the same fire he had seen in Sister Iris. In that, they were twins. And Bobby realized it was no accident he had wandered in that door. Nor was it accidental that this old woman had shown up to a Wednesday service this week. They had an appointment, and it was divinely arranged.

Bobby saw two very large angels accompanying the old woman. No celebrity or politician had ever been accompanied by a more intimidating bodyguard. But Bobby was not frightened of those fiery warriors whose eyes stared intently at him. They smiled at his attention, and their smiles shone as if they had halogen lights on their tongues.

"You better get a hold o' what's got a hold o' you." The old woman's hands rested on Bobby's forehead now.

Two large men stepped out of their pews and took up positions behind Bobby at the back of the sanctuary.

Bobby was only peripherally aware of the two men behind him and didn't associate them with himself particularly. He had never seen this woman lay hands on someone, though he *had* seen Sister Iris do something similar. Standing there in that strange church, he felt a completion—God tying the ends of a string or connecting the cables of an electric circuit. He had only a second to think about that.

After that pause, lightning came out of the contact between Bobby and Sister Pamela, the woman to whom he would only be formally introduced later. It made more sense to say that the lightning came from the contact, and not from Sister Pamela, because it wasn't Bobby who hurtled backward at the thunderous explosion.

Whether there was an audible explosion heard by everyone in the room was disputable. In Bobby's head, it sounded like thunder, and the flash of light that blinded his eyes reminded him of lightning. The wave that turned that little church lady into a projectile for Jesus looked to Bobby like a blast wave.

Bobby didn't fly backward, as those two bemused brothers behind him had surely assumed. But the boom did drop him to his knees, and it did start a flood of tears that made no rational sense to him in the moment.

While Bobby crumpled into a fetal position, wracked with weeping, he was vaguely aware of Sister Pamela vibrating noisily as she laughed. The worship around them rose to a higher volume, and a few people started stomping. But the room did not collapse into the bowels of the earth or launch into the stratosphere as it seemed it might when Bobby and Sister Pamela first met.

Two hours later, a time period that felt exactly like a minute, he was sitting in the back pew with a large woman fanning him with two hand-fans and saying over and over, "Thank you, Jesus. Thank you, Lord."

Bobby slowly leaned to his left and peered down the aisle. There, he could see the bottom of Sister Pamela's shoes. He looked because of a sound that resonated throughout the room, a room with only a dozen people left in it. The sound did not seem human at first. It certainly did not seem like something a one-hundred-pound granny could produce. It sounded like a cross between a bullfrog and a didgeridoo from the outback of Australia.

Sitting up straight now that he knew the source of that sound, Bobby began to hear a rhythm in it, like human speech. Only, the voice didn't fit the little lady on the floor. He leaned to his left again to check for one of those creepy critters he had seen hanging around people who spoke in strange voices. But he couldn't see anything like that. What he did see was more surprising.

Sitting next to Sister Pamela on the floor was a six- or seven-year-old girl, her eyes closed tight, and her right hand resting on the old woman's stomach. The girl seemed to be praying intensely. On the other side of Sister Pamela, in a similar posture to the little girl, sat one of those big angels. In contrast to the girl, however, the angel was drumming vigorously on the old woman's chest. The resounding beat Bobby was hearing came from that angel drumming on the old lady like she was a heavenly bongo.

He looked to the woman who was now only fanning him with one fan and who had followed his gaze to look at Sister Pamela. Someone had thrown a coat over the old woman to preserve some of her dignity, apparently. Only her shoes could be seen clearly from where Bobby sat.

"Do you hear that drumming sound?" His voice cracked like he was dying of thirst, which he just realized he was.

"Drumming sound?" The large woman turned an inquisitive eye on him, but seemed more curious than doubtful. "Are you hearing in the Spirit?"

Bobby had accepted the notion that he could often "see in the Spirit," as someone had once said. Perhaps no one else in the room heard the drumming or saw the angel. He did wonder about the little girl, whose hand pulsed in rhythm with that angel's music. The other thing Bobby realized at that moment was that the drumming was a signal, and it was calling *him*.

What does it mean when God sends an angel to drum out a message on the chest of a prone church lady at Wednesday night prayer meeting? Bobby was new to all this.

He felt obligated to wait for Sister Pamela to rise to meet him, despite needing to be at work at the docks early the next morning. As it turned out, he only had to wait another ten minutes. He greeted everyone else still present that late night while keeping his eye on the old woman and the little girl, who must have been up past her bedtime.

"This is how Sister Pamela started out." A man named Brother Bert held Bobby's hand in a prolonged shake. They both watched the girl next to the sister on the floor.

Bobby pictured the old woman as a small child, sitting cross-legged next to some saint who had been plowed over by an angel or two. He wondered whether the drumming had also been part of Sister Pamela's start.

Several hands reached to assist when Sister Pamela began to get up. The little girl had tried to help, but she was too small to raise the old woman. The large woman with the fans scooped up the little girl as Sister Pamela slowly rose and began to smooth her dress.

The others still waiting—standing in twos or threes, telling stories, and exchanging prayer requests—fell silent when Sister Pamela took a step toward Bobby once again.

Twice during her stiff walk toward him she looked as if she would crumple to the floor. She dodged and ducked each time, as if large birds were swooping toward her head. They seemed to be friendly birds, however, judging by the smile on Sister Pamela's face. She just said, "Oh, praise the Lord," when she ducked.

Finally reaching him, Sister Pamela offered Bobby her hand, but didn't speak at first. Instead, she laughed with her lips pulled tight over her slightly stained teeth. She swayed in place, perhaps tempted to get back on the floor with Jesus, the little girl, and the angel.

"I'm Sister Pamela. And you are Bobby, am I right?"

Bobby nodded, impressed by that revelation.

"The Lord is cleanin' you up for what he has prepared for you, young man. Them was washin' tears you had there. Them was for cleanin' out the wounds and makin' way for you to get all healed up."

Bobby nodded. Her words felt as true as any he had ever heard. He breathed a big sigh, feeling a new settling of his soul, as if Sister Pamela's words shuffled and sorted the things he heard during his floor time.

"You got to come back here and share what's on you with the brothers and sisters. They got the Spirit, but they need the power. You got to share what you're carryin'."

This, too, seemed to Bobby to be true and right. He nodded and stretched his lips into a tight grin.

From that day forward, for nearly nine months—a very long stint in one place for Bobby—he stayed in Oakland and attended that church. Though he had readily agreed to Sister Pamela's admonition, he had no idea how to do what she was prescribing. He knew he had something unusual, but he wasn't sure how he had come by it, and thus couldn't know for sure how to give it to other people.

That turned out to not be a problem. Sister Pamela and Pastor Kendrick's plan looked a lot like that first night. Generally it involved Bobby putting his hands on people's heads, and the husky young brothers standing behind the recipient of those hands.

Some nights, it looked like bowling in church, with some sincere saint playing the part of the bowling ball, and those young men being the pins. Bobby expected his assistants, Brian and Kyle, to get fed up with being knocked down so many times, but they seemed to enjoy it. Once in a while, Brian or Kyle would fall down laughing or crying so hard they had to be replaced by Rondell or Willie. But Bobby never ran out of volunteers to *catch*, as they called it. It seemed an appropriate description. And it was about as safe as catching a bowling ball. Somehow the bowling balls didn't get hurt, even on nights when they flew more like footballs.

As unexplained as most of what he did seemed to him, Bobby was learning during those months. He learned to associate different types of power with different types of spiritual accompaniment. Angels, such as accompanied Sister Pamela, would often take a ride into a pile on the floor with a human, and engage in the laughter. Bobby once thought he saw an angel sitting on the floor tickling a middle-aged man who laughed like he was going to burst. On the other hand, he often saw dark and treacherous spirits hanging on the people that received his touch. He witnessed those intruders being cast off as a man or woman crashed to the floor. Those falls seemed far less pleasant, and only resulted in laughter after the creepy parasite left. Eventually, he even learned things to say that would make freedom a more likely outcome from one of his lightning bolts.

It was at the Blood of Jesus Holiness Church that Bobby learned to *direct* his power. When he asked the faithful about this, the explanations involved so many religious terms that he mostly found them useless. "Slain in the Spirit" or "Out under the power" or "Baptized with the Holy Ghost" were all answers that demanded far more questions than he was inclined to ask. But he learned a great deal by simply experiencing the power of God flowing through him. His brothers and sisters in that church gave him confidence about what was happening to him. He grew less afraid of his own gift.

"I sorta felt like a man carrying a bazooka to kill a squirrel, at times." He looked at Anna and shook his head. "But it wasn't my doin'. Not my design, ever."

While in that church, he agreed to anything they asked him to do. That was how he raised a person from the dead for the first time.

In February of the following year, Bobby got a call on the phone in his little apartment, five blocks from the church. "Brother Bobby," said the voice he knew as Sister Marcella.

"Yes, Sister. You need a miracle?" That was not the first thing he generally said to someone who called him on the phone, even if miraculous power was the main thing people sought from him.

This phone call seemed to come to Bobby with a sort of movie trailer, a preview of what was coming. "A little girl?" he said, getting more of the details from that preview.

The woman stopped panting. "Oh, thank you, Jesus. He has already given you the call." Sister Marcella released a shout that she managed not to aim into the phone. "It's little Lashawn," she said, resuming the phone. "I think she's dead. You gotta come right away, brother."

Lashawn was the little girl who had sat praying next to Sister Pamela that first night. Bobby had partnered with the little girl for healing several times since then. He often seemed to need a partner when it came to healing common sicknesses or injuries. But no one doubted that he was the one to call for raising the dead. The calculus of why he was gifted for one miracle but not for another didn't hinder him once he started to trust that it was all from God.

"I'll be right over." He dropped the phone and burst out his front door, not even pausing to put on a jacket. Sister Marcella was Lashawn's aunt, and the little girl lived with her in an apartment next to the church building.

Bobby only slowed when he arrived inside the front door of her building. He stood panting in the small entryway and rang the bell next to Sister Marcella's mailbox. He caught his breath and prayed a straightforward prayer. "I'm gonna need some help on this one, Papa. I'm countin' on you." No "Thy will be done," no "if you can," and no formal opening or closing. Bobby just asked his Papa for what he needed, and left the theologizing to the seminary students.

He knew a few young seminarians who were more or less associated with the church, and who were fascinated by Bobby's power. He, in turn, loved to ask them questions about the Bible and about his experiences in church. Even though he often initiated the conversation, he felt no compulsion to believe anything they said. One great advantage to not assuming you know everything is not needing to change that status, or appearing to have done so in the eyes of others. That was, in fact, one of the things the seminarians seemed to like about Bobby.

When the door buzzer sounded, Bobby swung the inside door open and resumed his hearty pace toward the bedside of the little girl. Having no data on the history of resurrections—or instructions on the proper procedures—he simply assumed it was better to get to it as soon as possible.

Sister Marcella met him at the top of the steep, narrow stairway. She said something that made little sense to him at the time, but which he came to embrace—at least in part—as the years passed. Shaking her head and grabbing onto the bicep of his left arm, she said, "I just know that this is the reason you came to us. You gotta bring my little niece back to life."

For all Bobby had learned, and all that he had done, it seemed impossible at the time to see this one need as his entire reason for being there.

He shrugged at Anna in the relatively empty mall. "After some time, I sorta came around to thinkin' maybe Sister Marcella was right about that. But I'm not inclined to argue."

Sister Marcella led him to her apartment, where Brother Kendrick and Sister Carter met him at the door. Inside, Sister Patrice, the large woman who was Lashawn's other aunt, knelt praying next to the couch. The little girl's inert body lay swathed in blankets, as if she had been cold at the end. It was like a papoose, her head and face surrounded by the woolly blue covers.

Bobby didn't hesitate, still following that drive to attack death as quickly as possible, perhaps influenced by some unconscious thought about acting before her body grew cold, or before her spirit got far away.

Brother Kendrick addressed the others present. "Time to start prayin', sisters." And he led out in petitions for the life of the little girl. Brother Kendrick liked to pace when he preached, his Sunday morning striding only limited by the small stage at the church. As he led prayers for Lashawn, he strode back and forth from the living room to the kitchen. His voice rose, and the sisters moaned. His voice fell, and they shouted their amens and hallelujahs.

Bobby blocked out everything else in the room. He had no problem with the loud prayers surrounding him, but he felt he needed to focus on the little space occupied by the seven-year-old girl whose face had started to grow ashen, and who was inhumanly still. As he focused on that little universe, he knew there were three of them in that small sanctuary—him, Lashawn, and his Papa. The most reassuring part of that realization was that Lashawn was still around. He knew his Papa would always be present, and *not* just when he needed a grandiose miracle. But Lashawn seemed to be waiting for someone to bring her back.

Gently, Bobby put his hands on Lashawn, one on her cold forehead and one in the middle of her torso, as far as he could discern it under the thick blankets. Then he waited. Because he had no training in resurrection, he only did what he knew to do, and that was to wait for something to happen. The premonition that a little girl needed his help had just clicked into his head when Sister Marcella called him. He waited for another burst of insight about what to do next. He sat there like that for a few minutes.

Then an unusual thought came into his head—as if any thought coming to him while trying to raise someone from the dead would *not* be usual. He felt as if he were supposed to cough into Lashawn's mouth. Once again, he was liberated by his ignorance. No one was there to tell him that you shouldn't cough into a dead girl's mouth even if you want to raise her from the dead. He did briefly note that he wouldn't have to worry about giving her germs by this unsanitary method.

Bobby leaned down, not even pausing to check if anyone was looking. He heard a gasp when he bent down with his lips a fraction of an inch from Lashawn's, and then heard a small scream when he coughed into the girl's mouth.

After that cough, Bobby lifted his head a little to get a look at Lashawn. He thought maybe her color had changed, but he could detect no breathing, no movement at all. No one had countermanded the notion that he should cough into her mouth, so he decided to try it again. This his lips touched the cold lips of the little girl. He noted that they were not as cold as he had expected. Again, he coughed.

This time, the saints standing behind him remained silent. This time, it was Lashawn who gasped. Then *she* coughed.

"Yes!" said Bobby.

And Lashawn opened her eyes.

Her Aunt Patrice passed out on the nubby rug next to the coffee table, her thunderous landing shaking the entire apartment. Bobby was worried that another resurrection might be required, but Sister Patrice began to move again in a few seconds.

During those seconds, Sister Marcella squawked and praised and jumped up and down, her lesser weight only shaking the living room.

Brother Kendrick said, "Praise God. Praise God Almighty!" And then he began sobbing like an old woman at a funeral.

Lashawn was looking around, evaluating her surroundings. She seemed to be the wisest person in the room for those first seconds, observing and learning, considering, and perhaps remembering.

Bobby was stuttering in some language he had never heard before, though it reminded him of a thing he had heard coming from Sister Pamela. He didn't know why he was doing it, but made no more effort to *stop* it than he had to *start* it.

When Sister Marcella landed her last vault and shouted her last hallelujah, she scrambled past Bobby to Lashawn's side.

"What happened, Auntie? Was I dead?" Lashawn seemed relieved to have someone to ask.

For a few more seconds, Sister Marcella hesitated, as if she wondered whether it was okay to tell the child she had died. "Yes, dear. You was dead. But Brother Bobby brung you back."

She seemed to revert to her childhood grammar for that frenetic moment.

Lashawn turned her head toward Bobby, who was still look- ing at her even as he felt like he was speaking to someone else— or to no one in particular—in that strange language. The girl just looked at him, as if understanding now what was going on—why all the adults seemed to be simultaneously, but each uniquely, crazy. It apparently all made sense to her.

"I am so hungry, Auntie."

Sister Marcella blurted a laugh that turned quickly into blub- bering, giggling, and slurping.

Bobby started to laugh. He felt drunk, a feeling he had expe- rienced more times than he could recount, both from consump- tion of certain beverages and from prayer meetings at the church. He liked this kind of drunk, assured that there would be no hangover, and feeling no shame at letting his condition be ob- vious to everyone in the room.

That event sealed Bobby's reputation in that church and that neighborhood. One unanticipated consequence for Bobby was the way it sealed his sense of identity. Equally, however, it solidi- fied the degree to which he felt different, even isolated. He wasn't from the neighborhood. His skin was a whiter shade of pale than almost everyone in the church, and he was a natural wanderer. But his new loneliness was deeper than could be ac- counted for by all those things combined.

He needed to find someone who understood him, and who understood what God was calling him to do. He felt the need to find *his* people. He had no intention to settle down anywhere, but he was determined to find his own tribe along the way—peo- ple whom he hoped had a place in their land for such a wanderer as him.

Anna relaxed her hand holding the recorder. "So the people in Oakland taught you a lot, but you still felt like you didn't fit in there." The mall had gotten a bit louder, but a gang of noisy kids moved farther away.

Bobby glanced at those departing kids. "I loved them folks, but to them I was like a performer, or even like a circus freak. I needed to find folks that could just fit me in with them. I was just hopin' there was such people, somewhere."

Helping His Daughter to Know Him

Though Bobby had actually been somewhat annoyed at Mary, the woman in Minneapolis he'd dumped on the mall floor, he was grateful for the way that event opened the conversation between him and Tracy. For a woman who had gone to a lot of trouble to find her father, Tracy was strangely tongue-tied about asking questions his lifestyle surely demanded.

After lunch that Saturday, she started to ask those questions. "I just don't even know where to start." She was driving them home from the mall.

"Well, I could tell ya that people fallin' down like that is pretty common for me. And I see a lot o' people healed when I touch 'em, so there's that."

"And this is something you do in big meetings? That woman said something about holding meetings."

Bobby was relaxing into the comfortable seat of the new Toyota Camry his daughter drove. These questions were familiar to him. "I generally don't hold meetin's myself. Folks invite me to their church, or folks that are havin' meetin's sometimes invite me to tag along. I'm not a preacher or pastor or anythin'."

"Anything? I mean, you're *something*, right? Like a healer or evangelist or something?" Tracy had stopped hyperventilating, which was comforting to her passenger, given dense traffic around the mall.

"I don't have any title or position or anythin'."

"Why? Did something happen?"

Bobby guessed she was thinking of famous healers and ministers who had lost their position by virtue of a lack of virtue. But he stayed out of that pigsty. "I'm just not the kinda minister that wears a suit and has an office or a church or a TV show—or anything. That's not what God called me to."

"So, God called you to stay in the YMCA and wear Goodwill clothes?" As soon as Tracy said that, she winced.

Bobby laughed hard. He laughed for nearly half a minute. When he finally slowed to a chuckle, wiping at the corners of his eyes, he looked at his daughter. "The funny thing is, the answer is yes, sorta. It's funnier to me, though, to see how this all must look to you." He set off chuckling for another minute.

Finally he got back to the question. "Most people don't really take the time to try 'n' figure it all out. They either just call me names or ask me to heal their mother. There's not many that take time to ask real questions about what it all means, so I forget what it must look like to someone from outside."

"Outside? So you *are* part of a group of some kind?"

"I'm part of God's church, one o' his people, yes. But not really a member of any kinda organization." He snickered. "Reminds me of a Mark Twain joke. He said, 'I'm not a member of any organized religion, I'm a Baptist.'" Bobby tipped his head to try and remember. "Or maybe it wasn't Baptist. Anyway, I can identify."

He looked at Tracy, who drove silently with her mouth scrunched shut. "I have friends all over. Remember I mentioned places I've left some o' my stuff? Mostly it's people at churches that welcome me when I come 'round. I'm not organized, and I'm not religious, but there are some people and places where I feel like I belong."

"Like where?"

"Oh, like in Redwood, California, at Jack Williams's place. I'm welcomed at his house and at his church. They got other churches too, around the country, that agree with him and such. So they generally take me in when I'm around."

"They give you a place to stay?"

"They give me anything I need. I could ask 'em for anything at all, and they would give it to me, I think."

Tracy had a habit of quirking her head when she was surprised at something. "How do you know that?"

"They've always been generous with me—food, clothes, a place to stay, money, anythin'."

"Like, when would they give you money?"

Bobby almost said, "Whenever I need it," but he could tell Tracy needed concrete examples. "Well, ya saw me buyin' stuff with that debit card today?"

Tracy nodded. "Yeah, sure."

"Well, the account that money comes outta isn't my account. They just give me the card to use whenever I need anythin'. I don't use it much, but once in a while I feel like it's time."

Tracy nearly missed the turn onto her street with a sharp pump of the brakes and hard twist of the steering wheel. "Wait— someone just gave you a debit card to their account? How much is in that account?"

"I don't know. Never needed to know."

"Whose account is it?"

"Somebody in Jack's church, I think. I have no idea who, really."

"Your name's on the card, though?"

"Yeah, they just added me to their account and gave Jack the card to give to me. Like I said, I don't really use it much. I generally don't even carry it with me. Usually cash just shows up in my pockets if I need it, like at dinner the other day."

Pulling into her driveway, Tracy slammed the brakes abruptly.

That was when Bobby recalled he hadn't explained the origin of the fifty-dollar bill that paid for dinner the other night. Hiding things wasn't his specialty. Bobby couldn't read her mind, but he knew Tracy was spinning furiously at something—like trying to make straw into gold.

He added information without knowing whether it would help her mental struggles. "I didn't have the card with me the night we first met. I use it so seldom that I forget about it. I wasn't clear on whether I'd be payin' for dinner that night." That last part was a guilty confession. Seeing Tracy all discombobulated shouldered him toward vulnerability.

Tracy's vulnerability was flapping around her like a clown costume she was trying to hide under a trench coat. Her discomfort was contagious.

"I sort of knew it." Tracy had not moved from the driver's seat. Her voice was hushed.

Bobby thumbed back through what he had said and guessed she was talking about the fifty-dollar bill. "I do work a job when I can, but it's gettin' harder these days to get the kinda jobs I used to do—bus boy, day laborer, and such."

"What if you get sick and need a doctor?" Tracy finally reached for the door handle.

Bobby got out of his door and opened the back door to wrangle his shopping bags.

Tracy leaned into the back seat from her side and grabbed several of the brightly colored bags, both paper and plastic. She also grabbed his hat box, containing a new fedora.

He answered her question. "I haven't needed a doctor in more 'n ten years. Maybe longer 'n that."

"But you're getting older."

Her boldness to speak to him like that heartened Bobby. It was the sort of thing a grown daughter would say to her aging father. "I am getting older." He chuckled lightly. "But I have no plans on getting old."

For the first time, Tracy laughed at his carefree confidence.

Finding A Network

When Bobby left Oakland that spring of 1992, he traveled north, wanting to see the coast and the giant redwoods. His previous California adventures had never taken him north of the Bay Area. Hopping off a bus on the edge of Redwood, he hiked toward the center of town, not knowing exactly where he was headed. He passed a gas station with a Help Wanted sign in the window and turned back to inquire within.

A middle-aged man was coming in from the garage, talking to the kid at the cash register when Bobby entered. "You can stay till eight tonight, can't you?" He was a pear-shaped man with dark hair and a tentative beard on jowly cheeks. His tone was gentle and a little desperate.

The clerk paused his answer when he noted Bobby's entrance.

Bobby seized the initiative. "You need a cashier?" He spoke to the older man, who seemed to be the proprietor.

"Well, yeah. You lookin' for a job?" He glanced at Bobby's backpack.

"I am. Just got into town and need to find a job and a place to stay."

"What brings you to town?"

"The wind, and the Holy Spirit."

"What? Are you serious?"

"Wouldn't be much of a joke." Bobby was getting ready to regret his spontaneous answer.

"No, I guess not. I'm Kurt Voss." He reached his hand around the counter and received Bobby's hastily offered grip. "I believe in the Holy Spirit, and I believe he sends people to my door once in a while."

Bobby smiled, realizing the words that had popped out of his mouth were a setup by his Papa. He addressed the job. "I'm honest and hard-working, and I've done every kinda thing ya have to do around here, except I never changed a whole transmission b'fore."

"Well, I just need a cashier, and maybe a bit of sweeping up and stocking shelves."

"That'd be great."

"Eight dollars an hour good enough?"

"I can get by on that." Bobby would have accepted less back in those days.

"I can help you find a place to stay." Kurt added that as if it were part of the compensation package, and Bobby expected it would be welcome assistance.

"Sounds great!" Bobby offered his hand again, and they shook on their agreement.

Bobby had stumbled into dozens of jobs by this time in his life, but none more easily than that one. The ease of that connection felt like a confirmation that he was headed in the right direction. And maybe he had found a good place to stick around for a little while. One advantage of ad hoc job offers, sealed by only a handshake, was that Bobby felt little guilt about leaving when the current broke him loose to drift again.

He had just wandered past the brightly painted front of the church in Oakland, and his life had changed as a result. He felt from the start that his job at Voss's Service Station would be a much bigger event than finding temporary work.

True to his word, Kurt connected Bobby with a family in his church that had a big house with space to rent. A private entrance and kitchenette were included in the little studio apartment. As Bobby had said before the handshake, he could get by on the income from a full-time job at the service station. His hours turned out to be somewhat irregular, but generally averaged out to almost full time.

What Bobby discovered in his new job was that, as a manager and boss, Kurt was a nice guy. But he was a struggling businessman. It was hard for Bobby to tell why the service station struggled, but he began to add up the stories of disasters that had collided with the station and its customers as each of those tales came up in casual conversation.

One mechanic had reportedly forgotten to pull the emergency brake on a vehicle he had just finished repairing, and it rolled out onto the busy road. That left Kurt paying for the customer's car as well as the truck that plowed into it at forty miles per hour. An electrical fire had burned a mint condition '69 Camaro to the ground while it sat on Kurt's lot. A bull moose had stopped in one day to take a plate glass window with his antlers. And there were lots of other stories.

Maybe Kurt wasn't a bad businessman, but he wasn't good enough to make up for so much bad luck. Bobby didn't mind the irregular hours, mixed-up schedules, or unexpected odd jobs, but he was bothered that a man of faith and integrity should have such misfortune in his business.

One day, he prayed to his Papa about what was causing all those accidents. Not long after he asked that question, the mechanic who was in the supply room started screaming like his hair was on fire.

Bobby ran from behind the cash register to the storeroom to find Henry, the junior mechanic, thrashing his arms in all directions. To Bobby's natural eyes, Henry seemed to be alone in the storeroom, but Bobby's spiritual radar picked up a hostile presence in there.

He closed the door behind him. "What's happening, Hank?" he shouted over the boxes rattling on the metal shelves as Henry hit the floor.

For just a second, a case of air filters tottered on a high shelf before tipping and emptying its contents on top of Henry. Bobby couldn't stop the cascade of boxed air filters, but deflected some of them before they landed on the prone mechanic.

Henry was screaming intermittently, but managed to say a coherent word or two. His answer to Bobby's question was, "Get 'em off o' me!" His shout sounded childishly uninhibited. Any customers entering the station at that point would surely have turned and run for help.

Greater Things

But it wasn't a customer who entered then, it was Kurt. He flung open the storeroom door as if prepared to order his employee to keep it down. What he found, however, was Bobby wading into a pile of boxes that seethed and churned at the frantic flailing of someone beneath them—someone Kurt couldn't have recognized.

"What the flip is going on in here?" Kurt barked his favorite invective, given that he was a church elder.

Bobby turned to look at Kurt, a sheepish grin on his face. "No worries. Just a few demons. I think they're the ones that've been bringin' all the weird accidents." He turned back to Henry, where he could just see the top half of his face. "You get off him right now." Bobby was focused on a reptilian imp.

Kurt said, "Okay, you take care of it," and he closed the storeroom door.

Bobby assumed Kurt would cover for him at the register, glad to be able to fully focus on the fight. He wasn't surprised or offended at Kurt's retreat from the battlefield. His boss said, "Take care of it," and Bobby planned to.

"What is it?" Henry squealed, writhing like a man who has just discovered a snake in his sleeping bag.

"It's not yours," Bobby assured him, whether or not it was reassuring to know the monster pinning him to the floor belonged to someone else.

"*Whaaaattt?*" Henry shouted like a man falling off a cliff.

Bobby jumped back when three large creatures seemed to surge out of, or off of, Henry. They stood shoulder to shoulder, staring him down.

"It's him," said one.

"He's the one," said the second.

"Get him!" said the third.

That odd banter froze Bobby for only a second. With the three demons still staring him down, he stepped forward and poked each with his index finger. The result was something like three balloons deflating, retreating back onto Henry.

86

"What was that?"

Bobby bypassed Henry's question and continued to follow his inner promptings. He dropped to his knees, crushing a pair of air filter boxes, and placed both hands on Henry's chest, which had just become visible at the continued settling of the parts boxes.

Almost like he was giving him CPR, Bobby thumped both hands on Henry's relatively narrow chest and said, "Get up outta there right now!"

Henry struggled to get off the floor as though the command had been aimed at him. Instead of reaching an upright position, however, Henry only managed to sit up, his long black hair over his eyes, his teeth chattering, and flecks of spit flying in a little storm around him.

"Get 'em off me!" He flicked at his persecutors with both hands.

Bobby could see all three remaining attackers, and noted that they avoided Henry's hands by hooking talons into his ears and eyes. Bobby understood the significance. "Henry, you've been watchin' and listenin' to things ya shouldn't. You need to renounce those in the name o' Jesus, right now."

Henry responded immediately. "I renounce all the porn I been watching right now in the name of Jesus. Jesus, help me!"

The last bit was the most effective prayer Bobby had ever witnessed. As soon as Henry said it, two big hands swooped in and grabbed the three demons by the throats, hauling them out of sight in one struggling bunch.

As the three attackers rocketed toward the ceiling, Henry's lunch hurtled onto the pile of air filter boxes.

Bobby dodged just in time to save his shoes.

"Oh, man. Sorry about that." Henry wiped the back of his hand over his chin.

Bobby just laughed.

At the sudden quiet after Henry vomited, Kurt opened the storeroom door. "How's it goin' in here?"

"We're fine." Bobby laughed. "Clean up on aisle one." Then his laughter turned a bit hysterical. No matter how many times he'd been in similar situations—though certainly none exactly like this—Bobby shivered violently when the fight ended.

"Oh, I see that." Kurt sounded a bit sarcastic, but he started to laugh as well.

Bobby expected the mess in the storeroom would be the last damage those spirits exacted against Kurt. He believed his prayer had caused the spirits to become visible. That unmasking had caught Henry in the middle because of his spiritual vulnerability. And Henry had gotten free of something more familiar to him right after the three big spirits left. That last bit was the cause of the added mess among the fallen cardboard boxes.

Later that night, Kurt and Bobby discussed the excitement as they sipped sodas in lawn chairs next to the garage. They were facing the drainage ditch. That man-made creek hosted a motley collection of trees and shrubs that Bobby thought of as the side yard.

Kurt was clearly fascinated by the subject of spiritual warfare, even if he hadn't been particularly anxious to get into the fray in the storeroom. "So, did you know they were holed up in the storeroom?"

Bobby shook his head. "Had no idea. Didn't even know fer sure there was a nest of those critters around th' place. Usually they're on people, not buildings. But seems like they couldn't be on you, so they decided to be on yer business."

"Yeah, that makes sense. But I wonder how they got permission to be in the service station at all."

Bobby looked at Kurt, recalling a few confessions he had shared in the weeks Bobby had been working there. "You don't think there might've been some room for them where you were sayin' ya really didn't wanna be a businessman, but wanted to work for the church instead?"

Kurt pursed his lips, nodding. "That seems like a possibility." Kurt was as humble a boss as Bobby ever had.

As Bobby let that discovery settle, Kurt spoke again. "I gotta introduce you to our pastor. He'll get a big kick outta you."

Bobby chuckled. He had attended Kurt's church a few times, as well as a handful of other churches in the area. His odd work schedule reinforced his tendency to bounce from place to place. He had enjoyed what he saw of Jack Williams, the former hippie who was the pastor of that growing church in Northern California. Bobby's last impression of Jack, at his most recent visit, came after the service when he saw Jack's long-haired wife, barefoot, herding four little kids toward Jack.

On one of Bobby's earlier visits, he had also been intrigued by Jack's side comments about wishing they were seeing more supernatural power in their church—something they believed in but saw far too little of, according to that little rabbit trail during Jack's sermon.

The notion of a church that believed in a supernatural God but saw little supernatural activity reminded Bobby of the Holiness Church in Oakland. He heard an echo of Sister Pamela's admonition that he should stay and bring his power to the hungry folks gathered there. Maybe that was the reason he had bumped into Kurt after all. At least one of the reasons. Bobby was willing to test that notion when he got the chance to meet Jack, as Kurt proposed.

Moving Out of Tracy's House

After returning home from the Mall of America, Bobby sought to recover some normality between him and Tracy. That normality seemed to require Bobby to keep quiet about his gifts and experiences. He only hoped his Papa was going to cooperate with that truce.

On Sunday afternoon after sleeping in, and a big brunch prepared by Tracy, Bobby began to look at housing options in the area. He wanted to stay around, but not under foot.

"What d'ya think about takin' me around to look at one of these apartments?" He tapped on the newspaper in front of him.

Tracy had been busy in the kitchen and around the house, not paying close attention to what he was doing with the newspaper. She stood with a laundry basket gripped in two slender hands, staring at him. He knew it was a double-barreled surprise—that he was staying around for a while, and that he would do so in his own apartment.

The apartments he was considering were either month-to-month furnished units or ones that offered as little as a four-month lease. The selection was slender, and the search took them to neighborhoods in Minneapolis and St. Paul that Tracy was clearly nervous about. But she seemed to be getting used to his expectations differing from hers.

They sat parked outside a brown brick apartment building, two stories high, that advertised short-term furnished units. Before they even saw the interior, Bobby knew this would be his next temporary home. Perhaps it was what others would call intuition, or just a spontaneous decision, but Bobby thought of it as real estate help from his Papa.

"I might have found you a house to stay in short-term—some place that's not selling for one reason or another." Tracy craned her neck at the surrounding neighborhood as well as the apartment building with one boarded window and a sagging gutter.

Though there were options for as little as a one-week commitment, Bobby planned to pay for the entire first month at the Walnut Arms apartments in Minneapolis, twenty minutes' drive from Tracy's house in the suburbs. "I thought the housin' market was pickin' up 'round here." Bobby bypassed the lateness of her offer, knowing he hadn't warned her about his move.

"It is, but there's always someone with too high expectations for the sale price, or some family complications that keep them from closing a deal. Divorces cause that kind of mess sometimes."

Bobby sensed no bitterness whenever she mentioned divorce. He wondered if she wanted to talk about why he left her mother. That would be some tricky ground to cover, but he was game to try anything. "I hope ya don't mind me movin' out so soon." His thoughts about leaving Lori inspired a little cleanup with his daughter.

Tracy looked directly at Bobby. "No, I understand. You're used to your independence. I'm glad you're stayin' around for a while, anyway."

Bobby smiled. "I wanna stick around long enough to get to know my girl."

After a long pause, Tracy finally responded, low and breathy. "I'm glad."

A Lifelong Friendship Begins

"So, that was when you got to know Jack Williams?" It felt like finishing one of the connect-the-dots pictures Anna did as a kid.

"Yep. Kurt invited Jack and his wife Bernie over for a barbecue and included me on the guest list. Kurt's wife, Cindi, greeted me at the door. She'd already met me at the station. I'm thinkin' she was pleased to see me in something other than my work uniform."

Anna chuckled, letting Bobby continue with the story.

"Bobby, come on in. So good to see you," Cindy said.

"Thanks, it was good o' you to have me over."

"Well, Kurt told me about what happened the other day. I think it's time we get to know you better."

That was when Bobby remembered something Brother Kendrick had prophesied over him a few weeks before Bobby left Oakland. "Your gifts will always make a place for you." Bobby assumed Brother Kendrick hadn't fully anticipated what that meant, but here on the slate tiles in the Voss's entryway, Bobby had an inkling that prophecy was coming true.

Though he had met Jack Williams, shaking his hand at church, it had been one of those anonymous greetings one doesn't expect to be remembered.

When Jack saw Bobby coming through the dining room on the way to the back deck, he interrupted what he was saying and turned to open the sliding glass door for him. "There's the man I've been dying to meet." Jack grabbed Bobby's right hand in a brisk and firm handshake. "The storeroom exorcist." He added a big laugh.

Jack was about the same height as Bobby, but his big voice and proportionally large head made him seem larger on stage as well as face-to-face. His hair was still nearly shoulder length. It had begun to turn a medium gray, and he rarely appeared in a ponytail anymore.

Bobby smiled at the little joke about the storeroom.

"Tell the truth—were you scared in there?" Jack stood a few inches from Bobby, a confiding grin on his face.

"I was. All kinds o' weird stuff was happenin', and there were auto parts fallin' on us from all sides."

With eyes wide behind his silver-rimmed glasses, Jack shook his head and chuckled. "The spirits weren't throwin' things around, were they?"

"No, it was just Henry flailin' around, settin' the shelves to shakin'."

"Uh-huh." Jack stood close enough to study Bobby's pores. "I think you were scared, like you say, but I think you're a courageous man for steppin' right in there like that."

After closing the grill and setting down his spatula, Kurt joined them, a soda in one hand. "Unlike some of us who just looked for something else to do." He smirked and offered Bobby the cold drink.

Jack let go of Bobby's hand and slapped him on the shoulder. "I'm tired of talking. Had meetings all day. I bet Bobby has a very interesting story to tell about his life. I'd really like to hear that if you're willing."

The way Jack said that, it wasn't absolutely clear whether he was asking Bobby or Kurt. Maybe he was asking whether Bobby wouldn't mind being the entertainment for the evening. Bobby waited to see if Kurt answered.

Kurt said, "Yeah, I'd like to hear more. I feel like I hardly know ya."

That last phrase was one Bobby had heard before, and one he would hear many times throughout his life. Being known was not his top priority. His Papa knew him, and some folks gradually *grew* to know him, but he usually had to be asked before he uncorked his story.

He paused his telling there and grinned at Anna as if to check whether she had noticed where she fit into that bit of self-revelation.

She nodded and smiled slightly, but she let him continue his story about meeting Jack.

Cindy and Bernie, short for Bernice, joined the men out on the deck along with Kurt's two teenaged daughters. His daughters were both quietly polite, not sullen like some teens in that sort of situation. The coming and going of those folks, along with the arrival of salads, veggies, dips, and grilled burgers, delayed Bobby beginning his life story. The group settled down when the grill was turned off, the teens took their leave, and the adults looked satisfied.

"So, tell us where you're from." Cindi was probably in on the effort to extract Bobby's history, and her question was a good place to start.

Brief interruptions for coffee and dessert, a bit of cleaning up, and a small crisis with one of Jack and Bernie's kids over the phone gave Bobby time to breathe. Otherwise his story just flowed, the history of his thirty-plus years.

He told them about his early years in Topeka only briefly, lingering more on his life with Grandma Casey. He made no effort to avoid the failures and disappointments, being careful not to present himself as someone he couldn't recognize when he lay down that night to review what he had said. He expended a bit of energy trying *not* to prove anything with his story even though he sensed Kurt and Jack were particularly curious to know where he had caught his supernatural power. Bobby did indulge in some of his best miracle stories, hoping he was giving testimony, not just bragging.

Taking time to light the tiki torches around the deck, Kurt boosted Bobby's narrative. "So, you spent how long with the Holiness church in Oakland?"

"Longer 'n I expected. But I didn't expect to find 'em at all. It was about nine months there, I think."

"So how did they know you could raise the little girl from the dead? What else happened there after the big bang on that first night?" Jack was as eager a listener as Bobby had ever met. He sounded like a guy doing detailed research.

"Oh, there were some excitin' healings. I guess the one that impressed Sister Marcella the most was probably the man with the shriveled hand. He'd been born with it. He worked at the newspaper stand in the neighborhood, and everyone got to see how he made change with one good hand and one that was only half as big, and weak. He was at least fifty years old, so he'd had a long time to get used to just one good hand."

Bobby checked to ensure his audience was tracking with him, finding them hardly breathing. "I stopped by there on the way from church one Sunday and just had this crazy idea come into my head. It was about a curse on his family from when he was born, and that God wanted to break that curse. I didn't even know exactly what that meant, but told him what I thought I was hearin'.

"The guy, whose name was Frank, said he was born in New Orleans, and the lady who rented them rooms when he was little was a witch. Everybody knew it. He said he didn't know of anythin' in particular, but could imagine that his mother might've upset the landlady, given how his mom was. He didn't explain that, but I just wanted to do whatever it was I was supposed to do. I was thinkin' it was just chasin' off some bad spirit or other. But, when I prayed and told the curse to be broken, that withered hand started twitchin'. And then Frank started shakin'. He kept snappin' his bad arm like he was tryin' to shake a spider off. Each time he did it, he seemed to get more strength. Then he stopped and looked at that hand, and it wasn't yet the same as his other, but it wasn't the same as it had been before neither."

Again, Bobby paused to assess his listeners. He could sense how hungry they were, not just for his stories, but for the power of God displayed in his stories. "So I seen what was happenin', and thought I should tell the hand to get all the way whole, like Jesus did sometimes. And when I did that, he just stretched out his hand, and it looked like he just kept stretchin' it. Sorta like it was made o' rubber, like in a comic book. And it grew to be just like his other hand, only no scars and no cigarette stains. It was all the way better and brand new."

The smiles around him assured Bobby he was talking to the right people. He continued. "An' then Frank says, 'God healed my hand. I gotta go to church and get right with Jesus.' I didn't think to tell him he could get right with God right there next to his newspaper stand. So I took him back to the church where Brother Kendrick and a few others were still fellowshippin'. He showed 'em his hand, and everyone knew what his hand was like b'fore, so that started a big praisin' and shoutin' and repentin' service. Sister Marcella and Lashawn were some o' the folks that were there then."

All this was to answer why his church family would expect he could raise Lashawn from the dead. But Bobby knew there was more happening on Kurt and Cindi's deck that night.

It was Kurt that first blurted, "I want some o' that."

Bernie simultaneously started to weep uncontrollably.

Jack started to laugh just as uncontrollably.

That was uncomfortable for a moment, but Bobby knew it was all coming from his Papa.

Cindi asked Bobby plainly, "Can you pray for me to get some of that power?"

As soon as Bobby looked at her, ready to give it a try, Cindi pitched backward, flipping her chair over onto the deck. That tipping of the chair was particularly unusual because she was sitting in an Adirondack chair, low to the ground with broad back legs that didn't easily tip backward. When she landed in a great wooden clatter, Bobby was worried she might be hurt. But, upon standing up to check, he suddenly felt flashes of electricity shoot through his body, and his limbs all went wobbly.

Kurt tried again to say something, but it came out garbled and changed to some language Bobby didn't recognize. Kurt staggered up from his seat and grabbed one of Bobby's vibrating hands. The quaking seemed to multiply, as if the two of them had found a small fault line that was being torn by a tremor.

Jack tried standing up to join them, but he missed Kurt and Bobby and fell flat on his face.

Again, Bobby paused to look for blood. But he couldn't move and had to be content with hoping that the quivering man at his feet was having a good experience despite how hard he had hit the wooden deck.

One of Cindi and Kurt's daughters came to check it out. When the two girls saw how crazy the adults were acting, they turned to retreat into the house. But they both fell on the dining room floor and started to laugh drunkenly, their feet sticking out of the open sliding door.

For years after that evening, Jack joked that they had thought they were just inviting Bobby to dinner. They didn't realize they were inviting the Holy Spirit to come in and wreck their friends and family.

Bobby told Anna he took that as a compliment.

Loose in the Great White North

Monday evening, after showing a couple houses to a client, Tracy helped Bobby move into his new place. She drove him to the supermarket to gather some supplies to go with the large plastic bin of things she had already collected from her place. She knew her requirements for starting out in a new apartment were not the same as her vagabond father's. Tracy felt she was getting to know her dad, but still treated him like a visitor in her life.

Twice in the store, Tracy stopped herself from suggesting some item they passed on the way to what Bobby had on his mental list. She, of course, would have written the list down. She was proud of her restraint in not pointing that out.

Bobby glanced at her a few times when she started to say something and stopped herself. Perhaps he recognized that restraint.

By the time they reached Bobby's new apartment, Tracy was sliding rapidly into depression. She could see more of her dad's furtive glances, like he was trying to detect what was happening with her.

Between the two of them, they carried all Bobby's luggage and supplies up to the second-floor apartment in one trip. It was only slightly laborious. Just one chorus of "I'll Never Be Your Beast of Burden" cycled through Tracy's brain. She hung onto her load of dishes and food, stowed in a laundry basket, as Bobby fiddled with the unfamiliar key and lock. His array of bags and his suitcase lay on the ground at his feet. Cicadas sang their farewell song in the trees behind them, a note of regret in their tone as the first of the leaves had begun to turn red, orange, and yellow.

Bobby finally opened the door and pushed out of the way.

Tracy plowed through and set her load on the little table that divided the kitchen from the living room. Counting the bedroom and bathroom, the apartment consisted of four rooms. All but the bathroom were carpeted in brown, and the living room and dining room/kitchen were painted golden yellow. The bedroom and bathroom were both pale blue. Tracy breathed easier and tried a fake sideways smile.

Bobby settled his groceries on the kitchen table and turned to her with a concerned look in his eyes. "I'm not sure how much ya believe about this stuff or understan' it, but I think I can make things easier for you if you let me pray for ya just a minute here."

Tracy hesitated, but agreed to the prayer. Mostly she was hoping to get it over with. At the very least, she would submit to it as a father-daughter bonding experience. But when Bobby stepped up close to her, she suddenly recalled the woman in the mall, flopping on the floor like a tuna landed in a boat. Instead of calling a halt to the proceedings, however, Tracy just tensed up, squinting her eyes tight and crunching her shoulders up to her neck.

Bobby laughed—the last thing Tracy was expecting. "You can relax. This isn't gonna hurt." He sounded every bit the reassuring dad, amused at her childish worries.

Tracy and her worries were fully grown, however, and she didn't know as much about relaxing as she did about tensing up.

Bobby didn't wait for that to change. Instead, he reached up as if to grab hold of something hanging around her neck.

She saw her father pantomiming pulling something off her, which was odd. Stranger still was the feeling of something letting go of her neck as he made that movement with his hands. Then Tracy's experience escalated from odd to surreal.

"What the ..."

Bobby appeared to throw that thing away, but it seemed to snap back at her. When it came back, it was much nastier.

A sudden panic seized her.

"Let go," Bobby said to whatever was clinging to her.

Tracy struggled with a tight constriction of her throat. She worried that she was allergic to something in her father's apartment. The sensation reminded her of anaphylactic shock, which she had witnessed in a friend who was allergic to shellfish.

"Now," Bobby said.

To Tracy, his tone recalled childhood when her stepfather spoke to a misbehaving dog he didn't fear. The voice was stern, but not fierce or angry. Bobby apparently wasn't afraid of the thing that was trying to kill her.

Bobby pulled something else off her. This one seemed to be tied in, like he was pulling a whole rope out of her. As he finished, the atmosphere in that little apartment seemed to become rich and golden, like the light of a thousand candles. It felt as if that light had been there all along, but her dad had pulled away the blinds blocking it.

"I bless you with peace. No more depression, no more anxiety, no more fear." He wasn't barking at some invisible enemy now. He was talking to her.

It felt like she fully believed something profound and significant that someone said to her for the first time in her life. Not even her mother's declared love for her or her former husband's wedding vows sounded as true as Bobby's declaration of her freedom. It was as if she suddenly discovered the ability to believe. And her father had shown her where to find it.

See How Far We Can Wind This Thing Up

At their last mall interview in Illinois, Bobby explained to
Anna that he had brought the sort of fire Jack Williams had
longed for all his life growing up in his father's Pentecostal
church. Bobby brought the fire, but he knew that Jack, Bernie,
Kurt, Cindi, and dozens of others brought the kindling. Some of
it was charred from the past, maybe. Some was so dry that it felt
dangerous to get it anywhere near the fire.

To Anna, this was a profound look under the shiny lid that
was Jack Williams's public persona. She paused to wonder
whether she should write a story about Jack even if it was also
unlikely to be published. But she tuned that out and nodded for
Bobby to continue. He was growing more antsy. Anna assumed
that was about his daughter coming to pick him up soon.

Five days after that dinner at Kurt and Cindi's house, Jack
called the members of his church together for a meeting. Jack
had put out a call to all the leaders in the church. Apparently the
invitation got flung more widely than Jack intended, but the
agenda for the meeting was wide open, and the guest list may as
well have been. About a hundred and twenty people attended.

Bobby stood by as Jack cajoled one of the worship leaders to
take a guitar on stage and start the unscheduled meeting with
some songs. To Bobby, it seemed like the music was preliminary,
a mood setter. That was probably the plan.

David Radinsky, a thin thirty-something who had apparently
led worship in that church for some time, got to a mic with an
acoustic guitar that plugged into the sound system. He started
with songs Bobby had heard on Sunday mornings.

In the front row of seats, Jack stood with Bernie and some of
the other senior leaders of the church, including Kurt and Cindi
Voss. Bobby was seated between Jack and Kurt. He was relaxing
in his seat after a long day of standing on concrete at work.

Jack kept looking around as if to check if anyone else was hearing what he was hearing—or perhaps it was a feeling he was feeling. During the second or third song, he grasped his chest as if he were having a heart attack. He shook his hands in front of him a few times. Then he seemed to decide he had better sit down.

Bobby was ready to stand up to join in the worship by then. Without any intent on his part, Bobby's rising seemed to crash into Jack's sitting.

Jack didn't sit. He toppled over on his face once again. He later insisted that Bobby didn't touch him, and Bobby thought the same, but the motion of standing seemed to have blasted Jack off his feet.

For decades after that, Jack retold the experience of going to heaven that night, seeing Jesus, and seeing the plans God had for him and for their church. Bobby had a copy of that talk on CD in one of his stashes somewhere.

Of course Jack had organized that meeting, so Kurt looked at Bobby and then at Jack and seemed to feel responsible for carrying on. He conferred with Bernie.

Barefoot in church as usual, her hair streaming down her back and hands raised as high as possible, Jack's wife only reluctantly came down from her worship high to check what Kurt was saying.

Kurt simply touched her on the shoulder as if to speak into her ear, but that touch appeared to contain one of those hidden blasts.

Bernie did a dive and landed on her face not far from her husband. Now she was out too.

Kurt shrugged, looked at David at the microphone, and then checked with Bobby. He stepped closer to confer with him. When he leaned in close, Kurt started to shake. It was like no shaking Bobby had seen before. Kurt looked like he might launch off the ground. He stood on the toes of one foot, vibrating uncontrollably. And then he was down.

When the worship leader watched the third senior leader land facedown on the floor, he looked at Bobby. David and Bobby had not yet met, but David seemed to know that Bobby had something to do with the purpose of this meeting. Whether he had any idea what that purpose was, Bobby couldn't tell.

As he finished the fifth or sixth song, David glanced toward another person sitting in the front row. Maybe they looked more likely than Bobby to lead the rest of the meeting. But they didn't seem to take up the invitation in his pleading eyes. Lacking any other direction, he started another song.

Unfamiliar with the next song, Bobby watched the overhead projector. No lyrics appeared on the white square with rounded corners. Finally a hand shoved an upside-down transparency onto the projector, gripped the lighted surface for a second, and disappeared. The projectionist, a young girl probably not twenty years old, began to laugh like she was being mercilessly tickled by tireless hands.

Later, Cindi told Bobby that she had noticed a pattern by then. She was pretty sure that as soon as she decided to take over the meeting, especially if she said anything to Bobby, she would be knocked to the floor. In fact, in the years that followed, Cindi would crack up congregations with her telling of this story. She certainly was better qualified to tell it than her husband or her senior pastor or her best friend. Bernie was rolling around singing in a language that sounded Asian, which Cindi was sure Bernie didn't know.

Braving the expected consequences, Cindi stepped over next to Bobby. She reached out and gingerly touched his arm to get his attention. His eyes were closed, and he didn't open them when she touched him. Instead, he made a sort of barking sound and toppled to the floor, landing neatly between Kurt and Jack.

Her eyes wide, Cindi briefly looked at her hand to see if something about it had changed. Later she would claim she hadn't known it was loaded. In the spin of the moment, she had an idea. Her sister-in-law was sitting on the other side of her. Cindi slipped over next to Rhonda, her brother's wife, and touched her gently on the arm. Sure enough, Rhonda lurched, hooted, and then fell over, landing in front of her husband.

Before Cindi could touch her brother, he too tumbled forward, managing not to step on his wife as he fell to his hands and knees. Then he rolled over on his back to have a good laugh—a really good laugh.

There had been one other meeting scheduled in the building that evening. The midweek meeting of the high school group was going on in the recreation center. By the time Cindi had cleared out the front row and started to wade into the subsequent rows, her daughter, Martha, came staggering into the auditorium. Martha was there to alert the adults that something was happening in the youth group. When she saw her mom mowing down the faithful, Martha didn't deliver that message. As she had done at home after the barbecue, she tried to retreat from the scene, but was unable to get out the door, down on her face with her feet sticking over the threshold once again.

That meeting marked another new stage in Bobby's life and ministry. Those same emotional and spiritual reactions would accompany him wherever he was welcomed in churches around the country. He rarely made a big production of knocking people to the floor. It often happened without him doing anything at all. And, of course, knocking them down was not really what was happening. They were encountering the God who had also filled the ancient Hebrew temple when Solomon finished its construction. There, too, no one was able to stand in the manifest presence of God.

What to Do with Freedom

Bobby had learned over the years that people react differently to being set free from demonic oppression. Some go on a binge of some kind, unfamiliar with freedom and not sure what to do with it. For the rest of that week in Minnesota, Tracy seemed absentminded. That hadn't been his impression of her before.

"So, explain to me in words I can understand." She was dishing spaghetti at her kitchen table, where Bobby was more comfortable than either in his apartment or her well-appointed dining room. "What were those things, and how did I get them?"

This wasn't the first of these conversations since the night Bobby moved into his apartment. He had kept close tabs on Tracy to make sure she was adjusting—and that she didn't have any more critters he should pull off her. Though she seemed to him to be truly free, she also seemed truly confused.

"I like to think of it like a person is a house." Bobby swallowed a mouthful of salad. "Yer life is yer house. Ya get to say who comes and goes in yer house. But we all actually inherited our houses from our parents and other folks that raised us. So sometimes those folks leave us little souvenirs from before we're old enough to really be in charge of our lives." He stabbed some lettuce, his fork clicking on the bottom of the bowl.

Tracy was still looking at her father, her fork poised. Perhaps she was trying to picture her life as a house her mother had given her. "So I got those things from Mom?"

Bobby hummed while he chewed and shook his head. "I see these things more clearly than most people, and I still hesitate to say exactly where somethin' came from. My Papa tells me specifics once in a while, but I usually don't ask. I expect others are askin' about that after I leave the scene, like counselors and pastors and such."

Tracy nodded and began to eat.

Bobby added a note to her speculation. "Fact is, some of it might've even come from me—or come from me leavin' ya before you were born."

That stopped Tracy again. Her prospects for getting to the pasta and sauce while it was still hot were thinning. She shook her head and breathed hard once from her nose.

"But the point is, ya can't really account for all the stuff that accumulates on your life, 'cause some of it's inherited. Other stuff comes without ya knowin'. Some folks get cursed by others that don't like 'em, and they get hooked up with bad spirits that way." Bobby was not willing to let his food go cold. He fired off his answers as he loaded his fork.

"Will they come back?" The tightening of her eyes and hardness settling around her mouth implied Tracy had just thought to worry about that.

"They could try." Bobby had transitioned to the spaghetti, cutting the long strands with knife and fork in the interest of consumption, if not style. He chewed and swallowed the last of his salad before saying more. "That's why it's a good idea to fill up on God. That takes up all the space the bad guys would be fillin' in."

"So how do I do *that*?" She took a bite of spaghetti right after asking.

Bobby nodded while he chewed. "It's ..." he swallowed and took a swig of water. "It's not nearly as hard as some folks make it out to be. It's not like ya have to climb some high mountain on yer knees or somethin'. Ya just gotta open the door."

"Open the door?"

Bobby wiped his mouth with a cloth napkin, having caught his daughter checking the drips in his beard. He hoped he had improved the situation. "Ya gotta remember that it was God's idea to bring us along in the first place, and God's idea to reach out to people. Sendin' Jesus was his big invite for everybody. So, we don't have to get anythin' started. God did all that already. We just gotta say, 'Okay, I'm in.'"

"That sounds so different than what I've heard." Tracy reached for her garlic bread and furrowed her brow.

"Here, let me show you something." Bobby laid his hand on the table, palm up. "Just put yer hand there." He nodded toward his open palm.

Tracy set down her fork and reached over to her father's hand.

Within a few seconds, Bobby was feeling heat in the little space between their palms. Then that heat started to travel up his arm, and Tracy's hand started to quiver.

She pulled away, her eyes big and her mouth open about an inch. "What was that?"

"God." Bobby nodded and smiled from the side of his mouth. "What you've heard about God from religious people is what they came up with when they lost the power. All they got now is rules to keep ya dependent on the ones that make the rules. I'm offerin' you God, not a bunch o' rules."

Tracy stared at him, her meal forgotten again.

"You don't need to do anythin' right now." Bobby winked at her. "Just think about it a bit, and maybe ask God to show ya what's true. He has a way of doin' that so ya believe better than any human bein' can make ya believe."

More Like Leaving Home

Anna finally got a call from Bobby. He was in Minnesota and had even rented an apartment. Most importantly, he agreed to tell her more of his story. They talked on the phone for over an hour.

Anna was sitting in her apartment in Rogers Park, Chicago, wishing she could see Bobby's eyes as he recalled his life. She cleared her throat. "That leaders' meeting in Redwood is something I've heard others talking about. It's something of a legend among Jack's churches. I know how it changed that church and affected all of us who attend churches affiliated with them, but how did it change you?"

Bobby hummed for a second. "Well, let me tell ya, doing church with Jack Williams, Kurt Voss, and their friends and associates, was different than anything I ever experienced before that."

God was real to him because of the things he had experienced personally, and because of what he had seen God do for other people through him. But the accessible God with whom Bobby discussed his plans—and told an occasional joke—felt like his own personal God. His sense of his own uniqueness had been reinforced when he was with the Holiness church in Oakland. There were lots of expectations for behavior there, even down to calling each other "brother" or "sister." Bobby conformed, but he knew he wasn't speaking his native language.

In Jack's laid-back church, Bobby found something like the free faith he had discovered in the privacy of a freight car or a park or an SRO hotel.

"As strange as it may sound, finding out I was not so unique disturbed me for quite a while." He chuckled and continued, not waiting for a response from Anna.

He explained that, while he was upheld as some sort of saint by the church down in Oakland, "Brother Bobby" felt like an alter-ego. In Redwood, he was just a stranger who believed what everyone else believed. He also happened to *experience* more of what they all believed.

In those early days, Bobby had been no more inclined to figure out everything than he was currently. But he was more prone to be frustrated when things felt uncomfortable. His frustration over having to look squarely at his very private faith in the stage lights of Jack's church pushed him into his shell. He avoided people as much as he could without appearing to be impolite.

Cindi Voss had cornered him at the gas station one Friday night a couple months into his stay. "You have plans for the weekend, Bobby?"

Bobby was counting the money in the till near the end of his shift. It was almost eight o'clock. Mild September weather invited the outdoorsy types to hike and hunt, so there had been lots of visitors through the station. Bobby was struggling against the urge to travel too, to move on to the next job, the next town. He suspected the folks at the church were assuming he was there to stay. That made him even more itchy.

Maybe Cindy sensed that itchiness. "Kurt and I are just gonna watch a video and have some popcorn. You could come join us if you want."

Bobby looked up from the till. For some reason, Cindi felt like the sister he'd never had. But she was being an annoying sister that wouldn't leave him alone just then. His level of annoyance worried him, so he said yes to that invitation. It was probably a desperate move to counter his wanderlust and resist his anxiety about people getting too close.

Cindi looked surprised. "Oh, that would be great."

"Okay if I stop by and get some dinner to bring over? I haven't eaten yet."

"Oh, yeah. That's fine. Actually, you could just ride with us, and we can stop at Ronny's for carryout." She mentioned the popular dog and burger place near her house.

Bobby had been driving whatever loaner car was available, so a ride from the Voss's made more sense. But it also meant he'd be all tangled up with Kurt and Cindi for the evening and miss his breathing space even more.

That evening was no grand disaster nor a magnificent epiphany, but it did serve as the catalyst for his next move. Things just seemed too cozy. But this time he offered some advance warning to the people he had come to know instead of just saying goodbye the day of his departure.

"I'm not really surprised," Jack said when Bobby told him. They were sitting in leather chairs in front of Jack's desk. "I could tell you had your eyes on the door during a lot of your stay here. And I do think God has something different for you, not the traditional lifestyle most of us take for granted. What I would ask, though, is that you stay in touch. We're planting sister congregations in four other cities, so you could visit them if you're not coming back this way. And I'd like to hear your stories and know how to pray for you."

That last point was no surprise to Bobby. He knew Jack prayed for the people in his church, even if only briefly. But understanding that the offer wasn't unique didn't keep his throat from tightening.

At some level, Bobby knew that Jack didn't approve of his leaving so soon. Bobby thought of his urge to keep moving as something like the migratory instincts in animals. His understanding of his own unique migration had not yet seen enough light for Bobby to trust it. Nor had his ability to trust been expanded by these very trustworthy people. He was aware that he was running away. He wasn't yet ready to stop and figure out why.

After a stint in Portland, Oregon, another in Seattle, Washington, and another in Eastern Washington State, Bobby took a bus to Vancouver, British Columbia, in the days when crossing borders was easier. While in Vancouver, he followed Jack's advice and looked up the church that had been planted by Redwood.

One Sunday while attending the Vancouver church, he saw a young woman on stage who looked like a girl playing dress-up. She seemed to be wearing someone else's clothes. Her long hair and lack of makeup resembled a hippie from twenty years before. From the stage, she called people out, apparently knowing their names without having met them, knowing about their lives in ways that made some squirm. Mostly she demonstrated that God was watching and knew all about the people gathered there.

And she let them know, in the process, how much God cared. That young woman's name was Willow Pierce.

"Willow? Oh, wow." Anna stopped herself when she realized the fangirl she sounded like. "Uh, go ahead."

Bobby laughed. "I didn't get to meet her personally that time. I didn't know the church leaders who were leadin' Willow around by the hand. She was shy as an abandoned cat anyway."

The main thing Bobby learned from observing that frail young woman was the possibility of a sizable gap between the power of God on someone's life and their level of emotional health.

Anna was tempted to push into more of what Bobby knew about Willow in those days, but she had limited time with him, so she forced herself to postpone that curiosity.

Word Gets Out Bobby's in Town

Willow Pierce had been training young people in prophetic ministry for decades. Two young men who had been mentored by Willow had recently arrived in St. Paul. Jamie Cummings and Rich Oesterman had followed what they believed to be God's leading to go and live in Minnesota. But they didn't know why they were there.

They had four hundred dollars between them when they obeyed that call, and had been scraping by for five weeks on odd jobs and Jamie's new career at a fast-food restaurant. Meanwhile, they were still waiting to discover why they had been sent to Minnesota. Both being from Southern Texas, they hoped God would let them in on the plan before winter. They didn't even own a proper coat between them.

One morning while dozing between sleep and waking, Jamie's mind filled with an image of a beautiful city. Before him loomed a grand palace with a wide staircase leading up to huge ornate doors. While he stood at the bottom of those stairs in his dreamlike imagination, one of those huge doors swung open, and a man with a tray came walking skillfully down the stairs. There was a wine bottle and a glass poised on that tray, and the man sailed right down in front of Jamie without even rattling the glass.

When he reached him at the bottom of the stairs, the man with the tray smiled mischievously. "Do ya wanna know why yer here?"

"Yes, of course," Jamie said in his vision.

"Take a drink."

Jamie saw that the glass was empty, but the bottle was open. He lifted the bottle and poured himself a glass of the red wine.

"Drink it." The man seemed friendly, so that didn't seem a dangerous thing to do.

Hesitating in curiosity about why this stranger should want him to drink the wine, Jamie suddenly thought he recognized the man with the tray, though he hadn't noticed before. Believing he knew who was offering him this wine, Jamie drank boldly. The wine was warm and sweet and seemed to spread comfort throughout his body. He felt more alive, healthier, and more joyful than ever before. The wine inspired a brief giggle, followed by an urge to find a giant and fight him. Then Jamie looked at the man with the tray. "Are you the reason we came to St. Paul?"

The man nodded. "I'm not far away. Come find me." He nodded to the bottle. "There's more where that came from."

When the vision ended, Jamie sat up briskly, startling Rich, who was sleeping on the other side of the room.

"Huh? What? What is it?" Rich woke without sitting up, but made enough noise to convince his roommate he was alive.

Jamie was at the edge of his own bed, his feet on the floor. "Bobby Nightingale is in town. We're supposed to find him."

Bobby was sitting in the easy chair that came with his little apartment, his eyes closed, and a grin on his face. He was conversing with his Papa. As sometimes happened, he slipped from a waking state to a sort of dream. A little motion picture opened before his mind's eye. Two young men were looking for him. Their names and faces became familiar to him. One was tall and dark-haired, quieter and more serious. The other was shorter with blondish hair, and more nervous. And Bobby heard his Papa say, "*Go with them.*"

This was the sort of thing that reduced Bobby's desire for a computer or a social networking page or even a cell phone. He had all the communication tools he needed.

Later that day, Bobby felt like going out for something to eat, the groceries in his apartment holding no appeal. He pulled on his new fleece jacket and his fedora and headed toward the strip malls south of his apartment building. Though he couldn't name any, he knew there were little restaurants along the main road just outside his apartment complex. He planned to stop at the first one that looked good.

As he walked, he wondered at his freedom with his debit card, considering whether he had slipped into laziness about trusting God for his money. But that self-evaluation was interrupted by two young men jogging toward him and calling his name.

"It's you, it's really you!" The shorter of the two spoke, panting from the jog, and maybe from excitement at seeing Bobby.

"Jamie and Rich?" Bobby extended his hand.

"So, you knew?" Rich shook Bobby's hand, leaving a clammy residue.

"I can't believe this is really happening." Jamie spun halfway around and back.

"Buy me lunch," Bobby said when the sweaty handshakes had ended.

The boys nodded, a bit unconvincingly. Bobby assumed it was the part where he told them to pay for lunch. But he felt he was supposed to test them a bit. That's when he reinterpreted that little prompt about not using his card so much. That hesitation was probably just his Papa preparing him for this particular meal, not rebuking him for a lack of faith.

The three men were standing in front of a Mexican restaurant called Zacatecas Tacos. That sounded good to all of them. Jamie and Rich convened a secret meeting in the parking lot, involving opening their wallets and counting the bills before entering.

Bobby didn't make the meal an advanced test for them by ordering the Grande Fiesta with beer and appetizers. He just ordered a burrito and water—what he normally would have eaten for lunch. The young men followed his example, and they seemed to escape the register with a few dollars left.

While they waited for their food, Bobby felt inspired to strike up a conversation with the Mexican man who was assembling his burrito across the counter. "*Hola, qué tal?*"

"Hola," said the compact man who glanced up at Bobby.

When he saw the man's eyes, Bobby recognized his opening. At first it seemed the cook had a wandering eye, one that didn't follow the other. But Bobby caught an inner hint that the eye was glass. The man was missing an eye. Bobby asked him about it.

The answer was entirely in Spanish, and Bobby didn't understand all of it, though it seemed baseball had somehow been involved.

Switching to English, Bobby asked if he could pray for the man's eye.

The offer made the cook recoil, his brow furrowed and his head pulled back. But his friend at the cash register said the Spanish equivalent of "What can it hurt?"

Bobby motioned for the cook to come to the counter where he could reach him.

Jamie and Rich drew close in mute fascination.

Reaching up just briefly, Bobby said, "Let this eye be replaced with a new one, right here, right now." And then he waited.

The cook started to blink rapidly. He was looking at the counter, not at Bobby. In fact, he seemed to have forgotten about Bobby. Something about that counter seemed to have arrested his attention.

Jamie and Rich pressed up next to Bobby as if to get a better look.

At that moment, something fell from the cook's face, clattering as it bounced around the kitchen floor.

A confusion of curse words followed, then praise and inarticulate shouting. The cook started to stamp his feet and then bounce in place. Tears were wetting his entire face. He finally looked squarely at Bobby again, and there the miracle was apparent. Two good eyes, perfectly aligned.

"That's good, that's real good!" Bobby rejoiced with full-chested enthusiasm.

Jamie clamped both hands over his mouth.

Rich started laughing, which soon became a bit unhinged.

Once they had all wiped their faces with napkins and stopped their laughing and praising, they learned the man with the new eye was named Pedro. He came out of the kitchen, and Rich took video of his testimony. Jamie translated it into English as they recorded. When his testimony was done, the little cook hugged them each several times.

Eventually they got to sit down to eat their warm burritos and have the meeting for which the boys had paid. Bobby urged them to push past the shock of the miraculous eye to tell him the story of how they had found him.

The story of the dream with the tray of wine was quite entertaining, as if his Papa had arranged it just to give him a laugh. That was well within expectations, as far as Bobby's relationship with his heavenly Father went.

"So what do you think it all means?" Jamie paused before taking another bite of his burrito.

Bobby was interrupted from answering when three women came from the back room, accompanied by Pedro.

114

One of the women, younger and slimmer than the others, spoke English and translated for everyone. "I am Vera," she said. "I am Pedro's cousin. This is Pedro's mother. She wants to thank you for giving her son back his eye. It's a great miracle." She was talking over her aunt, who streamed words so rapidly that Vera was clearly translating only the key points.

"And this is my mother." Vera pulled the other woman forward. "She is Pedro's aunt, Louisa. She has cancer in her breast. She was hoping you might ask God for another miracle." Vera's voice crackled with emotion.

Bobby never stopped at a time like this to explain the difference between restoring a lost eye and healing cancer. With the input of several pastors and teachers over the years, he had come to accept the idea that one was a miracle and the other a healing. Bobby's gift was primarily for miracles—replacing parts and even raising someone from the dead. On more than one occasion, he had joked with friends that he should wait around until a sick person died, knowing that then he would be able to help them, and not necessarily until then.

In this case, Bobby had a sense of confidence that his Papa would provide the healing. "Okay," he said. "But I'll need some help." He looked around the room and found plenty of assistants. He could sense that several people in the room expected the woman's cancer would be healed. Certainly they based that confidence on what they had seen with the restored eye. Among those faith-filled folks, Bobby wasn't even in the top five. Without explaining any of this, he enlisted those helpers.

Vera, Jamie, Pedro, and Gio from behind the cash register all put their hands on Louisa's shoulders. She closed her eyes, made the sign of the cross, and muttered prayers in Spanish.

Bobby stepped up to the little circle of people and said simply, "Cancer, you be cursed right now. I declare healing in Louisa's body right now." He elevated his voice slightly and spoke more sharply than his usual tone, but without much drama. He was a bit distracted as he spoke, listening for some assurance from his Papa that the healing had happened.

When Louisa grabbed her right breast and began speaking rapidly to her daughter, Vera suddenly began to sob, tears now soaking her oval cheeks. She raised her hands to her face and watched as Louisa walked briskly away.

"She says she feels that it is all better." Vera spoke through her hands. "She is going to the ladies' room to check it out."

It took only a few heartbeats after the translation before they heard a cry and a series of Spanish praises from the bathroom in the tiny restaurant. Louisa came back, adjusting her blouse and undergarments in between raising her hands in praise.

"She is all better!" Vera said, providing a translation that no one needed. "Praise God, the tumor is gone!"

Bobby raised his hands and praised God along with Louisa.

Pedro and Gio jumped up and down, and Jamie and Rich whooped in celebration.

It was a good lunch, including the burritos.

Starting a New Journey

His voice sounded raspy and tired, but Anna didn't stop Bobby from continuing the long phone conversation.

"I found out that it was easier for me to hit the road and travel to unknown places, set up a life there and then move on again, than it was to explore my own heart. That was part o' the point o' all that travelin'."

He came to understand that truth more clearly while in Vancouver. But, after benefiting from emotional healing ministry at that church, he moved on once again. This time he knew more about the invisible luggage he took with him, but plenty of it was still there.

For most people, that was a metaphor—emotional baggage. But Bobby could often see, with his spiritual sight, manifestations of his wounded heart.

As he walked from the bus station in Minot, North Dakota that following spring, he glanced over his shoulder just the way he would check that his backpack was strapped shut. But this time he was looking at a little collection of heart wounds. In his mind's eye, they were like the trinkets, toys, pots, and pans tied to an old-fashioned tinker's wagon. He could even hear them banging together if he turned his attention fully toward them. Seeing them was not as difficult as getting rid of them, but awareness was progress, and it allowed him to check his headway.

While still in Minot, walking to his job in a restaurant along a main highway in town, he was talking to his Papa about that emotional baggage. He became distracted by the feeling that he had something stuck to the bottom of his shoe. Looking down, he saw a long strip of paper towel dragging from his heel. As soon as he saw it, a sandaled foot stomped that tail of towels and broke it free from his foot. Not until that intervention was Bobby certain he had not been literally trailing towels. He was seeing another revelation of his emotional woundedness.

There he was, dragging some deep hurt, this one having to do with his mother. And Jesus just said, "Nope, you don't have to drag that along anymore." With that, he stomped on it as Bobby walked on. And that freed Bobby from one more small hindrance. He could sense a new freedom from shame after that particular revelation.

His hurts each healed in a unique way. Not all were as painless as Jesus stepping on some paper towels.

He stayed in Minot for a bit longer than was his custom, listening for more of those healing revelations. While he was there, someone from the Vancouver church tracked him down.

Terry Holterman, one of the pastors of the Vancouver church, had heard stories from Jack Williams about the miracle man that shook up the Redwood church. Jack pointed her to Bobby Nightingale when she called him for advice regarding a terrible tragedy in their church.

Karla Warner had been attending the church for years. Recently Karla had married a young man with whom she had fallen deeply in love. She knew about his past struggles, but accepted his assurance that those struggles were behind him. But Tim, Karla's new husband, fell back into the drug use that had plagued him in previous stages of his life. Tim stopped attending church, spiraled into more destructive behavior, and kept Karla and some of her closest friends awake nights with worry and prayers for his deliverance.

One Thursday night, Karla returned from a prayer meeting to find Tim dead on the bathroom floor. Her friends from the prayer group responded to her frantic phone calls and swarmed her apartment. They prayed earnestly for Tim to be raised from the dead, but nothing happened. Eventually an ambulance took his body away to be examined by the county coroner.

When Terry heard what had happened, she texted Karla. **"Let me know what you need from me. I'm just a few minutes away."**

Karla texted back, **"Will you stand with me in faith for Tim's resurrection?"**

When Terry texted her offer of help, she had in mind pastoral comfort and logistical assistance, perhaps meeting with the grieving family and arranging the funeral. But when she saw Karla's request, she knew she had to agree. While it occurred to Terry that this request from Karla may have been a natural denial response to losing a spouse, Karla's fierce faith had inspired Terry before. Karla was not going to let death disarm her fighting faith.

As Terry started asking around among the church staff about anyone with experience raising someone from the dead, her senior pastor recalled stories he had heard about Bobby. That led her to call Jack Williams. Her phone call with Jack confirmed the identity of the stranger who had been in Vancouver for several months, but who did no extraordinary miracles while he was there.

Terry had an idea where Bobby had gone based on his request for the church office to forward some material to Minot, North Dakota. When she reached him by phone, he thanked her for the material.

She replied, "Oh, you're welcome. I'm actually calling about something else." And she told him Karla's story. "We'll pay to fly you out here if you're willing to give it a try."

Over the phone, on the call with Anna many years later, Bobby explained that he was not a flyer. He wasn't opposed to airplanes per se, and not particularly afraid of them. He simply had never had the need before that offer from Terry. Despite that hurdle, he felt a poke in the back to go back to Vancouver for this one thing.

"Beau used to talk about things like that—leadings and spiritual direction. I didn't really believe him until I started to hear them for myself." Anna allowed herself a personal reflection. It was getting late, and her weariness had dissolved some of her defenses, including concern about how long this phone conversation had gone on.

Bobby got back to explaining how he didn't enjoy his first flight any more than he had expected. He sat in an aisle seat, guessing it would be best for a rapid evacuation of the plane. Being a few inches under six feet tall increased his comfort in the coach seat, but nothing could settle his stomach at the thrust that lifted the hulking metal beast off the runway in North Dakota.

When he reached the Vancouver airport, Bobby had to apologize to Terry when he ran past her to the men's room. There he threw up violently. He expected Terry could hear him retching from the hallway outside the restroom.

"You okay?" She assessed Bobby as he emerged.

Bobby looked up at her and nodded. "Not a frequent flyer."

"Yeah, I see. Is that all your luggage?" She looked with raised eyebrows at the gym bag in his hand.

"It's enough for two days." He forced himself to stand straighter and breathe more easily.

Terry nodded and led him out of the airport. She was a tall woman and probably outweighed Bobby a bit.

She unlocked her minivan, and he tossed his bag behind the center console. He noticed a tarp over the bench behind him, a seat missing its back.

"This is my garage sale truck."

Bobby chuckled. He glanced at her once he connected his seatbelt. He hadn't spent much time with Terry during his stay in Vancouver, but felt that he knew her already.

His stomach was settling a bit, though he didn't expect riding in the van was going to help with that. He tried to distract himself by addressing the business at hand. "So, are ya sure about the young woman who lost her husband?" They were pulling out of the airport parking garage. "I'm not guaranteein' that he'll come back."

"She's strong," Terry said. "This is her idea. She's a fighter, and not likely to let the enemy take anything without resistance."

"That's good. But is she prepared to fail?"

Terry glanced at him as if to gain some assurance she could speak freely. "I've been asking myself a similar question. As a pastor, I wonder what my responsibility is in terms of encouraging Karla to accept what happened. As wise as that sounds, it just doesn't seem like it's time for that yet—not until we make our best try at bringing Tim back." She paused briefly, a small grin rising on her face. "Karla doesn't talk about failing regarding anything in her life, but she knows how things work."

"I didn't come all the way out here to fail, by the way." Bobby was recovering some of his strength, though the motion of the car kept his eyes focused outside to try to still his churning stomach.

Terry let Bobby's declaration sit between them for half a minute. "You didn't tell us much of your story when you were here."

"I was here to get some healin', and I got that started. It just didn't seem like the miracles were the most important thing to talk about then."

Terry didn't press him for more. She returned to the task ahead of them. "The plans for doing this are still in flux. Karla didn't even know where the body was for about twenty-four hours. Then she had to find a place that would allow her free access to Tim. Death in the Western world is a very controlled thing."

"She found him, and she found a place?"

"She did. And we have a tentative schedule. I'll drop you off at Ken's house and pick you up in the morning. That's when Karla hopes for an extended private visitation."

"Good. That sounds good."

After spending a night in the senior pastor's house, meeting his wife and kids, Bobby was collected and driven to the funeral home by Terry and a young man named Samuel Rice.

Samuel explained to Bobby that he had been on a long-term mission trip to Africa the previous year and had assisted one attempt at raising someone from the dead. "I'm also really good friends with Karla and Tim. She's literally like a sister to me. I don't have any natural sisters." Samuel was in his mid-twenties, a twitchy young man, but focused. He struck Bobby as a class clown who had given up the makeup and false nose at some point.

At the funeral home, they found the staff cheerful on a Friday afternoon, perhaps thinking of weekend plans. Bobby could sense Terry and Samuel's offense at the receptionist and staff teasing each other behind the front desk. Of course the assistant manager sobered instantly when he saw them enter. He solemnly ushered them to the viewing room.

Seats for a hundred people waited in rows on dark red carpet, the walls golden with lights casting elongated triangles toward the ceiling every few feet. Was that lighting intended to set a heavenly atmosphere? Bobby had seen heaven. He wasn't feeling it here.

What Bobby was feeling was death. He recognized it in the same way that a house fire survivor might regard the smell of charred lumber. He took a deep breath and hunkered down for another fight.

Bobby had heard people say they didn't want to be raised from the dead once they went to be with Jesus. From what he had heard, he was confident that Tim was with Jesus right then. Who would blame the young man for not wanting to leave heaven for this old world? But Bobby believed two additional things. First, he believed Tim was not being asked to come back to the same life he had left, the same woundedness that led to the drug relapse. Tim would return healed of those addictions. Second, Bobby believed forty-eight hours with Jesus in heaven had changed Tim. Of course Tim would be enjoying Jesus, but he would also know that Jesus accompanies his servants on the earth as in heaven. And Tim would know something about the things he was yet to accomplish on the earth—things he had been assigned that would be his joy—his and Karla's. Bobby believed Tim was willing and Jesus was willing. He was trying to get himself lined up with the two of them, and hoped the others in that room would do the same.

Coming into a situation where he didn't know the others led Bobby to assume little. He expected very little from the wife and her friends. He found an encouraging surprise, however.

Karla took charge of the proceedings—not what he expected of a grieving widow. She welcomed Bobby and introduced him but didn't turn the gathering over to him. Instead, she encouraged everyone to get quiet before God and to think of Jesus, not of death and impossibility. A guy with a guitar was there to facilitate turning their hearts toward faith.

That was a good start as far as Bobby was concerned. He took up a spot in the front row, several seats down from Karla.

Her friends, including Terry and Samuel, drifted to various places in the room, stepping into the worship.

The guitar guy was Andrew, a round young man with a dark beard and a baseball cap on backward. He wore jeans with big holes in the legs, and no shoes. Hardly anyone in the room was wearing shoes. Bobby hoped it wasn't important. He wanted to keep his work boots on.

They sang familiar songs from the Vancouver church, and Bobby easily floated into the worship. He diverted a bit of attention to Terry, who was walking up and down the aisle to his left, alternately praying in an unknown language and singing the songs. Something in the way she did that gave him a sense of peace and a feeling of home. He tucked that observation away for later, focused now on what his Papa had to say about raising Tim.

Without an announcement of any kind, Karla—and then Samuel, followed by Terry—moved toward the wooden casket at the front of the room. It was stained maple, a substantial and luxurious casket.

Bobby wondered if it would be too much to ask to open the lid. He was prepared for that not being an option.

Two other young women who had not introduced themselves moved toward the casket.

Bobby felt compelled to join the little congregation now forming.

Andrew continued to play guitar in the front row even when he wasn't singing.

Karla leaned on the casket, stroking it, and praying in her prayer language—a tongue of angels, it seemed to Bobby. Her sensual approach to that casket was unnerving. Her conviction about what they were attempting was undeniable. The pizza wafting powerful spices over the front of the room declared her expectations. She had brought Tim's favorite food for when he woke up ... hungry.

Then, once more, Karla surprised Bobby. She opened the casket.

He didn't know whether that was prearranged. It wasn't a proper viewing because the body hadn't yet been embalmed. When Karla opened the lid, Bobby discovered that Tim lay under a white sheet, so the living could barely detect the shape of a person inside. When he got closer, Bobby could see the body was packed in ice. Those were objective facts, but nothing to hold his attention. Nothing like the passionate determination of the grieving wife. Her fierce love for her fallen husband drew them together toward their goal.

Samuel moved to the head of the coffin and began to touch the white covering where it seemed Tim's head should be.

Bobby admired his boldness, recognizing something of himself at twenty years younger, perhaps. But Bobby wasn't ready to try raising someone from a coffin twenty years before this. Moving around the casket, Bobby landed next to Samuel. He put his hand on Samuel's back to pray for faith and power.

Within a minute, Samuel turned away from Tim, grabbed Bobby's hand off his back, and placed that hand on the corpse. "Your hands are hot," he said. "Let's get that heat on Tim."

Half a minute later, Andrew stopped playing guitar and spoke to Karla. "I feel like you have another name for Tim. Something only you call him. I feel like it's important right now."

No one in the room showed any sign of knowing anything about such a name, even though these were people who knew Karla well. But she looked hard at Andrew. "God gave me a name for Tim, to pray over him. It was Elisha. It means 'God is my salvation' or 'my rescuer'."

A chill covered Bobby's skin from head to toe. That seemed a clear direction from God—information Andrew couldn't have known, and a revelation that clearly supercharged Karla's faith. Bobby rode her faith, his hand still resting on what seemed to be Tim's head.

After listening to Karla and absorbing the impact of Andrew's revelation, Samuel placed his hand near Bobby's. "Hey, this is really hot here. I feel lots of heat all around here."

Bobby could feel it too. He looked at Karla, who was wiping tears at the confirmation of her secret name for Tim. "Karla, call Tim to come back, but call him by your secret name for him."

By the look on Terry's face—and everyone nodding around them—Bobby could tell this was what they all felt she should do.

Karla leaned into the coffin and stroked where Tim's chest must have been. She hesitated a moment, perhaps feeling the heat Samuel had reported. Then she spoke in a quavering voice. "Come back to me, my beloved. Come back, Elisha. God is your salvation. He is rescuing you from death. Come back now, Elisha. Tim, my Elisha."

Both Bobby and Samuel began to vibrate as she spoke. The coffin was shaking. The tremors began spreading to all the people in the room. Both of the young women Bobby had not met fell to the floor as if fainted. One of those girls, whose foot Bobby could still see from where he stood, was vibrating at the same rate as the casket.

"Death, you get out of here now!" Bobby spoke much more forcefully than he had since he had arrived. With his command, the room seemed to brighten. The vibrations did not diminish.

Samuel fell over backward and hit the carpet hard.

Karla was clinging to the casket as if it were a boat riding the rapids.

Bobby tried to stay connected to the body. It was moving, but not in the way a live person moves. Tim's muscles seemed to be flexing and loosening, as if being rejuvenated even before he took his first breath—the first breath of his resurrected life.

"Elisha, wake up now! Tim, wake up!" Karla shouted.

Movement. Definite movement. Bobby could feel a lifting. A rising.

And Tim sat up.

Bobby fell away onto his backside.

The sheet tumbled off. Ice packs scattered. Several people screamed.

The door to the viewing room burst open, and the funeral home manager staggered at what he saw. Then he fell facedown on the floor as if passed out cold.

Terry was on her knees at the altar rail next to the casket. She wept and laughed and thanked God.

Bobby's arms became limp, and he lay back on the floor, his heart overwhelmed with the victory.

Andrew sat in the front row of seats, his guitar dangling from one hand. He just stared at Karla and Tim.

A nimble and athletic young woman of not more than a hundred and ten pounds, Karla had leapt into Tim's lap. She sat with her arms around his neck, kissing him repeatedly.

Tim had wrapped his long arms around his petite bride and wept loudly through the hugs and kisses.

Bobby knew that no one in that room would ever be the same.

Anna took a long breath. She wiped tears from her cheeks. That story justified the long phone call, as far as she was concerned. But it was very late, past midnight. "Can I call you again? I wanna hear more."

"It's past yer bedtime, isn't it, young lady?"

"Ha! You sound like Jack Williams, calling me 'young lady'." She sighed. "And yes, it is past my bedtime."

"Okay. Mine too. Call me again. But wait this time for the Spirit to tell you when."

Anna agreed to that, perhaps only because she was so tired.

What Are You Doing in Minnesota?

Though he didn't admit it to Jamie and Rich, Bobby was surprised by all that happened in that one lunch at Zacatecas Tacos. He had only entered the restaurant with food in mind, along with a question about his role with these two young strangers.

"Where are you staying?" Jamie said, probably aware of the biblical echo.

"Come and see," Bobby said, letting Jamie know that his words had recalled that scriptural story.

Rich and Jamie followed Bobby back to the efficiency apartment, leaving their car in the strip mall parking lot.

Bobby peeled off his jacket as soon as he opened the door, and Jamie and Rich followed him in. They kept their light jackets on, though, as if uncertain what they were doing.

"May as well take off yer coats. We got some talkin' to do. Gotta figure out what God's arrangin' for the three of us up here in the great white north."

They obediently took off their jackets and joined Bobby at the kitchen table.

He tipped back in the upholstered wooden chair and eyeballed Jamie for a long moment, then gave Rich the same treatment. If he had asked them to open their mouths and say, "*Aaaahhhh*," he suspected they would have done it without hesitation.

Bobby laughed. "Lighten up, boys. It's just us mortals here."

Jamie slumped slightly and let loose a long breath. "So, are you here for some meetings? Did God send you here to do something? Or was it the guy's eye?" He said all that without a pause.

Bobby shook his head. "I'm just here visitin' my daughter. Don't have any meetin's planned. Just stayin' here for a while to get to know my not-so-little girl."

"Maybe we're supposed to help you *set up* some meetings." Rich was less breathless, more pensive.

Bobby shook his head slowly, a considering gesture, not simply a negation. "Doesn't ring true just yet. We can listen and see." He looked them over again, more briefly this time. "What d'you boys have goin' on? Jobs? Church?"

"Yeah, I have a job at a fast-food place," Jamie said. He glanced at Rich. "And Rich is taking temp jobs for now. We go to Heartland Church in Minneapolis. We're not doing much there, just waiting to find out why God sent us up here."

Instantly, Bobby felt he knew. He took a deep breath, overcoming a bit of self-consciousness about what he was about to say. "Well, I think I know what it is. You boys ever think ya might be called to do street ministry like the stuff I do, and like Brian Wright does?"

Brian Wright was an acquaintance of Bobby's, a much younger man who had escaped a life of drugs and crime in favor of healing miracles and making converts in unlikely places. According to Bobby's friends, there were numerous videos online of Brian healing people on the street, and one of him at a rock concert by a band with a less-than-holy reputation. Bobby had been instrumental in getting Brian started on that path. He provided a power upgrade, as Brian called it. Before that, Brian was hungry for more. He was sensing his calling but lacking experience with the kind of power that had made him famous since.

Jamie and Rich surely knew all about Brian Wright, a living legend in their circle of churches. But clearly Bobby had caught them by surprise with that suggestion. They just nodded numbly.

Bobby pursed his lips and assessed his new disciples. "I think we're gonna be spendin' some time together. Findin' some miracles to let loose. What do ya think about that?"

Their nodding became more controlled, but their voices remained mute. Jamie shivered visibly.

Bobby didn't understand what they were overwhelmed with, but hoped they were feeling inspired. He pointed to the wall. "I had a phone installed, so I can get calls." He leaned his chair back a few more inches and reached a pen and sticky pad on the kitchen counter. He swung them onto the table and wrote out his phone number.

The boys each reciprocated with their cell phone numbers.

"Let's not set a time or times," Bobby said. "Let's just wait for further instructions. Give me a call when ya think ya have somethin', even if it seems crazy. Crazy is usually good for this kinda stuff."

Jamie giggled.

The first call came from Bobby to Jamie. "You ever just get the feelin' God wants to see how much yer willin' to do for him? Just for the fun of it?"

It seemed to take Jamie a couple of beats to recognize Bobby's voice—or maybe it was the question that stalled him. Bobby knew his voice was pretty distinct.

He interrupted Jamie's bumpy silence. "Jamie, can you guys meet me in a couple o' hours?" He gave directions to an underpass on a highway along the edge of Minneapolis.

"That's right near us, I think." Jamie finally found words. "Uh, yeah. We can meet you in two hours."

Jamie texted Rich. **"Meet Bobby near here in two hours?"**

"Awesome!"

That was great, but Jamie's chest was resounding with a runaway heart rate. Here he was, an amateur trying to play in the big leagues. But he stopped that little gang fight of thoughts and declared peace amongst the warring factions long enough to call his assistant manager to see if he could come in an hour late. Even if the meeting with Bobby was right on time, Jamie didn't know how long this mission would take, and wanted to give himself a bit of leeway.

His boss agreed to call him back in an hour with the answer. That young manager was used to dealing with the whims and inconsistencies of teenage employees.

It would have been better for Jamie if the meetup had been in ten minutes. The two-hour lead time gave him a chance to worry and fret. He had heard a story about Bobby being shot by a crazed drug dealer after Bobby healed an addict of a knife wound and cleared the guy's mind of the effects of drug use. In a drug-altered state himself, the dealer thought shooting Bobby was necessary to protect his business. According to the version Jamie had heard, Bobby stood up, bleeding from a wound in his chest, and caused the gun to jam before a second shot was fired. He followed that by convincing the dealer that Jesus loved him and could forgive him for anything. It seemed that hearing about forgiveness from a guy he'd just shot in the chest was convincing for that dealer.

Though Bobby did have to take himself to the hospital for some stitches and a stay overnight for observation, the emergency medical staff all agreed it was a miracle that a thirty-eight caliber bullet could pass through Bobby's upper body and do so little damage. All his major organs seemed to have dodged as the bullet made its way through. That was the version Jamie had heard, anyway.

That day in Minneapolis, having too much time to think about such things soured Jamie's stomach. He was relieved when Rich arrived at the apartment, having left his work a couple hours earlier than scheduled. He was overqualified for the packaging assembly-line job. His confidence that he would keep his job was no surprise to Jamie.

Both young men changed clothes and then reconsidered their wardrobe choices. Jamie didn't have a Kevlar vest to slip under his hoodie, or he would have. Rich ended with a white button-up shirt under a light gray V-neck sweatshirt. Jamie took a moment to picture how blood would look on all that light-colored clothing. But he assumed Rich wasn't on that track with him and didn't want to drag him down.

Getting to the viaduct proved to be more difficult than Jamie had assumed. The chain-link fence that protected it on the side where they approached was ten feet high and unbroken. They could see Bobby on the other side of the drainage ditch and service road. He must have found a hole in the fence on his side—or had miraculously transported himself, as it was rumored he had begun to do in recent years.

Jamie and Rich were late after having to cross the bridge and then the highway to get to the opening that had allowed Bobby beneath the overpass.

Bobby waved them over. "Come on here, boys. I want ya to meet someone."

At first glance, Jamie thought Bobby was introducing them to an old man. But, when he reached for a handshake, he could tell the rumpled and stained person in those rags was a woman, and not necessarily a very old woman, though Jamie couldn't guess her age. Her hands were dark and greasy, but neither of the boys withdrew their offer of a handshake. And Jamie stopped himself from wiping his right hand on his pants after releasing the woman's bony grip.

"This is Candice." Bobby was talking like a normal person, clearly ignoring concerns about germs and dirt.

Jamie and Rich both muttered greetings.

Candice croaked a response, though the sound from her mouth was entirely unrecognizable as a word in any particular language. She then turned abruptly and flailed at something just behind her head. Her attacker seemed to pass her ear and then fly down her shirt.

For a second, Jamie feared she was going to extricate the invader by tearing her shirt off.

Bobby intervened. "Distraction, I command you to break off. You're not welcome here. Get out."

Candice jumped away from Bobby as if offended by his tone. She flailed her spidery hands around again, but it appeared her tormenter was on the way out instead of in this time. She started to speak in rapid gibberish. "*Suba somma fibber ta mimmy no fammy hoppa naw naw.*" Her gravelly voice was stern, if incomprehensible.

Before she could repeat that nonsense, Bobby spoke firmly again. "No tongues. No speech. Just quiet for now." As he said that, he was edging closer to Candice, even as she was backing away.

Jamie stood his ground, aware that Rich was also staring, mesmerized.

Candice was backing toward a little hut made of vegetable crates attached to a huge cardboard box, all covered in garbage bags. Instead of blindly backing into the little home, Candice spun and ducked inside like a prairie dog evading a hawk.

Bobby stopped at the entrance. Now it was his turn to speak gibberish, it seemed. The boys both stood passively while Bobby prayed in a language they didn't recognize. But Bobby made a gesture with his hand.

Jamie and Rich started praying in their prayer languages. How did Bobby know they could do that? Maybe just a lucky guess. Standing there jabbering in three unknown languages outside the cardboard home of a woman plagued by invisible bugs was weird, but that weirdness fit Jamie's expectations of what it would be like to work with Bobby Nightingale.

After nearly a minute of these incomprehensible prayers, the cardboard house seemed to explode. Candice came dashing out the other end and bounced off the chain-link fence. When she crashed into the fence a second time, it seemed that she was *not* trying to escape. It looked more like she was trying to hurt herself.

"Stop hurtin' my friend Candice," Bobby said. "If ya don't stop now, I'll make sure these angels torture you mercilessly."

Rich and Jamie looked at each other. They had been living together too long. They were surely thinking the same thing. Was Bobby referring to them as angels? That seemed even stranger than anything that had happened yet.

But Bobby interrupted that confusion as if he, too, knew what they were thinking. "Show 'em, Lord." He spoke to the air above the two younger men.

Instantly, Jamie saw a shining being hovering in front of them with a fierce focus to his fiery eyes. Then others joined, and they all turned toward Candice.

Jamie started shivering, his teeth chattering slightly.

Rich stood stone still. He was making a sort of low humming sound.

Bobby turned toward Candice just in time to dodge a direct assault. She lunged at him with one hand raised in a fist and the other in a claw. That claw seemed even more inhuman than before.

"*Aaahhhyeeeeeeiiii!*" she screamed as she attacked.

After Bobby's bull-fighter dodge, Candice wheeled around to face him again, but she suddenly seemed to faint, falling over backward.

Instead of dashing to her rescue, Bobby just stepped over to where she lay. "More distractions." He stood over her, looking down.

She opened her eyes and looked at him with the most human expression Jamie had yet seen on her face. She looked like a little girl caught playing a trick.

Bobby addressed her gently. "Candice, ya have the chance to be free now. I'm gonna call out all the spirits that're tormentin' you. Just sit back and watch 'em fly away. Don't worry, they can't hurt ya. Don't believe their lies."

Though he spoke those words to her calmly, and she seemed to be in her right mind for a moment, Candice's response was a blood-chilling scream. She screamed as if her heart were being physically torn from her chest.

Bobby didn't flinch. He just stood over her and watched.

To Jamie, it looked like Bobby was monitoring something, even counting. Jamie felt a sensation of traffic rushing past, as if they were back up on the highway with several large SUVs whizzing by.

Rich was shifting his weight so rapidly it looked like he was dancing in place, maybe deciding whether it was time to run for his life.

The scream must have lasted nearly half a minute. Given its volume and intensity, that seemed an impossibly long time. Jamie was certain that either his sanity or Candice's life would not survive that piercing cry.

Then there was silence. Candice appeared to be unconscious—or perhaps dead. But she coughed. And she started to shiver. It was not even near freezing, though they all wore jackets in the damp cool of early autumn. The shivering reminded Jamie of someone in shock.

Bobby knelt next to Candice and took off his jacket. "Come on, boys, we need to keep her warm until she comes outta this. We might need to call an ambulance." He pointed to the destroyed shack. "See if she has any decent blankets in there."

Rich dove into the mess of cardboard and plastic bags while Jamie held his phone at the ready.

Bobby gestured for him to come close, then grabbed Jamie's free hand to pull him to his knees. "We need to keep 'er warm." Bobby lifted Candice and cradled her as if she weighed hardly anything.

To say that Jamie was out of his depth would be to imply that he had an idea which way was up, and that he realized he was in danger of drowning. Some part of him was remembering the screaming maniac from a moment ago. Another was considering how truly dirty this woman was. Still another was thinking how inappropriate it might be for Bobby to be holding a strange woman so intimately close. One advantage of this bubbling cauldron of thoughts was that none of them held full control of Jamie's mind. Compliance with Bobby's instructions was the strongest direction Jamie could find.

Rich joined them, carrying an army-green wool blanket and a shiny emergency blanket that was somewhat less shiny than it had once been. They wrapped Candice in the two layers while Bobby prayed aloud.

"Papa, we need instructions here. Do we get emergency personnel involved?" He said this as if calling a friend for advice on an unusual situation.

At least, Jamie *assumed* this was an unusual situation for Bobby, though probably not entirely unprecedented.

"Call 911," Bobby said after waiting a few seconds.

Jamie blindly obeyed Bobby's command, his shaking hands finding the three numbers with some effort. Help was on the way. Certainly a different kind of help than Bobby had brought to the tortured woman.

Even if all of this was shocking and disorienting, the experience would certainly stick with Jamie and Rich the way every detail of a major accident sticks with a person—every second amplified into fine details of glass bits flying, pieces of flotsam tumbling, and a spectrum of noises that one doesn't normally hear.

Most of all, Jamie learned that being trained by Bobby Nightingale would be as unpredictable as had been the very fact that he and Rich would become Bobby's personal disciples.

Something About Terry

After raising Tim from the dead, Bobby developed a bond with everyone in that room. The one most natural for him to debrief with was Terry.

Anna found pictures of her on the internet. Terry Holterman was a round-faced woman with dark hair cut approximately in a pageboy style, streaks of white adding interest to her utilitarian coif.

Anna did wait to call Bobby only when she thought God was leading her to do so. She hoped she was hearing right and not just being impatient for Bobby to tell her more about that resurrection and what followed.

"Uh, I hope you don't mind me asking about … romance."

Bobby gave a long sigh. "I kinda gave up on that after things broke up with Lori. After that, I found a few women friends. A couple o' those tried to lasso me into romance, but I got clear o' those as quick as can be. Terry was different."

At that, Anna coaxed him to return to his story.

After Tim was raised, the entire staff of the funeral home emptied into the parking lot. Someone had called the police, apparently uncertain what to do when a person comes back from the dead. Deaths have to be reported, so the caller must have figured the reversal had to be recorded as well.

Bobby found an end to his energy by the time they filed out of the funeral home. In that void, he floated to Terry's van, weightless as a space walker.

Samuel arranged to drive Tim and Karla in their car after helping with some of the logistics, such as clothes for the formerly deceased man. Apparently the couple didn't feel up to driving just then.

"I'm glad he can still function in the face of all that." Terry was watching Samuel joke with Karla and Tim as they disengaged from the police and the funeral home staff and ducked into a gray Toyota Camry.

Nodding and grinning, Bobby was still struggling to find gravity and a place to settle down.

"You wanna get something to eat?" Terry was still staring out the front windshield as if unaware of who sat in the passenger seat. Or perhaps she was completely comfortable with him being there and didn't need to look at him.

Bobby agreed to the early dinner or late lunch, and Terry started her van with a turn of the key.

As they drove, it occurred to him that he hadn't put any thought into what he would do after the resurrection. His other dead-raising experience had come with little warning and no planning. This one was at least somewhat planned. But that planning had stopped short of any post-resurrection celebrations. That the participants had mostly dispersed to their various lives implied that all of them were sharing that disorientation.

Terry had originally agreed to pick up Bobby at the airport and taxi him around, including back to the airport the next day. So she was his obvious landing place when he did splashdown from that otherworldly experience.

"I forgot to call Ken about the resurrection." Terry's voice was dull and wooden as she mentioned the senior pastor. Then she burst out laughing. "I guess I better do that before long."

"Ha. Yeah. I supposed that is the thing to do." Bobby hummed a second. "The other time I saw this happen, the senior pastor was there intercedin' already, so I didn't have to make a call."

Terry parked the van in front of the restaurant. "Ken? This is Terry. It happened. It really happened. He woke up."

Bobby could hear the shouting and sudden burst of sobs over Terry's flip phone. He chuckled for a whole minute, a sort of purging laughter.

Terry just grinned numbly. That, too, seemed funny—in a twisted way.

When he and Terry finally sat at their table, having harvested a meal from the buffet, she stopped to look at what she had collected.

"Ya look like ya took someone else's plate." Bobby speared his first bite of au gratin potatoes.

"I feel like I did. I don't know what I was thinking." Terry surveyed the assorted dollops of various food groups, perhaps ten or twelve piles in all. It was a sort of sampler plate. "I guess I couldn't decide." She chuckled and shrugged.

"Yer still freaked out by what happened, o' course." Bobby lingered on her befuddled face for a few seconds. "I guess that's normal."

"Normal for raising the dead?" She picked up her fork and regarded her sampler plate.

"Only my second time. Third at the most."

"I've only heard the story of one other." Terry lifted her eyes from her plate after stabbing a pickled beet.

"Well, the first was when I was a teenager. He might not've been completely dead. There wasn't a doctor around to make a diagnosis."

At Terry's prompting, he told the story of his friend falling in the Big Blue River with a broken bottle jammed into his neck. Given that they were sitting at a restaurant, Bobby tried to sanitize the tale a bit.

Terry just ate and listened. Even though she was eating like a normal person, her silence seemed evidence she was still in shock.

Bobby expected he could talk on and on without interruption, but he was interested in the food piled on his plate. "I've seen some other pretty unbelievable things." Bobby started in on some roasted chicken. "It does mess with yer brain. I saw a guy git four missin' teeth back in a matter o' seconds." He looked at Terry, raising his fork. "I think yer head starts to stretch around this stuff, and it doesn't hurt so much the next time Papa pulls one outta thin air."

"Papa? Pulls one?"

"Yeah, God pulls a miracle out o' the air."

She nodded her acceptance of his explanation, but Bobby was hoping to get her to do some of the talking.

"So, what's the biggest miracle you saw with your own eyes before today?"

Terry swallowed a bite of Waldorf salad. Her big dark gray-blue eyes lodged into their corners for a few seconds. "I like watching legs grow out." She reached for her water glass. "But one time I saw this basketball player's *arm* grow out, like, two or three inches."

Bobby smiled appreciatively. "Yeah, I love watchin' that sorta stuff."

"So, do you have miracle meetings or healing meetings that you lead?"

Shaking his head slowly, he said, "I only sorta led one meeting down in Redwood once, and the whole crowd just ended up on the floor lookin' like a bunch o' kooks … including me."

Terry seemed to be settling into a more normal conversational mode, but looked a bit concerned, or maybe just curious. "Has anyone talked to you about taking your ministry on the road or anything?" She pushed the bangs out of her face with the back of her left hand.

"Nobody I would take seriously." Bobby tipped his head to one side as he chewed. He reached for his glass of water. "I'm not a public speaker."

Nodding slightly, Terry quirked one corner of her mouth. "You like staying under the radar." She would know that from the time he spent at her church. "But did you do any miracles while you were here before? Some things I don't know about?"

Bobby looked at her under his eyebrows and grinned sheepishly. "Papa doesn't generally let me stay 'under the radar,' as you say. There's always somethin'."

"So, what happened?"

"Well, I worked as a dishwasher in this place over by the airport for a couple o' months. And the guy I shared the dish machine with had terrible teeth. He had one that was all infected and needed to come out, but he had no insurance. He wasn't even legal, I think. His name was Juan. He begged me to knock the tooth out with a butter knife. But I figured if he was *that* desperate, then he would let me take a crack at healin' the thing. And he did." Bobby resumed his work on a pile of mashed sweet potatoes. "When word about his healed tooth got out, people would bring me every ache and pain, and their aunts' and uncles' too. I didn't heal everythin', of course. Never really been a healer like that. But got enough of 'em better that they kept comin'."

"And there was never a chance to invite them to church with you?" Terry was still pushing food around her plate.

"Most of 'em didn't speak English. Mostly they seemed to be Catholics." He knew that answer was incomplete. "An' I was stayin' under the radar."

Terry seemed to understand, at least as much as she could in her post-resurrection state.

Bobby liked the way the frayed edges of their personalities wove so easily together. He even started to think that if he was inclined to settle down with someone, Terry might be the kind of person he could try that with.

Bobby's voice was getting scratchy again. "But I wasn't there yet. Not even witnessin' a resurrection would change me that much."

Anna sighed into her phone. "I get that."

How to Explain This to His Daughter

When the ambulance took Candice to the emergency room, Bobby rode with her, claiming to be her close friend. He figured he was as close to a friend as any severely demonized homeless woman could expect to have.

Rich and Jamie had gone back to their apartment. Bobby had asked Rich to meet him at the hospital after he dropped Jamie off for his shift at work. Unsure of what would be required of him, Bobby wanted Rich to at least give him a ride home, if not to take turns staying with Candice.

Bobby told the emergency room staff that Candice had a sort of fit and then lay unconscious for a while, shivering. They seemed to confirm his impression that she was in shock. She remained unconscious for over an hour. When he saw her briefly in that state, she acted as if she were having occasional dreams—vivid, but not frightening, dreams.

The hospital staff sent him to sit in a small waiting area outside the room where they were monitoring Candice. He listened to the rhythm of the doctors' and nurses' voices in that room, professional and unemotional. Then someone laughed, and an animated conversation arose, including a new voice Bobby didn't recognize. Again, there was laughter.

A nurse came to the door and looked at him. "She's asking for you."

Bobby almost denied that that was possible, since he wasn't actually someone she knew, but he held onto that confession.

Just then Rich arrived, in a sort of rush that implied he'd had to fight his way in.

Bobby didn't ask for details, just gestured for Rich to follow him into the exam room.

They found Candice on an exam bed with her head propped halfway into a sitting position. A nurse had apparently just finished a sponge bath, which dirtied two pans of water. Candice wore a hospital gown that revealed a skinny woman with very tan arms. She was smiling at Bobby and Rich.

"Candice." Bobby reflected her smile, greatly relieved.

"Is it Bobby?" she said. "Sorry, I don't remember *your* name." She furrowed her brow at Rich.

Once again, Rich offered his hand and told her his name. Again, he seemed hesitant, but Bobby expected this time Rich's pause came from shock at the transformation he was witnessing. The woman before them seemed shy, fidgety, and awkward, but she seemed far too civilized to be living in a cardboard box.

"Wait till Jamie hears about this," Rich muttered, as if unaware he had spoken aloud.

Bobby chuckled. "How ya feelin'?" He stepped up close to Candice's bedside.

"I feel fine. But I'm so confused about how I got here. I know you did something—you helped me—but I'm not remembering everything clearly."

Bobby thought it was good that Candice didn't remember *everything*. But as soon as the last nurse left the room, he spoke frankly to his new friend. "You were under the power o' some big and mean spirits. I just made 'em leave ya alone. You don't remember because you weren't in yer right mind when I first found you."

"How did you find me?"

"I asked God to show me someone we could help, and he told me to look for candy. Then I realized he meant Candy with a capital *C*, or Candice. When I understood that, he showed me the viaduct under the highway—right where we found you."

Candice stared through Bobby as if she were sorting this explanation against her smeared memory. "I was screaming. I remember that." She zeroed in on Bobby's face again.

It wasn't just politeness that motivated Bobby to distract her from her more embarrassing past behaviors. There were more important things to discuss. Instead of answering her recollection, he asked her a question. "Ya wanna know how to stay sane and sober?"

Candice's deep green eyes remained on Bobby, though she seemed to be digging past him to something else. Maybe she was recalling why he was asking her that question. "I do. I wanna get clean and stay clean."

With Rich attending closely, perhaps taking a lesson, Bobby introduced Candice to the notion of a life lived with God inside her, explaining it much as he did for Tracy. They ended a little give-and-take with Bobby leading her through a simple prayer.

By this time, the hospital staff had collected their files on Candice and called a social worker to come see her.

Bobby and Rich left eventually, promising to stay in touch with her. They got the phone number of the social worker and left Bobby's home phone number in exchange.

It was dark outside, and Bobby suspected Tracy had been trying to reach him. He had promised they would talk that evening.

Rich drove him home so he could check his voice mail. "So, was that what you wanted us to see?" Rich stalled Bobby's exit from the car with that question.

Bobby stood and then bent to look in the passenger door. "I never know exactly how things are gonna work out. We'll keep workin' on it. They won't all be like that." He stepped back half a pace. "Ya gotta admit ya did learn a thing or two—even if ya don't know what yet."

Rich just smiled and nodded.

"Well, stay in touch. Gotta go connect with my daughter." Bobby took his leave.

As he expected, there were two messages for him in voice mail. He called Tracy. "Sorry I wasn't home."

"Oh, it's okay." Tracy's voice dove deferentially.

"I could use some supper. Wanna come by and pick me up? I'm buyin'."

"Sure. I'll be over in fifteen minutes."

"Great."

Bobby hung up and turned to cleaning up his place. He talked to God as he worked. "So, how much do ya reckon I should tell Tracy about what I was doin' this afternoon?" He put dishes in the dishwasher. "She already thinks her dad is an alien from a far-off galaxy." He chuckled lazily.

Listening as he rinsed and stacked, Bobby thought he heard only permission and freedom, no warnings about sparing Tracy the bizarre details. As he listened, he hummed a Tchaikovsky piano concerto he had forgotten the name of. His voice bounced along with the scales, though perhaps not quite on key.

By the time Tracy arrived, Bobby had made enough headway to forget how the apartment looked and to focus on greeting her. He had even had time to spiff himself with a clean shirt, a face wash, and a quick trim around his beard.

"Did you eat anything?" He let her in the door.

"A little of this and that. Not a real meal." Tracy did a realtor's glance about the place. Her eyes settled back on him. "So, what have you been up to?"

Bobby began to tell her about meeting Jamie and Rich. He turned out the lights and followed her out the door. As he climbed into the car, he filled her in without heavy redactions. Starting with the first encounter with those two young men, he told her about the string of healings and miracles that eventually led to his direct answer regarding what he had been doing that day. "I felt like I was supposed to train those two guys, though I don't have any kinda plan for how. Just show and tell, is all I could think of."

"Show and tell?"

"Yeah, ya know—show 'em what I do and then answer their questions. That usually works good enough."

"You've trained others like that?" Tracy was driving toward an Italian restaurant she had proposed.

"I've been sorta travelin' between a bunch o' churches associated with my friend, Jack Williams. They're all over the place now. I sometimes agree to do some show and tell with young folks in those churches."

"They ask you for this?"

"Yeah. Their pastors or healing ministry people or such. Sometimes old friends get their noses into it and set me up for this kinda trainin'. I don't mind. Usually it's fun to see what the kids do with it."

"Do with it?"

"Well, when someone comes into new power for healin' or miracles, they react a bunch o' different ways."

Tracy looked at him, but then focused on changing lanes, her hands tight on the wheel.

"There was this little girl in Dallas ... I say a little girl, but I mean a young woman. She wasn't much more 'n five feet. And she was like a cute little kid to me. Anyway, she sees me put this guy's ear back together. It'd been busted up in an accident, and he could hardly hear anything outta it." Bobby snickered as he recalled the incident. "She was real impressed, and, like, overcome with compassion to help somebody. But it was just me and her and this young guy who was her friend. The guy with the ear was goin' home to tell everybody his good news. So she looks at me and sees this big scar from the car accident when I was a kid. And she says, 'We should heal you too.' And she stands on her tiptoes and reaches for my forehead. Now, I wasn't sure what she was up to, so I stepped back half a step, and she kinda lunged at me. She ended up with her hand on my eyes instead o' my forehead. What she didn't know was I'd been puttin' off gettin' glasses, 'cause o' the bother and expense. So, she accidentally zaps my eyes with her good intentions. And my eyes cleared up like that." He snapped his fingers as Tracy turned off the car and sat with her hand on the door handle.

"Your eyes were healed?"

"Yep. No need for glasses now. And that was, like, five years ago." He followed her lead and got out of the car but continued speaking over the roof. "I just laugh at how she healed me by accident."

Tracy led the way into the restaurant.

Bobby checked to make sure he had his wallet, still conscious of how important that was to Tracy.

The hostess showed them to a table under a dim Tiffany lamp.

Bobby kept pouring out his answers to her smattering of questions. Not until the main course was on the table and the salad plates removed did he finally get to the story of Candice, the answer to the original question.

Tracy's food was probably a useful shelter for her, especially when he described the parts where evil spirits spoke to him and he told them what to do. She was more tongue-tied than preoccupied with the food, he was pretty sure.

"So I have her social worker's phone number." Bobby just remembered he had written it down, but wondered where he'd put it. Setting his fork on his plate, he checked a few pockets, finally locating it in the breast pocket of his newish flannel shirt. He pulled the slip of paper out to confirm he had found it, then put it back.

Tracy stared at his pocket for several seconds as if she had seen evidence there that her father was not simply delusional.

Bobby grinned at her. "Pretty strange stuff, huh?"

Tracy half nodded and half shook her head, as expressive a nonanswer as anyone could have offered. She strained a brief grin and then returned to her pasta and Alfredo sauce.

Bobby paused for an internal check with his Papa. Had he missed a signal to go slow and omit some of the details of that day? He couldn't find evidence of that, so he just smiled again at his daughter and picked up another piece of garlic bread.

Turning the Water into Drinking Water

Anna urged Bobby to tell her more about his partnership with Terry. She had found evidence that it continued to this day.

He told her that, in his forties, he allowed Terry to talk him into joining her and a group from her church on a trip to Haiti. All expenses paid sounded good to him, and his itch for new horizons made him vulnerable to her missionary invitation.

Her church was connected with a small group of Haitians and North Americans living on the coast not far from Port-au-Prince. They provided medical services, health education, and filters for drinking water. While there, Terry's team would hold evening meetings for the folks in the area—folks who attended a variety of churches as well as patronized a variety of voodoo practitioners. The latter she especially emphasized in her invitation to Bobby.

"Sounds fun." At that point in his life, he was only being half facetious about such things.

The missionaries had carried themselves in a way that didn't antagonize the local witch doctors. Terry assured him she was not advocating a challenge like Elijah on Mount Carmel. But she said she hoped Bobby's power might reach some of those who were impressed with their own.

At their first evening meeting in a little church with a mud floor and a tin roof, a voodoo priest did attend. He sat in the back.

Bobby was sitting in the front row listening to Terry preach—and trying to sense what his part was in that service. Terry had left that undefined. He felt free to listen to his Papa for instructions.

She and Bobby were aware of the priest because the pastor who served that little church in the hills had pointed him out. Terry didn't appear to be focusing on the leathery-skinned man with his dreadlocks piled high atop his head. She was carefully pacing her words for the translator, concentrating on her preaching.

In those years, Bobby was seeing fewer vivid spiritual revelations—spirits almost as visible as people—but there in the humid interior of that church packed with a hundred people, he caught sight of something that swooped over his head and began circling Terry. It stretched a claw toward her neck. When Bobby saw that threat, Terry began clearing her throat as if suddenly coming down with a cold.

Bobby resisted the urge to jump up and try to rescue his friend. During his internal tussle, he felt his Papa telling him to head for the *back* of the church instead. That twisted against his instincts even more, but Bobby suspected he would be glad he followed his Papa's advice.

Rising from the bench, which rocked slightly when he stood, he kept his head low and turned up the aisle in the half light of early evening. Immediately he could see his destination. To him, it looked like the voodoo priest was sharing his seat with a dozen other critters of various sizes. The largest creature was a giant skeleton that hovered over him.

When Bobby drew near, he reached his hand up and snatched a chain that was as clear to him as if it came from the hardware store. It stretched toward the front of the room. Bobby reeled in the spirit circling Terry, pulling it back toward the priest.

The priest muttered something in French and then gibbered in another language, but he didn't seem surprised to see Bobby interfering with his games.

Hearing the various languages, Bobby hoped he wouldn't need a translator for what came next. He tried speaking to the priest in English. "I come to keep ya contained right back here, not to chase ya out. Ya need to hear with she's sayin', so I don't want ya to leave. But I'm shuttin' down yer interference right now."

A dozen or so people had diverted their attention to the odd little white man approaching the priest. An eight-year-old girl, sitting on her mother's lap, spoke up. "He's grabbing the priest's friend." She spoke to her mother in Creole.

Bobby was impressed with the girl's sight, but more impressed with his sudden ability to understand Creole.

"You cannot stop me." The priest spoke in a raspy old voice.

Though Bobby had understood every word, he suspected the priest wasn't speaking English. "I can, and I have." Bobby stuck with his native tongue as far as he could tell.

The priest tried to stand, but abruptly sat back down. It was the sort of move he would have made if Bobby had pushed against his chest as he tried to stand. But Bobby's hands were at his sides, and he wasn't leaning close enough to push the priest.

Bobby gestured to the man sitting next to the priest, an even older man who appeared to be heavily inebriated. Compliantly, the old man pushed over, allowing Bobby to squeeze in next to the priest. Bobby was hesitant about squeezing so close to the voodoo master, but he felt he was supposed to do just that, demons and all. He took a deep breath and trusted his health and safety to his Papa and to the angels that seemed to be crowding into that little church.

Again, the priest tried to stand, only to be pressed back into his seat. This time Bobby saw a shining hand reach down and settle him.

Bobby could feel the priest resign himself to staying seated, slumping slightly. Bobby hoped the old guy was focusing on what Terry was saying.

When Terry began to wrap up a few minutes later, Bobby heard the priest sniffle. He did a furtive check and saw a tear rolling down the old man's face.

When Terry issued her invitation to anyone who wanted to start a life of communion with Jesus, the priest was the first one on his feet. This time he was not pushed back down. He headed unhindered to the front of the room, not even slowed by the glaring attention of everyone around him.

Bobby felt a magnetic pull to follow the priest. He arrived at the front just in time to see the old man wracked by spasmodic seizures. An invisible opponent jerked at all the priest's limbs simultaneously, twisting and crumpling him. What looked like it should have landed him writhing on the floor instead held him suspended in an awkward crouch.

Terry was observing the priest much the way a mother watches a toddler pitching a fit in a busy store, both aghast and unperturbed at the same time. When she turned toward Bobby, her expression changed to relief.

Just when it appeared the circus had arrived in town and there would be a spectacle to behold, Bobby shut it down. He placed a hand on the head of the oddly twisted priest, and the man hit the ground with more force than mere gravity could account for. He even rebounded slightly when he hit the hard-packed mud. After one more spasm, he lay perfectly still, not even breathing hard after the invisible wrestling match. His eyes were wide and unresponsive, his mouth agape with white flecks of saliva dotting his beard.

Then he smiled and blinked. "Praise de Lord," he said in heavily accented English.

The congregation had sucked all the air out of the room more than once during the man's spasms and the violent landing. Now they gave all that air back with a cheer and a chorus of praise. Dozens surged toward the front of the room where Bobby and Terry and others met them for healing, deliverance, and salvation.

When the pastor of that little church, a converted army officer known in the area as Colonel Pastor, saw the raw power of God at work, he came to Bobby. "Mr. Bobby," he said in his deep voice, "you must help us with one more thing. Our water is cursed. It kills the babies and makes big people sick."

Bobby was just standing up from touching a boy's leg to make it grow. Growing out legs he had done. Freeing people from monstrous spirits he had also done. Healing a community's water would be a new one.

He and the rest of the visiting team had listened to a briefing on the water issues with which Haiti struggled. Chemical, medical, and social explanations for the poor quality of the water had all been presented. No one had mentioned a curse. The one explanation didn't negate the others, of course. Much about Haiti seemed to be cursed as far as Bobby could tell, seeing more manifest demons than he was used to in most places.

He saw that Terry was guiding a dozen people into a relationship with Jesus, with the help of a translator. Thinking she might meet up with them later, Bobby agreed to go with Colonel Pastor and half a dozen other men from the church. On the way out the door, they collected Paul McDermott, one of the missionaries from Canada. He raised his eyebrows high when they explained the nature of this new mission.

Outside, the inky night sky glistened with reflections off the ocean, scattered starlight, and dispersed electric lights. Bobby focused on the immediate task—not tripping and falling from the path.

The pastor led the small procession snaking up the mountain to a scraggly grove of trees and shrubs. Taking one of the two flashlights carried by the group, Colonel Pastor shone its beam on a small polished bit of driftwood roughly shaped like a man. Red strings with bones and bits of metal tied to the ends hung from the childish sculpture's neck and arms.

The pastor kicked the little man over without much drama. "The shrine is not the power. The power is the curse left here many generations ago. We must break the power of the generations that this shrine is here to worship. Tonight I feel the power to defeat this enemy."

Bobby wasn't feeling much in particular, but he turned his attention to a sort of green fog he perceived on the hillside above them. A smell of rotten eggs intensified as he measured that eerie presence. Without warning, Bobby belched. Then all the men around him began belching, a couple of them uncontrollably.

"Okay, cut that out!" Bobby aimed his command at the green fog, not the dismayed men around him.

One of the locals turned and ran back down the path, a dangerously hasty retreat in the dark.

Staring into the night, Bobby saw that green presence form into a face, then coalesce into an animated figure that lunged at him with violent intent.

Bobby just put up one hand as if to break the attacker's nose. "Jesus has come to take this ground. It belongs to him. All your claims here are broken." He didn't raise his voice much despite the rush of adrenaline. He was tired after a long day. Bobby turned to the pastor and his friends. "It's broken. Now it's time for us to bless this water."

Even as he spoke, that green monster lunged at him again, as if to ambush him from behind.

Bobby merely flicked at it with one hand and said nothing. "Just start blessing the water," he said. Then he surveyed the dark hill. "Where exactly *is* the water?" The batteries in the flashlights were being reserved for emergency use only.

Colonel Pastor took two steps to his right and pointed to a rock partly obscured by grass and weeds. "It comes out of the ground here."

Bobby squeezed past him and ducked to see some sign of the flow. When he saw starlight reflecting on a thin stream, he put his hand in it. "I bless this water in the name o' Jesus. He makes it good from now on." He gestured for the others to follow his example. "Go ahead," he said to the pastor.

In his travels to all sorts of churches, Bobby had observed a wide variety of ceremonies and practices. He had never seen anything like what they were doing tonight. Not a ritualistic person, he nevertheless felt that a sort of ceremony was needed to recover from the curse.

When the last of the men, Paul McDermott, touched the water and declared it blessed, Colonel Pastor let out a shout, and the others followed. This was not part of Bobby's newly invented ritual. To him it felt like a shout of relief as much as a shout of triumph.

From that day forward, the villages that received their drinking water from that little spring saw no more deaths by waterborne disease. They had only to treat their water with common filtering techniques to keep it pure and healthy.

Bobby joked to Terry the next morning, "I woulda turned it into wine, but I don't really drink wine. Never got a taste for it."

The Women in His Life

One morning, about his fourth week in Minnesota, Bobby received a phone call from Terry. She had moved to Florida, retired from full-time church work. Apparently she still had the ability to do a miracle or two, managing to locate Bobby.

"Well, you found me."

"Your two new disciples have been all over the internet with the news of their experiences with you. What was the last one? The boy on crutches in the mall with metal pins in his legs?"

"Sounds familiar." Bobby was anxious to hear why Terry was calling, sensing it was *her* who was in need this time. "What's up with you, girl?"

A weary sigh came over the phone before Terry answered with words. "Well, I hate to bother you with this, but I got some serious news, and I felt like I should call you and just let you know."

"Cancer?"

"Mm-hmm. I've been prayed for by folks down here at the church, but I felt like you would have something for me."

Bobby was still getting information from his supernatural source as he listened to her. "Yeah. I think this is a spirit that latched onto you at that last ministry trip to Mexico."

"Hmm. That makes some sense. We did confront a local healer—some guy who called himself 'The Power of God.' It did occur to me that I might not have been as protected as I should have been."

"It's comin' off right now." Bobby thought his authority would travel over the phone connection and set his friend free. What happened, instead, was something his friends called "Bobby Airlines."

Instantly, Bobby was in Naples, Florida, with Terry, and she was falling on the floor laughing at the surprise—a surprise to both her and Bobby.

Tracy lay on the floor in her bathrobe, cackling like a crazy woman.

Bobby could see an iron hand releasing its grip on her. He didn't even get a chance to address the demonic disease—it just ran away. Maybe the surprise of his arrival had loosened something in Terry as well as in himself, allowing the power of God to blast through.

Sitting down on the pale green carpet next to Terry, Bobby crossed his legs and gently placed a hand on her head, which stopped rolling from side to side and rested into his touch. This gentleness between them was unique in Bobby's experience. With no other woman would he feel free to touch her like that, alone in her home. He was also aware of the authority he had in Terry's life—something she had granted him uniquely, as far as he knew.

Bobby had been at Terry's condo for two hours when he started to feel an internal pull back to his place in Minnesota. They were seated at the kitchen table by then, looking every bit the old married couple—Bobby in his socks, his hair rumpled and beard untrimmed, Terry in her white floral-print robe with her dark gray hair matted to one side. He could tell she worried about the way she looked no more than he did.

"I'm supposed to have brunch with my daughter, Tracy, today." He settled his coffee cup on the table. "Feels like I'm headin' back there real soon."

"I'm so glad you're getting to know her. I feel like you *both* need this."

Bobby nodded, reached across the table, and patted Terry's hand. "You're one o' the most generous people I ever met. Gotta go."

Terry nodded, as if giving him permission for another miraculous flight across the country. "See you soon, I hope."

"Soon."

Then he was back in his apartment. He set to finding his shoes and picked up a message from Tracy. She had reported being on her way ten minutes before, which meant she would be downstairs in her car any moment. "Good timing, there, Papa." Bobby chuckled.

As soon as Bobby settled himself in the passenger seat next to Tracy, she noticed something.

"So, I see you've been eating already. Couldn't wait?" She wasn't scolding, just teasing.

After a puzzled moment, Bobby reached up to his beard, which often contained a historical record of past meals. He glimpsed a crumb tumbling to his lap out of his mustache. A sheepish grin served as an apology as well as a pause, while he considered how much to say. "Had a muffin at my friend's house this morning."

"Those guys that follow you around?" Tracy pulled out of a parking space, checking her mirrors.

"Ah, no. Someone I haven't told ya about yet."

Tracy slowed the car and took a good look at her dad. "You have a girlfriend?"

Bobby guffawed. "Whoa, that women's intuition thing is real!"

Tracy laughed along with him. "So, tell me. Who is she? You haven't said anything about any women since I met you."

"Her name is Terry. I met her in Vancouver many years ago. We've been friends for decades now. Good friends."

"Really? Good friends?"

"I know what yer thinkin', young lady. Just good friends." He tipped his head to the right. "But, if I *was* to think o' marryin' again, I would start that conversation with Terry."

"So, just friends, but with possibilities."

"Yeah, that's right."

"So tell me about her. What does she do? Where does she live?"

Now Bobby was back at that original door mat on which he had hesitated before, like a guy wondering whether just wiping his feet there would be enough, or whether he had to take his shoes off to really come clean. "She's retired." He started with

155

the easy part. "She was a pastor for, like, forty years. She's a bit older 'an me, but not so's you'd notice."

"Older woman, bakes muffins, a caring person, right? Pastor and all?" Tracy sounded approving, her tone still light and cheerful.

Bobby loved the sound of her approving voice, her teasing acceptance. In hopes of staying there, he prayed he wouldn't have to tell Tracy about his morning transport. He wouldn't lie, of course, but he didn't have to tell everything to everyone.

"So ..." Tracy prompted.

"Well, we've been on some great adventures together, and she still calls me when she can find me. We don't see each other too often."

Just then, Tracy had to slam on her brakes to avoid a delivery truck that had begun to enter the left turn lane on the five-lane road. It had stopped short, leaving her blocked. She just missed the rear bumper of the big square bread truck, as well as the little red compact car that buzzed past on her right. Tracy swore.

Bobby laughed.

"You think that's funny?" Tracy scowled but let out some slack, ending with a bit of a snicker. "You have a foul-mouthed daughter. You okay with that?"

Bobby chuckled as Tracy finally made her transition into the turn lane. "I recognize more evidence that you're related to me and yer mom, is all." He kept his eyes forward with a satisfied grin. He was thankful for the women in his life. Both of them.

In Jail a Time or Two

From scattered reports on various websites, Anna could tell that the late 1990s inserted a series of swerves and crashes into the story of Bobby's life. Some might have been easy to see coming, others more like being T-boned at an intersection. Mostly those were messes of his own design, according to Bobby.

In 1999, he was in New Orleans working as a dishwasher in an old eatery near the French Quarter. His aggressive insistence on trying to heal cervical cancer in one of his fellow employees was misinterpreted, and he lost his job. The one-room apartment in which he lived was paid through till the end of the month, ten days away, so he set himself that deadline for finding new work. A couple ditch-digging jobs outside the city were all he could rummage in the next two weeks, and that shortfall landed him on the street.

By this point in his life, he was thinking of himself as a missionary to anywhere he was put. The homeless population of New Orleans seemed as good a mission field as he could imagine.

Sleeping in a rusted 1964 Ford Fairlane in a vacant lot, Bobby made a few acquaintances, if not friends. He had no money to steal, and his possessions were just enough to use for a pillow and covering at night, so he fit in with the desperate and depressed folks around him. Many of those were African American men who had HIV/AIDS.

At various points in his experience, Bobby had felt a sort of divine supply of power to heal a particular illness. He still didn't think of himself as a healer, but when the scope of his life focused crosshairs on a specific need in his neighborhood, he fired at it with confidence.

He told Anna about the time he healed Grady Thomas, an AIDS patient being kept alive by a federal program and an angelic presence in his life. Bobby had first noticed the angels.

Walking on a cobblestone street on his way from a soup kitchen, Bobby was celebrating the feeling of warm food in his belly when he was surprised to see what he thought was an illuminated sculpture next to an abandoned corner store. Two bright white figures sat close together, still and vigilant, their faces as bright as their clothes, their hair gold and luminescent.

Bobby was used to being the only white face in these parts, though his sunbaked skin could hardly be described as truly white. But these guys were different. Shaking himself free from what felt like a web of dullness, he realized he was looking at two angels. He rarely saw things like that in those days, and was surprised to have the privilege reinstated, if that's what was happening. He turned from his walk toward his temporary residence to see what the angels were doing there in the weed-lined parking lot.

They stood up when he turned their way. They were over eight feet tall. When he was just about to ask them a question, both angels looked toward the ground near their feet.

A darker figure lay there in a fetal position on the cushions of an old pink couch. Only the cushions remained, no couch frame in sight. There lay Grady Thomas. He might have been dead, but Bobby had dealt with that before, so he didn't stop his advance toward that critical spot, even in the face of the two intimidating guardians.

Grady was shivering when Bobby knelt next to him, unusual for June in New Orleans. Then Grady rolled onto his back and started to choke, his dark brown face turning ashen gray, then purple to nearly charcoal black.

Bobby told the spirit of death to let Grady go, but the seizure continued until Grady finally made the noise old timers call the death rattle. His lungs seemed to be filling with liquid, his frail frame overcome by the ravages of AIDS. Then Grady was silent, though his eyes stood open wide.

Bobby searched for a pulse and could find none. For a brief moment, Bobby wondered why the angels bothered to call him to Grady's side. But that was where he picked up more fuel for his joke about it being better to call him *after* someone died than to call him for the healing. Setting aside his brief indignation at being called to Grady's side too late, Bobby leaned into another battle with the spirit of death. He grabbed Grady and held him to his chest. He commanded life to go from his body into Grady's. Why exactly he did it that way, he couldn't explain. But, after about a minute, he heard Grady gasp for breath.

Grady's wide eyes came back to life, his huge pupils returning to normal size. His face faded to a more natural brown. When Bobby let go, Grady sat up and began to cough.

Bobby patted him on the back, continuing to mutter commands to several unfriendly spirits that swept up and out of Grady's body.

Then Grady looked at Bobby. "I think I was dead. And I don't think I'm gonna die anymore. I feel fine." He struggled to stand, pressing his right hand against the crumbling curb on one side and his left hand on Bobby's shoulder. "I feel good!"

Bobby stood up as soon as Grady finished his rise to full height. Grady was a few inches taller than Bobby. Looking up at him from close range, Bobby let out a laugh. He extended his hand, and the two men introduced themselves. "I think you just got healed o' whatever killed ya," Bobby said.

"Was AIDS. That's what the doctors said."

"You feel good?"

"I feel better 'n any time I can remember, even before I got that damn disease."

Bobby clapped Grady on the shoulder. "God sent two angels to call me to yer side, and then the devil tried to take yer life before I could do anythin' to help ya. But God raised ya from the dead just to stick it to that old devil. And I do believe he healed you of the AIDS along with it."

"I believe everythin' you're sayin' there, brother. I surely do." Grady hopped, clapped his hands, and then danced a little softshoe on the gravelly pavement. "Praise the Lord!"

Bobby remembered the two angels and looked up to see them laughing. They started to dance with Grady. This struck Bobby as uproariously funny. He started to cackle in high-pitched peals.

Grady caught the giggles and began to stagger around instead of dance.

The two of them were making so much noise that a police cruiser, doing its rounds in the neighborhood, slowed to see the drunk and disorderly pair.

After the cruiser parked, a barrel-chested female cop climbed out. The driver followed.

As they approached, Bobby began to point at them and laugh. He found it funny that he was so full of God the police thought he was drunk.

"Put your hands on your heads," the male officer said.

Grady didn't seem to understand, doubling over and laughing harder.

Bobby tried to raise his hands over his head.

Simultaneous with that attempt, the male officer suddenly spilled over backward as if Bobby had struck him under the nose, though the officer was still twelve feet away.

The female officer watched her partner hit the pavement. She sprinted at Bobby and tackled him.

Bobby went down like a scarecrow in a hurricane, still laughing at the top of his lungs.

Grady started clapping his hands and guffawed as if impressed with the skillful tackle.

Once on top of Bobby, the officer pointed her service pistol at Grady. "On the ground, now!"

Grady complied by falling over backward, still laughing.

Four more police cars arrived within minutes, surely alerted by the fall of the first officer. New Orleans cops charged into the vacant parking lot and then slowed. Bobby and Grady were still laughing. A few yards away lay a uniformed police officer doing the same. The female officer stood in the middle of the three men, her pistol held in two hands, a look of intense confusion on her face.

Bobby and Grady spent that night in jail. It was the best Bobby had slept in months.

A detective interrogated Bobby while he was in custody. "What did you hit the officer with?" The fiftyish cop had a brown paper bag complexion and greased back gray and black hair.

"I didn't touch 'im." Bobby was having trouble stopping his smile. Though the giggles had passed by then.

"The officer reporting the incident saw you raise your hands, and her partner fell over backward at the same time."

"But I didn't touch 'im."

"Did you throw something? Why did the officer seem drunk when units arrived on the scene? No trace of alcohol was found in his blood."

"It was the Holy Ghost."

"What?"

"When I raised my hands, the Holy Ghost hit 'im and made 'im drunk in th' Spirit." All this was language the officer could have heard in a number of churches in the parish, if he ever attended one.

"Why did you do that?"

"Have ya asked the officer about this?" Bobby was truly curious.

"I'm asking *you* questions. Just answer me. Why did you do it?"

"I didn't mean to. It was an accident."

"What was?"

"The officer gettin' hit."

"So you *did* hit him."

"No, the Holy Ghost hit 'im."

"What is that? The street name for some new drug?"

"No ... not that I know of."

"And what were you doing in that neighborhood? It's just drug dealers and prostitutes down there."

"I live down there."

"What's your address?"

"It's a vacant lot. Don't think it has an address."

"So, you're homeless?"

"Yes, sir."

"And on drugs?"

"No, sir."

"Why did you seem drunk when we brought you in?"

"Did they test the urine sample yet?"

"I'm asking the questions."

"What was the question?"

What impressed Bobby most over the years of recounting that story was the bull-headed persistence of the detective. He seemed to be pursuing answers he was determined to ignore.

Bobby stayed in jail for two more days until a judge declared he had to be released for lack of evidence of wrongdoing.

Grady stood waiting outside the police station when Bobby finally stepped out the front door.

Bobby smiled grandly at his new friend. "Ya look like a new man."

"I am *exactly* that. I am a new man." Grady chuckled. "Wasn't much left of the old one, so it's a good thing I ain't him no more."

Bobby started to laugh, but reined that in for fear of another arrest. He wasn't sure he could endure another interrogation like that ... without laughing his butt off.

The Time of My Life

A few days after his brief trip to Florida, Bobby called Rich and told him it was time to meet up for what would be their fifth ministry venture.

"Where?" Rich swallowed noisily.

"You tell me," Bobby said.

"You want *me* to tell *you* where we should go?" He made a noise somewhere between "huh" and "aha." Then he answered simply, "The plaza by the Minneapolis Central Library."

"Right. What time?"

"Half an hour." Rich paused. "I'll text Jamie."

Bobby hopped on a bus, which would likely get him there a bit late. But he felt confident their appointment was going to work out just fine. He read a paperback novel as he rode, depending on the height of the buildings in his peripheral vision and the frequency of stops to alert him when they reached downtown.

Jamie was blindly following instructions again. This time they came from Rich. Jamie had the added distraction of driving in Friday morning traffic. That traffic surely included tourists seeing the city or escaping for a weekend with the fall leaves, whose colors were at their height.

It was eleven thirty in the morning when Jamie left his car in the parking garage and headed for the plaza. He felt no compulsion to stay clear of ground zero before the other two arrived. He thought he might scout the area in advance of the main assault. He wandered toward the bicycle racks—steel poles embedded in the pavement like giant staples. Looking around with a wide view of the place in mind, he nearly stumbled over a young man of about eighteen years old struggling with his bike lock, his face toward the ground.

"Hey," the young man said, marrying a greeting to a warning.

"Oh, sorry. I didn't see you there." Jamie stepped back a bit.

"Yeah, that's *my* line." The kid grinned in Jamie's general direction.

That odd reply and silly grin set Jamie's brain into reset mode, trying to figure out what he had stumbled into. A white cane with a red tip, folded in one saddle bag on the bike, the sunglasses on a cloudy day, and the young man feeling around on the ground without looking at his hands, added up. "Oh, sorry." The second apology was supposed to cover not realizing the young man was blind. Then he looked at the bike and the young man again. "Wait, you ride a bike?"

"Ha. Yeah. Aren't you glad it's not a bus?" He stood up. "I'm Gerry." He extended his hand into empty space near Jamie.

Jamie took that hand. "Jamie. You must be some kinda stunt rider to do it without seeing."

Gerry took a deep breath, obviously accustomed to explaining himself. "I gotta get around, and I like the feeling of the air in my face. I use echolocation to test what's around me, clicking with my mouth as I go, especially in unfamiliar territory."

"Dang. That's awesome." Jamie remembered Gerry feeling around on the ground. "But you lost something?"

"My key to my lock. It's on a yellow springy thing with a yellow plastic tag on it. At least my friends tell me it's yellow. They could just be BS-ing me."

Jamie almost laughed at the joke as he searched the ground. "I don't see it here. If it really is yellow, it would stand out on the dark gray pavement."

"I'll take your word for that. I've never seen anything yellow or gray."

"Yeah." Jamie was in problem-solving mode now. "Do you have another key at home? Maybe I could drive you there so you can pick it up and bring it back."

"Really? You would do that?"

"Yeah. We just have to wait a minute for a couple friends I was supposed to meet here."

"That would be great. Are those friends hot girls? That would be even better."

"Not hot, not girls." Jamie snickered at the juxtaposition of that question with Bobby Nightingale.

"Too bad. How old are you, about twenty-three?"

"Whoa, that's scary. Reminds me of this friend of mine who knows stuff supernaturally." That last bit of extra information tumbled out like a troop of clowns exiting a tiny car. "Yeah, he can heal all kinds of stuff too, like even blindness." That came along like the clown on the tiny motorcycle catching up to his companions.

Gerry fell fully silent.

As if on cue, Bobby strode up, followed thirty seconds later by Rich. The timing allowed Jamie to make leisurely introductions for each in turn. Jamie hoped Gerry couldn't sense the knowing glances being exchanged by the coconspirators.

"Which one is your friend who heals blind people?" Gerry said after meeting Rich.

"He is." Rich and Bobby simultaneously pointed to each other.

"Either you both are, or neither," Gerry said.

"Well, ya could let us give it a try and find out if either of us can," said Bobby.

"Definitely not a hot girl." Gerry had cocked his head to the side to listen.

Bobby seemed to ignore the joke. "What could it hurt?"

"Uh, you could smack me in the forehead, and that might hurt." Gerry shopped a broad smile around at the three others.

Jamie kept laughing, appreciating Gerry's humor and only beginning to consider the stall tactic it constituted.

"My friend here can tell ya somethin' about yer childhood that'll make ya believe this healing is possible." Bobby looked at Rich, who looked back with his eyebrows as high as he could arch them. It was more than a question. It was more like a rebuke. But Jamie was learning to expect Bobby to put them on the spot.

"Go ahead, tell 'im." Bobby spread half a smile and nodded very slowly.

Rich's face morphed through a variety of scowls and puckers. Then his eyebrows shot up again. "I see you very nearly drowning under a bridge as a kid—in a river near your house. And your mother had to actually be admitted to the hospital because of the emotional stress that put on her."

Gerry had no wise crack for that. He stood still, turning his head slowly from side to side as if sweeping the area with a radar dish.

"We can heal those eyes." Bobby spoke in a low, reassuring voice.

"Actually, it's your brain that needs healing, or the part that connects your eyes to your brain." Rich seemed to get another news flash over the wire.

"Okay, this is freakin' me out." Gerry's smile had turned rigid.

"I'm gonna pray for just a few seconds," Bobby said. "Then Rich can gently touch ya on the head, if y'er willing."

"No smacking." Gerry said it with less comedic energy than his earlier jokes.

"No smacking." Bobby prayed briefly for direction and power, and Rich stepped up to Gerry.

"Okay if I put my hand here?" Rich touched Gerry on the forehead just below his brown bangs.

Gerry nodded slightly.

Bobby motioned for Jamie to get around behind Gerry. Then Bobby said to Rich, "Just tell his optical nerve to be restored, and the part o' his brain that's supposed to see."

"Okay. Eyes—I mean, optical nerve and brain—be healed now." Rich's voice quavered just a bit.

Bobby put one hand on Rich's free shoulder and let out a puff of air.

Instantly, Gerry shouted, "*Aaaeeeeeeee.*" He flew backward into Jamie's hands.

Jamie just avoided tumbling over, managing to keep Gerry on his feet.

As soon as he was standing on his own again, Gerry reached shaky hands to his dark glasses. He pulled them off. The plastic-framed glasses slipped from his fingers and clattered to the pavement. Gerry shook his head. "I don't know. I don't know what's ha— happ— happening." He whipped his head left and right. "What is this? What's happening?"

"Hit him again." Bobby pushed Rich forward a step.

As Rich reached up to Gerry's face, the teenager flinched, as if responding to the proximity of Rich's hand. Then something snapped between that hand and Gerry.

The teen staggered backward again. His hands out to his sides, he vibrated from head to toe and stared straight ahead. Now he was staring like someone who could see. "I ... I ... I ... I," was all Gerry could say. Then he started to cry like a little kid, even as he surveyed his surroundings with a look of wonder. "You really did it."

Jamie and Rich were both laughing hysterically.

Bobby just grinned at them and at Gerry.

Jesus in the Gumbo

Bobby got into the habit of visiting New Orleans every couple years, mostly to see how Grady was doing. Four years after those days in jail, Bobby was back in the Delta with very little cash, but with a strong sense that he was supposed to be there. He found Grady employed at a barber shop where he had worked his way up from sweeping to cutting hair, thanks to a community college course.

Grady had moved in with his sister and her kids in those days, and Bobby was invited over as his honored guest.

Loraine, Grady's sister, seemed happy to thank her brother's healer, but she also seemed nervous about something. Something with the food, perhaps.

Bobby had lost twenty pounds since Grady had seen him last, the result of two long fasts and too few jobs. Maybe he looked hungry to Loraine, and that worried her about the amount of food she had. His visit hadn't been planned in advance.

Three adults and three children ages eight to fourteen sat down to the meal. Grady insisted Bobby give the blessing.

By this time, Bobby had figured out the house was not flush with funds or food, so he whispered a request to his Papa before uttering the prayer over the meal. Never an orator, and not trained as a preacher, Bobby kept the prayer short and unembellished. But he felt a great weight lift off when he said "amen."

On the momentum of that liberated feeling, Bobby attacked the biscuits and gumbo like a fireman who can smell the smoke of a distant fire when he sits down to eat. When he scraped his bowl clean, coming up short of licking it, Bobby looked up with a smile. "That was some o' the best gumbo I ever ate, Loraine. I'd really like to have some more, if you don't mind."

Loraine looked at Grady, her big brown eyes pleading for rescue.

Tommy, the fourteen-year-old, spoke up. "I'm not hungry. Bobby can have the rest of mine."

That nearly broke Bobby in two, so he stood up from the table to relieve his hosts of their pain. "Sorry I surprised ya like this, folks—not expectin' a hungry guest and all." He made his way around Earline, the youngest of the kids, and squeezed past the kitchen counter toward the stove.

Loraine had knit her brow tightly, her eyes following him in shocked silence as he lifted the lid to the gumbo pot. A column of steam rose from the pot, and Loraine gasped. Her head shook, and her jaw dropped when Bobby began filling his bowl with hot gumbo.

"Lord Jesus." She pushed away from the table.

"That's right." Bobby wound his way back toward the table. He set down his bowl and then doubled back, grabbing a couple more biscuits.

Grady and Loraine sat in stunned silence.

Earline spoke up. "Momma, did Jesus make us more gumbo?"

Bobby laughed and laughed.

Winter on the Way

By the time he was in his sixties, Bobby knew one thing about Minnesota. When you mention it anywhere besides Minnesota, people say, "It's cold up there." His dedication to getting to know Tracy was all that kept him in the Twin Cities through October and November. Whether he could do December and January was yet to be seen. He followed his Papa's leading as a rule, but that leading seemed to generally tend south around this time of year.

Tracy had developed the habit of picking up little items for Bobby's apartment when she saw garage sales as she traveled for her real estate work. Bobby accepted each gift gratefully, starting with a framed black-and-white photo of a Chicago street scene from the 1950s. "You know I'm just gonna give this back to ya to keep for me when I hit th' road again."

She didn't look surprised. "I just want you to be comfortable while you're here. And I love to browse garage sales. My place is full up." And she continued to visit Bobby's place with something new in her hands each time.

With Jamie and Rich, Bobby's relationship had evolved to one of mission control. He would call the boys and tell them what he thought the Spirit was leading them to do that day or that weekend—or whatever time period seemed to be in play. Once, he told them he thought they were supposed to sit quietly in their apartment, picture Jesus coming into the room, and then stay there until Jesus gave them instructions otherwise. Later he heard how that night ended with two teenage boys being healed of broken bones and then committing their lives to following Jesus.

Bobby expected Jamie and Rich would get a message to move on before winter hit. He envied them that escape.

"You probably should get a warmer coat," Tracy said. They were out shopping in the middle of November.

Bobby had taken a couple temporary jobs in light manufacturing to help pay his expenses, not completely comfortable using his blind debit card for the long-term—which three months was for him. Tracy had begun to invite him over for home-cooked meals more often, and even paid for an occasional meal out. But her buying him a winter coat seemed to suit his soul even worse than his current jacket would suit a Minnesota winter.

"We'll see. I may not be around for the whole winter." Bobby was careful to only mention that when absolutely necessary. He didn't want to drag around a cloud of imminent departure when he was with Tracy.

"How about socks?" Tracy stopped at a display of wool socks in the department store they currently perused.

Something—or someone—told Bobby it would be good to let her get him a couple pairs of socks. It seemed an odd concession, but it felt important. "Yeah. I suppose those'd be good at night. Gets cold in my room."

"And you might even have a day when you need to wear them outside. Some days in November can get real cold."

Bobby picked up two pairs of socks and nodded approvingly, happy with his choice and at peace with Tracy paying, if she offered. He liked it better when he coasted along, spending the invisible cash in the bank account from Redwood, California. But that strategy had a short half-life.

When they made their way to the cash register, a line of early holiday shoppers already formed there, Bobby settled in like a retired guy with nothing better to do than shop. As he parked in that contentment, he suddenly knew something about the older woman standing in front of him.

"You have a metal right hip." He said it as soon as she glanced in his general direction.

"I beg your pardon?" She puckered her lips for a second. "Hey, as a matter of fact, I do have a metal hip. I had replacement surgery three years ago. How did you know? Are you a doctor?"

"Still hurts ya some, 'specially when the weather changes like this, huh?" He kept his tone sympathetic, a low hum to his voice.

The old woman's painted-on eyebrows did a quick dip. "How do you know these things?"

Bobby caught a glimpse of Tracy in the corner of his eye and thought he saw her smile briefly, like someone who was in on the joke. "Sometimes God tells me things like this just before he does a miracle—like replacing a metal hip with a painless, natural one."

"You do? I mean, he does?" The woman's last question almost sounded like the squeak of a dog's chew toy. Her watery eyes, behind thick glasses, drifted upward, and her head tilted back a little, as if she were looking past Bobby at something more fascinating. Her expression turned from contemplative to savoring, her eyes brightening and a smile beginning on her dark red lips. Then she began to cry.

Bobby gently took the woman's elbow, her silky purple winter coat soft to the touch. He led her two steps forward to keep her place in line.

But she wasn't paying attention to that. "Did you do something to me?"

"God is giving ya a new hip right now."

"But why? I had surgery already. I got a titanium one, and it cost thirteen thousand dollars."

"This one's for free."

Now the woman seemed to connect her conscious mind with something happening to her hip. She lifted her right leg, bent at the knee. Once she put her foot back on the ground, she shifted her weight from left to right. She twisted, then looked at Bobby. "You know, I suddenly feel much younger. It's like I'm remembering what it was like to have my own regular hip before it hurt so bad. I think you're right. Or, I should say, I believe. I do believe."

"It started happenin' before ya believed," Bobby said.

The woman looked at Tracy now. "It feels really good. Much better than before. And better than the other one."

Bobby looked at Tracy. "Go ahead and put your hand near her left hip and say, 'Hip, be healed.'"

Tracy had followed the still-nameless woman toward the front of the line. Now she seemed to be following her into her dreamlike state. Her hands moved in slow motion. But she was awake enough to remember her manners. "I'm Tracy, and this is my dad. Okay if I put a hand on you?"

The woman nodded. "Alice."

Tracy placed her right hand near Alice's other hip, which was obscured by her puffy purple coat, and she approximated Bobby's instructions, uttering something like a command for healing.

"Oh, that's nice." Alice's eyes grew wide. "Oh, my dear." And she did another round of shifting weight, lifting knees, and waggling hips.

Bobby noted that nearly a dozen people were now attending to the strange goings-on. "Both of 'em better now?" Bobby asked.

"They *are*." Alice's slide-trombone reply implied that Bobby's question constituted the strangest coincidence with what was happening to her hips.

"That's God showin' ya just how much he loves ya, Alice."

With all the attention on Alice as she continued to test, proclaim, and chuckle, Bobby was probably the only one who noticed Tracy sniffing and wiping at tears.

They had reached the head of the line. While Bobby was looking at Tracy, Alice snatched the socks from his hand and threw them onto her pile of goods. "I'm payin' for these, and you can't stop me." She punctuated that with peals of laughter.

That settled the issue of who would pay for the socks.

A Very Windy City

"I found a couple of small publications that mention you, or someone very like you, in the early 2000s." Anna wanted to test Bobby's long-standing commitment to anonymity. "There were a couple of videos too. One was you lengthening a woman's leg by a full two inches so that it was perfectly obvious to the viewer. The other miracle video involved interviews with a man and his wife after you restored the man's severed spine so he could walk."

Bobby cleared his throat. "I didn't know about those. Never looked on the internet. Don't expect to start now."

When she prompted him about those days, he recalled that he had survived a couple northern winters in the past, including one in Chicago in about 2003 or 2004. Bobby was hiding from his growing fame. He didn't have to turn down invitations to various churches and revival conferences if they didn't know where to find him. He had no ties with Chicago, and thought it would be a good place to hide for a while.

For his daily bread, Bobby worked at a meat-packing plant, cleaning up after the butchers had done their worst to the doe-eyed cattle and squealing pigs. The low man on the totem pole, Bobby usually worked the nonkosher side of the business where the old joke proved not to be true—that the resourceful meat company used every bit of the pig except the squeal. He survived a job like that by knowing the pay was better than many alternatives, and that he wouldn't be staying long, just as he wouldn't be staying long in the cold winds off Lake Michigan.

Sitting in his hotel room where he paid three hundred dollars a month for one room and a bath, Bobby was missing Terry, or maybe just regretting being in hiding. Though he still traveled extensively, rarely staying anywhere for more than a few months, he had accumulated acquaintances all over the western half of the continent from Nebraska to California, from Vancouver to Juarez.

His room was cold, the neighbors were loud and uninviting, and his book was boring. Bobby decided to wander—a dangerous thing for a single man on a Saturday night, he knew.

He walked fast enough to feel warm after a couple blocks, pushing past the initial shock of ten-degree windchill. He passed a more reputable hotel than the one he was staying in and thought he recognized someone—a young man he had worked with on the West Coast. It seemed such a longshot coincidence that Bobby was inclined to see it as a divine arrangement. On the other hand, his old acquaintance seemed preoccupied and might not even remember him.

After walking on past, Bobby scolded himself for that fit of bashfulness and turned back. His turn resulted in direct eye contact with Stevie Collins, his old friend. Stevie was wearing all leather from head to toe, including a leather fedora and a long leather coat. It appeared he had achieved some part of his dream to be a rock star, or at least to dress like one.

"Bobby?" Stevie had short, artificially black hair, and what looked like black eye makeup. "Bobby, is that you?"

A voice called from inside the limo Stevie was about to enter. "Hey, Stevie, your groupies are looking older these days."

Stevie cursed at the owner of that voice and kept his focus on Bobby. "How ya doin', old man?"

"I'm good, kid. You look like ya found a band ya can go somewhere with." Bobby recalled lots of dreamy conversations with Stevie about what he wanted to be some day. Bobby had heard him sing back then and thought it likely the kid could make it in the business, about which he admittedly knew very little.

"Yeah, it's the big time. Goin' to play over at the Pavilion. Headliners. But I wouldn't be here if it weren't for you, Bobby. You saved my life."

The owner of that other voice stood up out of the limo to see the cause of their delay.

Stevie was referring to a drug overdose he had survived when Bobby found him in the basement of the restaurant where they'd both worked. Stevie had taken one too many of the wrong kind of pills. When Bobby took him to the emergency room, doctors said he was allergic to something he had taken. Those doctors also claimed Stevie would have died without Bobby's intervention. They couldn't quite get their heads around exactly what that intervention was, but both Bobby and Stevie knew that God had saved the young man's life that day.

"Hey, are you still doing the miracle stuff?" Stevie asked.

"Miracles?" His friend turned toward Bobby.

"Bobby, this is Karl. He's the lead guitarist in the band." Then Stevie turned to Karl. "This is the guy that saved my life back when I was messing with those pills I told you about. He's a real miracle worker, literally."

"Awesome." Karl shook Bobby's hand. He was a skinny kid who looked like he would fit in a college math department. "Hey, bring him with us. We could have him do some miracles and freak people out."

Stevie laughed.

Bobby thought it was a stupid idea and was sure it wouldn't be seriously considered.

A woman in leather pants and coat joined the three men, rising out of the limo. "Hey, Denny is ready to go. Let's get the f— out of here."

"Deirdre, this is Bobby, an old friend of mine."

She looked at Bobby with carnivorous eyes that made him look away.

Stevie interrupted that moment. "You wanna come with us? It'll be a blast. And who knows? You might get to save someone's life. Lotsa people getting high at our concerts."

Bobby's travels were not limited to hopping trains and riding buses. He also traveled in his spirit, wandering beyond the street on which he stood. In that moment, he saw two young men lying on the pavement, bleeding. He knew then that he was supposed to keep them from dying. Based on that revelation, Bobby accepted. "Sure, I'll come with. Don't have anythin' else goin' on tonight."

Deirdre looked doubtful.

Bobby was probably as uncomfortable with the notion as Deirdre, but he was used to accepting assignments that made him uncomfortable.

Riding in the back of a limo was not one of the uncomfortable parts of the night's activities. Bobby refused the champagne, but sampled the snacks and stretched his legs. He met Denny, who had been lounging quietly in the car during the introductions.

Denny's floating attitude hinted at stimulants consumed by one means or another. Dark glasses concealed the exact disposition of his eyes, but the things he was saying inspired the image of spinning pupils.

Bobby pretended not to notice.

The University of Illinois at Chicago Pavilion, known as the UIC Pavilion by the locals, seated thousands of people. Stevie and his band had hit the big time without Bobby knowing anything about them. Tchaikovsky was the only music he pursued, with only passive tolerance for anyone else's music. Bobby hadn't learned much about the metalcore or hardcore punk music Stevie liked to talk about. But here he was, arriving at the Pavilion as the designated miracle worker for the band called Sister Sweat.

When the limo pulled up to the stage entrance, they were greeted by security guards in yellow coats barking into walkie talkies, many of them sporting dark glasses under the streetlights.

Even as Denny stumbled out of the car and the others helped him make it over the low curb, a mob of fans burst through wooden barricades. Four hefty guards intercepted the first wave and bounced two skinny young men off a metal post next to the building.

Bobby saw the moment when those two boys crashed into that unforgiving pole. He watched them crumple to the pavement. Their collision stopped nearly everyone where they stood.

While others gawked, Bobby saw his cue. He pushed past Stevie and Deirdre to the two boys. Only one of the boys was moving, and he thrashed like a squirrel half crushed by a passing car.

"Okay, son, calm down. Just lie still a minute." Bobby knew he had only a short time before professionals intervened. He didn't intend to make the bystanders think he was a doctor, but probably benefited from that assumption for a moment. He placed his hand on top of the boy's head and closed his eyes for a moment.

"Hey," said one of the security guards behind Bobby.

Bobby noted two police officers pushing through the crowd.

But Stevie spoke up. "Give him a second. He can heal stuff like this."

As those around him seemed slowed by confusion, Bobby began to see results. The boy who had been thrashing lay still now and began to breathe normally. Then he opened his eyes and looked curiously at Bobby through bangs hanging past his nose.

"Better?" Bobby was pretty sure of the answer to that question. He gave the boy a hand in sitting up.

"Yeah. What did you do? I feel fine."

Bobby slid over to the other victim, using the distraction of the first boy rising from the pavement to seize the initiative with the second young man. The wiry young man lay motionless, apparently unconscious. A pool of blood was forming in the gutter. Bobby spoke a brisk command. "Bleeding, stop right now." That produced another stunned freeze among the people hovering over him. Bobby put his hand on the top of the second boy's head. "Cuts be closed and brain restored." He could hear murmurs and small gasps around him, but still no one tried to stop him.

One of the officers spoke into his radio, presumably to an ambulance on its way.

Bobby stayed focused on the two injured boys. It was just as he had seen in his mind's eye before agreeing to go with the band.

The second boy began to rouse even as the first got to one knee. He was still swaying, so one of the cops assisted. Though he wasn't bleeding as profusely as the second boy had been, the side of his face was crimson, his hair matted, and the collar of his gray T-shirt dark under his black jacket.

"You better take it easy there, kid. Just sit for a minute while the paramedics get here." The officer settled him back on the curb. "You know him?" The cop gestured to the boy still lying on the pavement.

Bobby could see from the corner of his eye when the first boy shook his head. That boy leaned over and picked up a CD case and a spilled CD from the pavement.

"Hey, kid, I'll sign that for you." Stevie crouched near the boy.

Producing a pen from his pocket in dreamlike slow motion, the boy handed Stevie the CD case with his other hand.

The second boy was rising to a sitting position by the time the paramedics broke through the crowd. "What the—" One of them responded to the surreal scene—two young men sitting over a pool of blood with no one looking as severely wounded as the pool implied.

At this point, Denny vomited near the limo. When he was finished, he stood slowly, apparently sobered a bit. He pulled off his sunglasses.

Bobby made eye contact with the drummer for the first time, getting an internal glimpse at what the semi-stoned musician was experiencing.

Then the stage door burst open, and a broad-chested man bellowed in their direction. He waded into the crowd around the band.

Stevie did the introductions. "Bobby, this is our manager, Foster. Foster, this is Bobby, an old friend of mine. He just healed two nearly dead kids. We're gonna let him have a go at it later in the concert."

Denny crowded up next to Stevie, leveling his dark-circled eyes at the manager. "We have to let him do it. It's God, man."

Foster's bushy eyebrows rose high for a second, then he seemed to find his way back to his reason for bursting out that door. "You guys are late. Get on stage for a check. The other bands are both done, and you guys gotta make sure nothing got screwed up from our settings this afternoon."

Bobby checked with the two boys who were both sitting up and wiping blood off their faces. Then he followed the band into the venue, with a backstage pass on a bright green lanyard dropped over his head.

He watched the final sound check and watched one of the warm-up bands take the stage. By the time the second band was under way, a sort of riot was brewing, apparently inebriated young men pushing at each other and shouting at the warm-up act. One young man screamed, "I wanna see Stevie do a miracle!"

Bobby squinted at Foster, who was looking at his watch.

Returning Bobby's silent inquiry, Foster just shrugged.

Certainly the healings outside had not been done in private. Dozens of people witnessed something. And Bobby expected the two healed boys were spreading the message of what had happened to them. He snorted at the idea of Stevie doing miracles.

The second act ended their set to weak applause and some sarcastic shouting. Bobby wasn't sure how normal that was. He did recognize the big roar of the now-capacity crowd when Sister Sweat was finally introduced.

Stevie gave him a thumbs up on his way out to the bright lights.

Bobby didn't know exactly what Stevie had in mind, but at least he felt welcome there in that very unfamiliar setting.

When Stevie, Denny, Deirdre, and Karl took the stage, the fans' energy seemed to supercharge the first song.

During the second song, Bobby saw those two boys being ushered toward him. Foster had just strode quickly away in response to some sort of crisis.

"Hey. How ya doin'?" Bobby shook the boys' hands.

Against the wall of sound around them, the boys introduced themselves as Kyle Ross and Matt Bower.

Bobby noted that they were now wearing clean black Sister Sweat T-shirts. Both wore leather jackets that seemed to have been wiped down, and their hair had been mostly cleaned up. "They gave you backstage passes?"

Matt nodded and leaned in close. "I think they were afraid we would sue them for getting bashed by the security guards." He laughed cynically, beer breath filling the small space between him and Bobby.

It was hard to hear, so Bobby just nodded and smiled at them.

Stevie spotted Kyle and Matt during a lull and looked around at the rest of the band, then checked the wings. Was he looking for the manager? Foster had seemed uptight about Bobby being there. Had he approved the two young men being on stage?

Stevie grabbed another vocal mic and waved Bobby onto the stage. He was definitely looking right at him, as much as Bobby hoped it was the two boys he was calling out to the lights.

Bobby's feet wouldn't cooperate, but the two boys gave him a push. His feet followed their gentle momentum. His foam-like knees moved without giving out on him entirely. Bobby blocked the spotlight from his eyes and grinned involuntarily at Stevie when he reached center stage.

Stevie tried to hand Bobby the other microphone, but Bobby shook his head.

"I'll heal people, but I don't talk." He pointed to the front of the stage off to one side. "Just give me some security guys, and I'll meet kids over there. Especially if they have broken bones or deaf ears or somethin'."

The venue was loud, and Bobby was forcing volume through numb lips, but Stevie apparently got the idea. He turned toward the crowd and then toward the security guards along the front of the stage. "I wanna see some *bleeping* security guys over by this side of the stage." He looked at the audience. "And any of you that have *bleeping* broken bones or deaf ears or some sh— like that can come over there and get healed." Stevie didn't say *bleeping*.

Bobby had never heard a more compelling invitation for ministry in all his life.

Stevie's weird instructions resulted in security guards just looking at each other, but Stevie reiterated his instructions with even more expletives.

Kids milled and looked at each other as well, but several started to push through to where Bobby posted himself along the front of the stage. He figured he could avoid getting crushed by staying above the crowd. He sat on the edge of the stage and reached down to touch heads, shoulders, and raised hands.

A half-dozen kids ripped braces off. One girl got out of a wheelchair when her spine was apparently restored.

Of course the security staff were used to catching bodies surfing over the top of the crowd, but they also did pretty well at catching kids who fell backward when Bobby touched them. After confusion over what to do with the fallen youngsters, the security staff decided to line them up along the end of the stage next to Bobby. As that row of feet pointing toward the rest of the audience grew, more of the concert goers turned from listening to the band to watching the healing.

After the concert, Stevie met Bobby backstage. It was well past midnight. "You gotta come with us. We're in Columbus, Ohio tomorrow night."

Bobby shook his head. "I don't think that's right for me. I ain't cut out for all this. I gotta keep it low-key, I think."

Stevie didn't try to change his mind. That was no surprise to Bobby. He could sense the discomfort of the other band members, sneaking glances at him as he spoke to Stevie.

He ended the night by praying for Stevie's health and protection, and getting a limo back to his hotel, or at least close to his hotel. Bobby didn't want any of his neighbors to see him get out of that sleek black vehicle.

"After that night, I couldn't really hide in Chicago no more." His voice was gravelly by this point. Time to end their call.

"Thanks for telling me your version. It's much better than the article I found." Anna snorted a laugh. It was past her bedtime too.

No Fifteen Minutes of Fame

Tracy and Bobby were sitting in her living room. Bobby planned to sleep in the guest room, too late for Tracy to drive him home.

She was drinking wine, a pleasant pink glow to her pale cheeks. Her eyes were as glossy as polished marble, and her words came with languid ease.

Bobby liked this kind of conversation. No longer a drinker himself, he had grown accustomed to ruminating conversations with those who had raised their blood alcohol to the point of abandoning their defenses.

"So, ya gonna go to that church that keeps callin' here?" She had kept him appraised of the ten or more messages on her answering machine. How that church had found *her* number and not Bobby's was a mystery. Jamie and Rich were gone back to Texas, and the boys had known Bobby's number but not Tracy's.

"I guess I will," Bobby answered. "With those young guys gone, I may have one more mission while I'm here."

Tracy pushed herself up a bit straighter on the slope of the couch. "You mean one more mission besides converting your daughter to the straight and narrow?"

Bobby laughed. "You look at my life and think I know anythin' about the straight and narrow?" He relaxed into the big easy chair. "Ya best forget any notion o' straightenin' yerself out, my girl." He waited a second and then continued. "An' run like mad away from anyone who tries to stick ya into anythin' about God that's narrow." He looked toward the yellow light cast by the lamp across the room, a three-quarters circle on the ceiling providing most of the illumination.

Bobby crossed his legs and leaned back a bit more. "God is way bigger than anyone will tell ya. God is in everything. God is everywhere. And the secret is that most people spend a load o' energy trying their best to ignore all that. They feel him creepin' up on 'em, and they get all into their heads and *think* it away.

They feel his love drippin' on their hearts, and they analyze it to death. They get a glimpse o' his greatness, his depth, and they scramble around for somethin' to hold onto, to keep 'em from fallin' into that deep place that's really God himself." He gazed at his daughter. "No, girl, this is not just a straight and narrow God, but also deep and deeper, more and more. If you find some o' that, grab it and don't let it go."

"What about Jesus?" Tracy seemed to rouse herself from the lull of the wine.

Bobby nodded. "Jesus was a mess for the religious people to deal with in his day. He wouldn't play by nobody's rules, 'cause he knew his Dad was way bigger than their straight and narrow little boxes. He offered what was way better. The narrow path he offered was himself. One person. He didn't make up some new religion with a new set of rules. No, he offered just one law— love. That's the Jesus you're lookin' for, not straight and narrow rules. Just one guy who still lives, and heals, and talks to us inside our own hearts." He expected she wasn't going to remember much of what he said, but he said it anyway. "Just take a moment and listen, and you'll hear him."

Not much later, Tracy said goodnight with a contented smile, and Bobby she would absorb at least some of what he had said.

Tracy was cheerful and not hungover the next morning. "That might be a sort of miracle." She grinned at him in the kitchen.

That weekend, Bobby agreed to be part of a revival service at one of the largest African American congregations in the Twin Cities. He thought he felt his Papa leading the way to this particular church.

Brother Carter Hinds would give the sermon that Sunday night in his big, lush church. Bobby wasn't going to take the pulpit anywhere. "I can take it out back and make sure the nails are all fixed." He smiled apologetically at the pastor.

When the service began, Bobby noticed an unusual number of white people in the church. And they didn't strike him as church people. Many of those folks remained in the foyer when the seats filled up. Bobby didn't know whether Maranatha Church was usually so full, or if the pastor had done a remarkable job promoting the meeting. But he detected some surprise in Brother Hinds's puckered lips and long stare toward the back of the sanctuary before he opened the service.

By the time Bobby was standing at the front of the room touching people lined up the aisle and around the back of the sanctuary, the organ blaring and the worship team crooning, he could tell that many of those nonchurch people were reporters. Cameras and microphones sprouted, not just phones for personal recording.

He tried to ignore all that digital recording and those craned necks and scribbled notes, but he did allow his attention to rest on one young woman. A sympathetic face. Anna Conyers had found him. Or maybe just followed the others when they declared they had found him. He sent a smile her way, and she adjusted her big glasses and grinned back at him.

The service ran on for hours. Bodies stacked in the aisles and front pews, dozens celebrated restored health and freedom. But Bobby was planning his exit. Among those still standing, the people with the cameras and microphones were a growing cohort. He didn't want to wait for them to mob him at the end of the ministry.

Brother Hinds slipped up behind him. "You know about the reporters?"

"I guessed it. Can I git out the back way or somethin'?"

"Yes, you can. Is your daughter still here?"

Bobby had to search for Tracy. She had faded into the crowd hours before. But he did pick her out at the far end of the front row. "She's over there, if ya wouldn't mind showin' her where to meet me." He only glanced in her direction to avoid tipping off the reporters.

During the quick scuttle off the stage and out the back door, a pair of men caught up to him. "Mr. Nightingale, what do you think about what Beau Dupere said about you?"

"Bobby, are you the greatest miracle worker in America?"

"Mr. Nightingale ..."

He dodged toward Tracy's car in the alley behind the church.

And there was Anna. She was looking at him more like an old friend and less like a predatory reporter.

Pausing by the passenger door, he spoke across the top of the car. "Good to see ya, young lady. I got yer number. I'll be hittin' the road, but I'll give ya a call."

She seemed only slightly surprised by his quick escape, as if she knew she was there in the alley just to get that commitment from him. He maintained eye contact with her as Tracy drove him away.

Tracy was shaking with tension as she eased the car past the pressing mob growing in the alley. "Why don't you wanna talk to them? I thought you would want people to know God can do miracles." Tracy only spoke after they escaped the last shouted question, muffled by the closed car windows.

"I do. I want God to be known. But those people were there to see if *I* could do miracles, not God. I don't wanna be a celebrity. It did no good for Beau Dupere or anyone else I know of." Bobby had to pull himself back from the edge of frustration. That anger probably had more to do with the murder of Beau Dupere than with what had happened at that church.

Part of what soured his mood was that his visit with his daughter had been ruined. "How long d'ya think it'll take 'em to find yer house?" He wasn't really asking her as much as thinking aloud.

"I don't know how the church found my *phone* number."

There was still no crowd at Bobby's apartment when he packed his things the next morning. And Tracy reported seeing no sign of reporters around her house. But they escaped both residences, opting for a buffet lunch. They found a restaurant serving a holiday meal just days before Thanksgiving.

"This'll have to be our celebration, I guess." Bobby sat in the back corner of the popular restaurant.

Tracy shook her head. She was clearly not happy, but she didn't seem surprised that he was leaving. It certainly helped that she had seen the mob of press the previous night. She would at least know what he was running from.

"Where will you go?" She poked at her turkey and stuffing.

"I'm gonna head south, of course. Winter. Maybe Kansas City for a while—on my way down to Florida to see a friend."

"Do you have enough money?"

Bobby had given that some thought, having already discovered that hitchhiking or freight-car jumping didn't suit him so well in his sixties. While he contemplated the answer, an Asian man approached the table with the smooth manner of someone making an illegal drop. And indeed, the man laid an envelope on the table. Then he bowed and scooted away.

Tracy stared at the envelope on the table as if she expected it to do something. It was stuffed with something the size of US currency.

Bobby followed the mysterious gentleman with his eyes, trying to decide if he was just a man, or perhaps an angel. He looked at the envelope for a moment, then turned back to Tracy. Her wonder was childlike, her eyes wide, her mouth parted slightly, her jaw free of tension.

Bobby was going to miss her.

"Is that what I think it is?" She set her fork on her plate.

"If yer thinkin' it's my travel money, then yer thinkin' the same thing I am." Bobby shrugged one shoulder and kept digging through his mashed potatoes and gravy.

"Who was that man?"

"Don't know. I usually don't."

"Usually?"

Bobby held onto a belly laugh, still intent on getting the best out of his buffet investment. "Mm-hmm."

"Does this mean God is okay with you running away from the publicity?" She winced a little, as if regretting her wording.

Bobby drank some water, not annoyed at being accused of running away. He had heard it before in a dozen different shapes and sizes. Her question seemed like a good chance to tell her more about how his Papa worked.

"It don't necessarily mean God is endorsin' it. I've learned over the years that my Papa takes care o' me even when I make mistakes." He allowed an internal flash of regret at not getting to tell her these things when she was younger. "Parents bail their kids out o' trouble sometimes, even when that trouble is the kid's own fault."

Tracy just studied Bobby's face.

"I don't associate Papa's providin' for me with endorsin' everythin' I do. I learned that by trial and error ... especially error."

Tracy nodded slowly, picked up her fork, and returned to her food.

In Bobby's eyes, it was as if the girl he had glimpsed a moment ago had put her grown-up face back on. Yet it wasn't so much that she shut down her childlike wonder, it was more like she had grown up a bit during that conversation. At least that's how it seemed to him, not exactly an expert at kids growing up.

That afternoon, Tracy dropped him at the train station.

He had called his building manager with the news of his departure to see what he owed. He gave Tracy his keys to go and collect some of the odds and ends he left behind—mostly décor she had bought for him.

"I'll be back to visit, of course. I have yer phone number now." He said it firmly, forcing his promise past a rolling sense of loss. They stood in the station, an announcement about a departing train pausing their conversation.

She nodded at him confidently. "I know you will."

They hugged for a long time before he headed for his train. Saying more was simply impossible. He had to wipe tears away before and after waving goodbye to his daughter.

Heading South for the Winter

Bobby took a train from Minneapolis to Chicago, and a bus from Chicago to Kansas City. He was on the run. But, rather than ask his Papa to hide him by not doing any miracles along the way, he asked that he be sent to people so far off the grid that they would know nothing about him or about Beau Dupere.

At the bus station in Kansas City, Bobby felt a pull to talk to a blind woman who was sitting with her back to the wall, her head held high as if she were on sentry duty, attending to every little thing that passed in front of her.

"Hi, I'm Bobby." He stopped directly in front of the vigilant woman.

"Are you the one I'm supposed to be listening for?" She turned her face approximately toward where Bobby stood. "I had this really sure feelin' that I was supposed to listen here for someone who could help me out with somethin'."

He listened for instructions about healing the blind woman, but heard nothing about that from his Papa. Bobby answered her question, however. "I had a similar feelin' when I laid eyes on you sittin' here. Don't know what it's about yet. I expect it's somethin' good."

"I don't usually talk to strangers."

That reminded Bobby of the woman with the bent back he healed that summer. "I generally *do*, which makes it possible for us to meet."

"Mm-hmm." The woman didn't sound entirely convinced of this arrangement.

"You have a brother named Terrance who has a place for me to stay." Bobby received that intelligence on the spot.

"How do you know that?"

"Same way I knew to stop and talk to you."

"Angels." She nodded.

"What's yer name?"

189

"I'm Mabel. How come you know my brother's name, but you don't know mine?"

Bobby snorted a laugh. "I been askin' that kinda question all my grown life. If ya git the answer for me, be sure to let me know."

For a meeting laced with more questions than answers, Mabel was doing well to keep up. "Well, help me up, and I'll take you to Terrance. We gotta get on another bus."

"How'd you know I got off a bus?"

"Smelled it."

"Makes sense." Bobby helped her to her feet and stepped out of the way so she could lead him to the local buses.

Forty-five minutes later, they arrived in a neighborhood that looked like it was waiting for the bulldozers to arrive. If there was urban planning at work there, the plan was neglect.

Mabel signaled Bobby to follow her, pulled the cord for the bus to stop, and headed out the side door onto the street. "Terrance lives over in that building there, but you'll find him sittin' at his cousin's barbershop over there." She waved up the block toward a barbershop that looked twice as old as she did.

"*His* cousin?" Bobby said, noting the odd construction. "I thought he was yer brother."

"Half-brother. Different daddies."

"Oh, I see. Okay, so ya need any help?" Bobby assumed he was saying goodbye to Mabel.

"I ain't leavin' ya yet." She aimed her forehead toward the barbershop and led the way. "I gotta introduce ya."

"Oh, thanks. That'll be good." Bobby was used to making his way with or without introductions.

They walked past a tall man talking on a cell phone in front of the shop, Mabel clearly as familiar with the lay of the land as if it were her living room. The tall man paused his phone conversation to simply say, "Mabel."

She returned the greeting with a wave of her hand, striding through the barbershop door.

"Terrance," she called as soon as she stepped into the sunlit shop. "I brung someone to meet ya."

The conversations in the shop stalled. Bobby expected not many white men came in. Certainly not many led by a blind woman.

"I think God sent him to us. That's what I think."

A slender man, who looked as if decades of hot sun and the pressures of life had melted away his natural fat, stepped toward Bobby. His dark brown face looked like a creased leather jacket. "God sent him?" He eyeballed Bobby.

"Hi, I'm Bobby."

"Terrance," said the older man.

Mabel spoke up. "He come up to me and said, 'You got a brother name Terrance who has a place for me to stay,' jus' like an apostle sent by the Lord."

"You wanna stay in *this* neighborhood?" Terrance's yellowish eyeballs shone all around his dark irises.

"I just try to follow what I think God's sayin' to me. It don't matter to me what neighborhood, so long as I'm doin' what he says." Bobby could hear a few chuckles from the other men in the shop but stayed focused on Terrance. Then Bobby felt he had the go-ahead for something he had expected earlier. He turned toward Mabel. "Before anythin' else, Mabel, I feel I'm supposed to heal yer eyes."

She squawked. "Heal my eyes? Nobody can do that. I ain't got no eyes." She opened her wrinkled lids to reveal two empty sockets.

"Jesus," said one of the men seated behind Bobby.

"Had cancer," she said. "Had to get 'em took out when I was young."

Bobby pushed ahead. "Guess God wants to give ya some new ones, then."

"You serious?" said Terrance.

Bobby nodded. Then he spoke to Mabel again. "Can you step over toward the wall behind you a bit, so we're outta the way of the door?" Bobby felt this was going to take a while and didn't want to be interrupted by traffic in and out of the shop.

"Can I sit down?" said Mabel.

"Of course. I'll sit here next to ya."

Terrance just stood where they had left him, pivoting his head toward the far wall. Finally, he unstuck his feet from the tiles and scuffled to the seat on the other side of Mabel.

Bobby began by praying—not something he did in all healing situations, just something he thought he should do to start *this* one.

The shop was silent except for the sound of clippers humming as a young man got a trim around his ears and on the back of his neck. The barber was watching Bobby in the mirror perhaps as much as he was looking at his customer.

After finishing his prayer, Bobby said, "Okay, I'm gonna start by pulling off the trauma of losin' yer eyes. It's sittin' on you like a vulture waitin' for you to die so it can pick yer bones." While that sounded gruesome, Bobby expected Mabel would recognize what he was saying.

She just nodded.

Telling that beast to get lost was standard stuff for Bobby, and he made little show of it.

Mabel puffed a bit, like someone who'd just walked up a flight of stairs, and that part was done.

Bobby followed with a prayer of healing for her soul, where she felt she was abandoned by folks that should have been protecting her, even if they really couldn't protect her from cancer.

Mabel received this blessing with no more than a nod of her head and another "Mm-hmm."

Bobby next called for the eyes to be rebuilt. He talked that through like he was sculpting with words, pausing to go back and repeat himself a few times, as if each stroke laid another layer, and then another.

The entire shop stayed still through the process. All haircutting had ceased. Bobby could feel faith in the room, though he didn't know who was carrying it. Though he hadn't calculated that effect in advance, Bobby understood the impact of his method as it was happening. His Papa's careful approach was nurturing an atmosphere of faith.

Bobby commanded the new eyes to fill the sockets, replacing all scar tissue. A chill awakened his spine when he saw Mabel's eyelids start to bulge. He encouraged Mabel to open her eyes even though he suspected she couldn't see yet.

Several men gasped at the sight of those eyes. One even blurted a screamed before capping it off. The tall man from outside was inside now. He was on his phone again.

At the point where Bobby was calling the new, shining brown eyes to *see*, three men and two women rushed through the door. The crowd was growing, as was the faith in the room. "I command these new eyes to see perfectly."

Mabel blinked. She had adopted a smile for the last few minutes, her head shaking with excitement. The smiling, blinking woman looked twenty years younger than the old woman who had sat in that chair before the miracle started. "It's light. It's all blurry, but it's light." She scanned the room and settled her gaze on the front windows.

"I can't believe this." Terrance was clinging to the arm of his chair, leaning toward Mabel.

"More," Bobby said. "I command clarity to them eyes, both of 'em, and right now."

Mabel's whole body was quivering, her hands up to her face, her head turning more rapidly. She looked at Bobby, then at Terrance. "I see you both real good. I can see close up." Then she looked across the room. "Still blurry out there." She reached toward the mirror on the opposite wall.

Bobby persisted, blocking out the weeping and swearing from the two dozen folks now filling the barbershop. In all, it took about fifteen minutes to recreate those eyes and speak sight into them. Bobby enjoyed it more than most healings, more than most of the creative miracles he had seen. He enjoyed it so

193

much, he was willing to accept that it might spoil his plan to hide out in this neighborhood. It was well worth it.

People showed up with champagne and snacks, with cheap wine and equally cheap cigars. It was Bobby's first barbershop dance-and-praise-party. But how else were they supposed to celebrate someone getting her eyes back? Bobby felt right at home.

By the end of the night, Bobby had a place to stay for free in a building owned by Terrance and his cousin, the barber. Bobby had made some very grateful friends.

Bobby Meets Willow

Anna flew to Kansas City to meet with Bobby. This time her magazine was paying the fare. Bobby had become a story. He'd agreed to meet with her as long as she didn't reveal where she found him.

He smiled broadly when she approached him in another suburban mall. "I still say you ain't gonna get this published, but I'm glad they're footin' the bill fer ya."

She laughed, amazed at herself for how casually she could receive his warning. She wasn't wasting her time. Being with Bobby was different than meeting with Beau or his family, but it was equally inspiring. Perhaps inspiring in just the way she needed it at this point in her life.

"Tell me about how you met Willow Pierce. I interviewed her in jail last week." Anna was walking with Bobby in that mall in Kansas City. He said he needed to walk to keep from dozing off.

He told her about a time when he was sleeping on a park bench in Decatur, Georgia, about ten years ago. He was stretching his back to slough off the cramped soreness of sleeping outside, his thoughts turning toward breakfast. Just as he stood up from situating his shoes on his feet, a minivan pulled to the curb by the park. A slender, pale woman stepped out of the sliding side door, her long legs appearing first before her penetrating eyes caught Bobby's attention. She was looking right at him.

"Bobby? Bobby Nightingale?"

When she said his name, Bobby recognized Willow Pierce. They had crossed paths twice before without really meeting each other. Bobby was pretty sure Willow wasn't from Decatur, Georgia, and wondered what she was doing there. "Hello, Willow. Do I finally get to meet you face-to-face?"

Willow laughed a low laugh. "Yes, today is your lucky day. I woke up this morning and heard Father tell me to go and find you in this park. I didn't even know this park was here."

Bobby smiled broadly. That sounded just like his Papa.

Willow introduced the driver, Dan, and the other passenger, Pirya, before she followed Bobby into the van. "You're sleeping in the park?" Willow asked as Bobby settled his gear behind the seat.

"Oh, just when the weather's good and I don't have any connections in town. What're ya doing here?"

"A church affiliated with ours is just launching down here. I came to do my thing at a weekend conference."

Bobby knew Willow's "thing" was to prophesy to people. He had seen it in action on stage and had heard several stories. He hadn't, however, heard any stories of Willow following her inner voice to scoop up strangers in a city park.

"I didn't know Jack had a church down here," Bobby said.

"It was planted by our church in Colorado, but it is part of the same network." Willow was looking out the windshield. "Do you normally check in if there's a church that might know who you are?"

Bobby smiled, straightening out his shirt, which was still bunched up from his open-air sleeping. "Well, I don't know who knows me or cares to admit they know me, but I do like to visit around the network, kinda like home-away-from-home."

"Sort of a spiritual home, you mean?"

"Exactly." Bobby was wondering about being in the closed van with other people, having not showered for a few days. He didn't want to presume on the grace of his fellow occupants, so he addressed his own elephant in that little space. "I could use a shower before hangin' out with too many people."

Willow smiled. "Want breakfast first?"

"Sounds good."

Over breakfast at a fast-food restaurant, Bobby agreed to stow his stuff at Dan's place, where he could get a shower, and then go to the conference for a Saturday morning session. He wasn't agreeing to *do* anything there, and Willow didn't ask. He knew she was following directions to pick him up in the park, but she hadn't shared any further instructions with him.

The morning session of the conference began at ten. Willow wasn't speaking at that meeting, but was in charge of the ministry time afterward. They arrived in plenty of time after the brief stop at Dan's place. Willow and Pirya had stayed in the van and made calls to let others know of Bobby's presence.

In those days, Bobby was generally clean shaven—that was, when he had a chance to shave. He did a hasty job of it at Dan's place, keeping in mind the women waiting in the van. But he certainly smelled better, and he had time to remove the bits of tissue from a few nicks on his face before entering the conference venue.

Jackson Sanders was the first to greet Willow and Bobby. He was another of the speakers listed on the poster for the conference. He had met Bobby in California a couple times. "Bobby." Jackson wrapped him up in a big hug. Jackson originated in Australia, but had been in the US long enough to fake his way through American English. "What a pleasant surprise. I hope you're gonna help with ministry time, mate."

Grinning at Jackson as he slipped out of the rangy Aussie's embrace, Bobby said, "I might be persuaded."

"Excellent! Now I feel like we're loaded for bear." Jackson chuckled and stretched a smile that sent creases in all directions around his mouth and eyes.

The morning session in the main hall featured Debbie Schwarzenbach, a teacher with a winning sense of humor. As her talk wound to a conclusion, Willow pulled Bobby up with her to wait along the side of the stage. Standing there listening to Debbie, Willow turned to Bobby. "I think I have something for you, and I don't think it's supposed to wait."

Bobby expected she meant she had a message from God for him. He had no objection to hearing from his Papa through one of his other kids. "Go ahead."

"I see you coming along the street and looking in the window of a beauty salon. And there's this person sitting in the chair, their back turned to you, and you notice the woman doing the hair styling instead of the person in the chair. And you get all infatuated with the woman with the comb and scissors, but you don't notice that *Jesus* is the one sitting in the chair. And I think Jesus is telling you not to feel bad for missing him there. He knew you would fall for that woman. He's just letting you know that he was with you all along, and happy you started to see him more clearly once you left the camper." She stopped. "Yeah, that's the word—*left the camper*. I hope that makes sense."

She didn't need to ask if the word connected with Bobby, because his face was contorting and his eyes filling with tears. "Oh, I didn't realize ..." Bobby's voice trailed off. Then he crumpled to his knees before falling facedown on the stage.

After running away from the scene of his grandmother's death, Bobby had also run away from the death of his marriage. Through the years, he had wondered whether the brokenness of the first escape had made the second one inevitable. And he carried a lot of guilt about leaving both his wife and his grandmother. And, though what Willow said only addressed leaving his wife, what Bobby heard from his Papa while lying on the floor dug deep into that time when he escaped the foster care system by leaving Grandma Casey's house, leaving her body alone on the kitchen floor. He had not realized how much he needed assurance regarding those things, that he needed release from his self-condemnation and from fear that he had made two monstrous mistakes.

Bobby only regretted briefly that he wouldn't be able to help Willow with the ministry time. He just couldn't stop crying.

After lunch, Bobby joined Willow in one of the smaller seminar settings where she had the floor, and Bobby hoped to stay off the floor.

Though more than a dozen people saw major healing miracles in that session, and many more in the evening session, what Bobby remembered about that day was his time on the carpet. That purging which started with Willow Pierce and her humbly presented word from God.

"I figured I owed her one after that." He grinned at Anna.

I Was in Prison and You Visited Me

In December, after leaving Tracy in Minnesota, Bobby was tucked into his couch in his Kansas City apartment on a windy night. He was thinking about what Anna had said about Willow Pierce being in jail. His John Steinbeck novel lay in his lap when he felt a tap on his shoulder. He knew there was no one else in the room, but turned his head that direction anyway. His Papa sometimes caught his attention that way. Without that past experience, he might have assumed the apartment was haunted.

"What is it?" He spoke aloud.

In his mind, he heard, "I want you to go and encourage Willow Pierce."

"Where is she, in jail?"

"Yes, jail. In Colorado."

This was one of those points where Bobby was more certain that the words he was hearing in his head were from God and not just his own make-believe. He would never have come up with that plan on his own. He waited a beat, wondering if he should ask any more questions.

Then he said, "Okay, let's go."

In a split second, he flipped from that apartment to a jail cell. As he did so, it occurred to him that it might be inappropriate for a man to just pop into a woman's jail. A brief internal glance at his Papa only revealed the same merry laughter he so often heard in response to his thoughts, especially thoughts about challenging God's choices.

Bobby was sitting on the bottom bunk. His arrival seemed to stir someone sitting on the top. He held his breath briefly, hoping Willow wouldn't scream, though he had a hard time imagining her screaming.

A face, upside down, appeared over the edge of the bed. In the low light, she looked pretty calm. Willow broke that impression, however, by swearing under her breath.

Bobby laughed.

Her head disappeared as she pulled back a bit, her hand just dangling over the edge.

He teased her for the profanity. "I knew you had it in you, kid."

After a brief pause that might have included a small snicker, she said, "Why are you here?"

Bobby didn't flinch at what might have seemed a rude question. He and Willow both knew that his presence here was not his idea. "'Cause all yer angels are busy fightin' the whole US government to get ya outta here, of course." He laughed. Part of the joke for him was the way he was just now learning what was happening. The first he had heard that Willow was in jail was from that brief mention by Anna. His Papa was still filling him in on the details.

Before she replied, Bobby made another joke. "Actually, I was so desperate to get another prophetic word from you, I got myself arrested and thrown in jail."

Willow had recovered from her shock, apparently. "And the miracle is that they believed you're a woman."

Bobby climbed out of the lower bunk and took the small step to the opposite wall of the cell. From there, he could see Willow on the bunk a bit above his eye level. She sat smiling wryly. The earlier thought about this visit being inappropriate encouraged him to be careful how close he looked at a woman ready for bed in the privacy of her own cell. He decided that leaning back against the wall would afford her more cover. He smiled at the creases on her pale cheek where she had been lying on her pillow.

"Are you here to tell me jokes?" Willow asked.

Bobby was wondering exactly what he *was* doing here. In those brief seconds, he heard his Papa explain the situation. Willow was in jail because of a tip she'd given to the police regarding an abducted girl. Her information was so detailed and accurate that they suspected she was part of the abduction. His Papa had already told Bobby he was here to encourage her. That was enough to know.

Bobby sobered. "Well, I assume it was 'cause ya needed some company. My thought is that ya been prayin' by yerself too long, and Papa wanted me to have a little prayer meetin' with ya. He'd a sent someone ya know better, but none o' them are ready for a trip like this."

"What about transporting me outta here with you?"

"You assume I'm leaving? No, I think this looks pretty nice. I may stick around." He chuckled low and slow. He hadn't answered her question, even though he had, in fact, transported another person once. That wasn't in his instructions this time, however.

Ignoring that joke, Willow moved on to another question. "Did some of them refuse when offered the opportunity?" She was clearly referring to friends who weren't ready for miraculous transportation yet.

Bobby laughed. "I don't think so. Papa knows what us kids can take without askin'. On the other hand, I suppose some might've had the thought and just assumed it came from watchin' too many science fiction movies."

Willow nodded for a moment. Then she responded to another thing Bobby had said. "So what are we supposed to be interceding for, do you think?"

"Oh, I leave that to you. That's closer to yer realm than mine."

Willow didn't take long to find an answer. "For its own good, the government *has* to allow that there are sources of knowledge beyond what their investigations can discover. We can't have prophetic insights disabled in the fight against pain and death. We're on the same side."

"Sounds right to me." Without further introduction, he started talking to the third person in the room. "So, Papa, did she get it right? Is that what we're bringin' today?" They both paused to listen for the answer.

A chill ran down Bobby's back, and Willow wriggled her shoulders at exactly the same time, clearly feeling the confirmation.

"All right, Father," Willow said. "I accept your assignment, and I release freedom and acceptance for your truth, your words, and your revelation, even at the highest levels of law enforcement. I accept, for all of the prophetically gifted brothers and sisters, courage to take the risk and willingness to see into the messiest messes people are making around the world."

"Mm-hmm, Mm-hmm. Yeah, that's the thing. I feel it. Yep! Let it come!" Bobby thought he felt the jail cell shift as in a minor earthquake—or at least a tremor. He had felt that a few times before when he thought his Papa was shaking the world around him just to remind him of the one who built its foundations.

They both stayed silent for about a minute. The Spirit alive in each of them recognized the same Spirit in the other, and that allowed them comfort with each other. Though he didn't know her well, Bobby recognized Willow's family resemblance to his Papa. For Bobby, at that point, words weren't necessary.

He took a deep breath. "Ya passed the test, kid. Ya know Papa wanted exactly what ya prayed, but ya didn't have the authority to pray it until you submitted to this nonsense." He gestured to the cell around them.

"It's so generous of him to send you in here to be with me. He's so good to me." Willow leaned forward and reached out her arms.

Bobby knew an invitation to a hug when he saw it, and guessed Willow's reasons for not leaving her bunk. He stepped up to the edge of her bed. It was an awkward hug for Bobby. And the exchange of smiles afterward was a bit less comfortable than the prayers had been.

Bobby cleared his throat. "Well, this is where we find out if I was just kiddin' about staying in here." He chuckled, feigning uncertainty, his lips tilted and one eyebrow raised. "What happens if I can transport *in* but can't transport *out*?"

"I think you can do it." Willow had on a peaceful smile.

And with that, Bobby waved at her once, and saw her smiling face no more.

Most of Bobby's life was shared only with his Papa, but he checked the clock when he arrived back home and guessed that Terry might still be awake. He had an urge to tell someone of his little adventure. She was the perfect person to tell.

As he listened to the dial tone, waiting for her to answer, Bobby thought about the feeling that Terry was the perfect person to share his life with. He wondered whether it might be time for him to stop running—once he reached Florida, that is.

A Circle Completed

Anna stood on her small balcony with her cell phone to her ear. "I just heard about Willow Pierce getting out of jail. She said you visited her there. How did that work?" It seemed like a lot of travel for an infrequent flyer.

"Oh, that's another one o' those stories I expect yer editor ain't gonna wanna publish."

"But you can still tell *me*, right?"

"Ya think there's a story to tell?"

"I have a feeling."

"That's good. I think yer supposed to follow those feelin's more than you do already. Though I think you been doin' that more than you allow yourself credit. Some o' what you call instinct is really God's Spirit leading you."

She drew a long breath. "I believe that." She chuckled into her phone. "Are you gonna tell me, or what?"

"Ha. Sure."

And Bobby told her another story about being transported. This one seemed the more believable just because Anna had also visited Willow in jail. She visited in a more conventional manner, of course. Another visit paid for by her publisher. Her boss was thinking Willow's was a case of religious persecution.

"What does it feel like, being popped from one place to another?"

Bobby gave a gravelly hum. "Kinda like wakin' up from a nap, I guess. Sorta disconnected from what was happening before."

"Huh. I don't know what I expected you to say, but it all sounds so ordinary when you tell it. And that's like a lot of your stories. Just everyday people seeing miracles in their lives." She turned back toward her apartment. It was too cold outside to stay out long. "I guess that's what's so challenging to me about all your stories—and Beau's and Willow's. If God is willing to work with ordinary people, then I have to ask myself, why not me, right?"

He chuckled. "I think you jist hit it right on the head, Anna. Right on the head."

That turned Anna back to Bobby's connection with Jack and Beau. "How often have you gone back to Jack's church in California?"

"Every few years or so. That's where I met Beau the first time,'o' course. I always liked him, though we were nothin' alike, as you know."

He saw Beau again in about 2011. Bobby was back at the church in Redwood, appearing at Kurt Voss's class for young miracle workers. Kurt had recently accepted the job of developing classes for people who wanted to learn how to do the things Jesus did. He invited Bobby to do some of his show and tell—mostly show. Bobby was glad to do it as long as Kurt didn't ask him to teach. Showing was not the same as teaching.

The class grew to almost a hundred people that fall. Kurt said the growth came from word spreading that real miracles were as common as PowerPoint slides. Kurt's assistant, Danny, brought the PowerPoint. Bobby brought the miracles. And Kurt kept it all heading in the right direction.

On a Sunday evening in November, Jack and Beau had attended the class. They sat in the back row where Bobby expected two class troublemakers—the cool boys who might mock the nerdy ones leading the class.

Kurt had been demonstrating words of knowledge—supernatural hints about what God wanted to heal next. He called out TMJ and jaw pain in general, and two students raised their hands to acknowledge they had that ailment. Beau raised his hand too.

Bobby and Kurt received Beau and the other two jaw pain sufferers at the front of the class, and Bobby got a case of the giggles. In Jack's church, that wasn't unusual. They had been dealing with that phenomenon ever since Bobby first visited. Bobby's giggles, however, seemed to jump to Beau, whose bright white smile lit the front of the room before he bent over to grab his ribs.

Kurt seemed to be fighting it, but he lost his ability to speak. And then the first rows of students started to titter.

What the others didn't know was that Bobby's giggles started when his Papa gave him very strange instructions for how to heal Beau's jaw. Getting a bit drunk in the Holy Spirit, like the folks at Pentecost, limbered Bobby for following those crazy directions from his Papa. He staggered to where Beau was bent over in hysterics and tapped him on the shoulder, still laughing.

Beau tried to stand up straight, his head weaving upward and his shoulders alternating on the climb to uprightness.

As soon as Beau's face was fully visible, Bobby cocked his arm and aimed high. He punched Beau in the jaw.

Anna stopped him there. "Wait—you literally punched him?"

"Yep."

She paused. "Some critics accused Beau of punching people in the healing lines. Do you think he might have actually done it?"

"I wouldn't be surprised. Though I was plenty surprised that day."

Part of what made it funny to Bobby was how unqualified he was for a real fight with hale and hearty Beau Dupere, years younger and in much better shape. Add doing it right in front of a bunch of impressionable students, and it was plain crazy. He had heard relevant stories from the history of healing movements, but he wasn't recalling any of those very clearly when he socked Beau.

For Beau, his drunkenness might have been helpful. The sock in the jaw probably didn't hurt so much. In fact, when Bobby landed the right cross, Beau fell over backward, laughing even louder. He hit the ground howling hilariously.

Kurt stopped his own laughter when the punch landed. The solid smack seemed to pause a lot of the noise in the room. Kurt renewed his belly-busting guffaws, however, when he heard Beau howling on the floor.

By then, Jack was at the front of the room. Bobby wasn't clear what Jack's intention had been when he rushed up there. Was he there to stop Bobby from belting anyone else, or was he hoping for a punch in the jaw himself? Whatever the case, Jack didn't make it all the way up the aisle before falling on his face.

Bobby had seen lots of people on the ground like that, including Jack. But that kind of drunkenness was rare for the famous senior pastor. A brief hush among others in the room probably reflected that.

During that hush, Bobby felt he knew something about a man sitting in the middle of the group of students. The man was from Mexico. He had been a member of one of the Mexican drug cartels and had been dramatically converted. He had not, however, gotten rid of all the clinging remnants of his past life. When the laughter spread to that part of the room, the man did not laugh. Instead, he began to roar like a lion—perhaps a demented lion.

When Bobby allowed himself to see in the spirit realm, he saw a huge beast rise up over the students. It was a coal black monster with red eyes. Bobby understood that it was a spirit of immense power, both in the life of the man who was carrying it, and in the life of his hometown in Mexico. Bobby stepped toward the roaring man, but paused to poke Beau with his toe and gestured for him to follow.

Beau responded as if he *wanted* to follow Bobby, rousing from his place on the floor, but he struggled to get to his feet.

Bobby bent and tapped Jack as he went by as well, sensing they were entering a high realm of conflict, and hoping for reinforcements.

The students on both sides of the man from Mexico were on the floor laughing, either undisturbed by his animal noises or finding them hysterical. That made it easier for Bobby to make eye contact from the aisle, several chairs away from where the man sat, his hands gripping the chair in front of him.

The man suddenly stopped roaring, looking at Bobby with a plea in his eyes. But he seemed unable to speak. Bobby saw the beast on that man respond to his plea for help by squashing him into his chair.

Jack arrived at Bobby's shoulder, his laughter gone.

Beau was still trying to get control of his feet. He staggered up behind Jack and grabbed the backs of two chairs.

Bobby nudged laughing students out of the way and climbed over others. When he arrived, he addressed the man by name. "Are you Carlos?"

For a second, the man looked at Bobby and nodded. Then it was no longer Carlos's face that Bobby saw. The eyes, especially, seemed alien.

Bobby prayed a quiet prayer, and the creature holding Carlos screamed. At that, all the lights flickered, and the Emergency Exit signs on three sides of the room exploded, sparks flying.

That seemed to sober Beau, who began following Jack and Bobby through the rows of chairs and piles of students.

The students seemed sheltered from Carlos's monster. Jack and Beau assisted with clearing a space around Carlos, Beau literally carrying a petite teenager to a spot farther from the fray.

Looking at Jack, Bobby explained something he was seeing. "The thing on this guy is connected to something all the way back in Mexico, which must be where this guy comes from."

Jack explained. "This is Carlos Garcia, pastor of a church down in the battle zone between drug cartels. He used to be with one of the gangs and did some bad stuff for them. I thought we got him free of everything though."

"I think this is different," said Beau. "This isn't just about Carlos. This is about his village."

"Yeah, that's what I'm seein'." Bobby was grateful for Beau clarifying the meaning of the unusual manifestation.

Jack looked at the two others and nodded, as if absorbing their discernment. He stepped toward Carlos.

Bobby felt it was right for Jack to take the lead, though he didn't stop to catalog why.

Beau leaned toward Bobby. "My jaw feels great, by the way." He chuckled just briefly.

Jack addressed Carlos in Spanish for a while, then switched to English.

A stout man in his early forties, Carlos was now scrunched in his chair as if a great weight were trying to drive him through the floor.

Bobby pushed through the row of chairs to get behind Carlos. He prayed and watched as the weight seemed to lessen.

Jack asserted his authority, in the name of Jesus, over that room and over what was happening to Carlos. He forbade any spirits from disturbing anything else in the room, glancing toward the ruined Exit signs. He then told the big spirit on Carlos to grab any smaller spirits and get ready to take them out of that room and off the continent.

The lights did flicker once more, but nothing broke. Bobby gave the spirit's name to Jack after getting that information downloaded to him.

Beau took Carlos's hands and said something that started Carlos weeping.

When Bobby saw the spirit launching out of the room, dozens of the students cried out, a few coughed, and one began to wretch.

Kurt was near the latter student and intervened to stop that attack. For many, their laughter turned to purging tears or to a sleep-like state.

The three men attended to Carlos for the next twenty minutes, ensuring he was unharmed and totally free.

Kurt had students come to the front to give testimonies of being delivered from seemingly unrelated ailments and oppressions corresponding with the departure of the big spirit.

Bobby's voice was staticky when he paused his story. He was probably as tired as Anna. "What seemed to impress Jack the most was what happened back in Carlos's church in Mexico. Seven diff'rent people felt a great weight lifting off them. One boy, who had been mentally handicapped and violent, was suddenly changed that night, his spirit calm and his mind clear. Two women in the church separately reported seein' angels sweep through the village. And one of the houses where drugs were being cooked exploded into flames that night. Everyone escaped alive, surprisingly, but the house and thousands o' dollars of drugs were destroyed."

Anna sighed into her phone. Was there any end to the miraculous gifts of this man she could picture slumped on a couch in a Midwestern mall?

A Slow Trip South

Bobby had hoped his trip from Minnesota to Kansas City was just the first leg of his journey to Naples, Florida, where he wanted to spend time with Terry. It turned out the journey south took nearly a year. He stayed in Kansas City for several months doing various odd jobs and even more odd miracles.

The most controversial miracle recalled that night in Redwood and the burning of the drug dealer's house in Mexico.

Terrance had been Bobby's guide to the neighborhood in Kansas City for those months. He employed Bobby as a handyman in his building when Bobby insisted on making a financial contribution. In the course of that job, one of the harshest realities in the neighborhood stabbed close to Bobby's heart. He had to break open the door to one of the apartments in his building to help Terrance determine whether the tenant was inside, and whether she needed help. They found a twenty-something woman, her face purple-black, lying on the living room floor with a needle still stuck in her left arm. She had been dead for days.

Terrance cursed the drug dealer he held responsible for the young woman's death.

Bobby knew a house where drugs were being processed and distributed from. He had a feeling he was supposed to go to that house and do something, as surely as he knew he wasn't going to raise that girl from the dead.

After dark that evening, Bobby walked up the street where the drug dealers lived, accompanied by Michael Jessup, a young man well over six feet tall and weighing more than three hundred pounds. The neighbors joked that Michael was Bobby's bodyguard. It was a joke because Michael was a gentle and sensitive soul. He followed Bobby on his adventures not as bodyguard, but to learn how to do miracles.

"So, have you decided what your gonna do when we get there?" Michael was checking around them, adept at spotting trouble before it spotted him.

"I feel this angry thing inside me that ain't mine," Bobby said. "I think I gotta just let it go on that house. Not sure what that means or what it'll do, but that's what I got."

Standing on the uneven sidewalk in front of the pale green house, gray now in the streetlights, Bobby paused to listen to his Papa. Then he simply released that angry feeling. "I let this hot anger go now and tell it to land where God wants it, and do what God wants it to do."

Bobby saw a flame rush out of his chest and into the house. That flame burned more intensely in the house than the light that had been leaking from cracks around the boards and shades covering the windows. He watched in his spirit as the fire penetrated to the basement of the building. At that point, something told him to run for cover.

Michael picked up his walking pace to keep up as Bobby scooted away.

They were halfway down the block when the first explosion sounded. A heat wave touched Bobby's bare neck, and shards of wood and glass provoked Michael to shelter his head with one big arm. When he glanced back, Bobby sped up more as a flaming board bounced just ten feet behind them.

"Bobby? Did you do that?" Michael had stopped to watch.

When Bobby looked past Michael at the house, three figures, dark against the flames, ran staggering out the front door, followed by a barking dog. Bobby prayed that any other occupants would escape as well. He felt assurance in his spirit that no one had died in the explosion. "I didn't touch that house, as you know yerself. I just have to think it was God's doin', not mine."

Though he didn't suspect Michael of telling the neighborhood what happened to the meth house that night, Bobby detected a change among the folks around him—suspicious glances and a fearful reserve when he spoke to both friends and strangers. Perhaps what he was sensing was more awe than fear, but the rising barrier was disruptive nevertheless.

Salinas, Kansas and then Fayetteville, Arkansas, followed by Memphis, Tennessee and Jackson, Mississippi, each hosted Bobby, and a few miracles, over the following months. As much as any time in his life, Bobby was on the run. He knew he couldn't run fast enough to get away from God, and that wasn't the goal. But he kept moving, ahead of the echoes from healings, financial blessings, lost treasures found, and another resurrection. Bobby wasn't afraid of being found, just certain he didn't want fame.

He was running, but he was not running straight to the destination he had in mind. That would have to wait. Along the winding way, his Papa was having his fun, using Bobby to whip the enemy's behind in one state after another.

At night in a fleabag hotel in some southern city, Bobby lay by himself remembering some of the smiles and some of the tears he had witnessed. The healed arms, restored ears, and broken addictions tended to lose their fascination. But the look in the eyes of a mother whose child would now live, or the eyes of a deaf person who could now hear, or a sickly boy who would now grow up to be strong—those eyes never seemed to lose their magic for him.

Months after leaving Kansas City, Bobby arrived in Tuscaloosa, Alabama. Sitting in a diner along the highway, he heard a TV news report of a hostage situation in a farmhouse not far from where he sat. Like most people, he usually heard the news as someone else's story, something removed from him. But a sense of closeness, like a good friend sliding in for a hug, interrupted Bobby's lunch.

Inside his head, he was saying, "*Hostage situation? Papa, are you sure about this one? This seems too crazy for even you.*"

Again, in his head, he heard a very distinct answer. "*Yes, but not too crazy for you.*"

Bobby laughed aloud at that response. Fortunately, no one was sitting close enough at the counter to wonder what he was laughing at. He stopped chuckling and took a deep breath, speaking again to his invisible accompaniment. "*Okay, how do ya wanna do this?*"

To Bobby, it seemed that he heard laughter all around, both inside and out. At least God was having a good time. In answer to his question, Bobby felt he should go outside.

"*I don't want 'em to see you disappear.*"

Bobby chuckled and headed for the back side of the diner.

As soon as he got out of sight of the windows, he transported from that parking lot to the living room of a run-down house. He noted the ragged rug on the floor and an old tube TV blaring the news right next to him. Bobby expected he knew where he had landed, but was hoping he was wrong.

"Where in hell did you come from?" A man spoke with a heavy southern accent, such that the word "hell" came out in two syllables, "hay-ell."

Bobby turned slowly to face that voice. When he did so, he made eye contact with a pump-action shotgun. Bobby laughed a nervous sort of laugh. "Nowhere in hell." His voice cracked a little. "Somewheres in Alabama."

The man holding the gun made a skeptical noise, which attracted Bobby's eyes to his face. Perhaps ten years younger than him, the gunman seemed much the worse for all fifty-some years. He wore a bushy mustache that concealed his lips when he wasn't speaking. And he had bushy eyebrows that looked like junior versions of that mustache. His hair was slicked back and about the color of a cloudy sky.

"I'm Bobby." He reached his hand in greeting. "God sent me to help ya."

When the man with the gun stepped closer, Bobby caught sight of a woman and a small girl tied to chairs behind the kidnapper.

Bobby hadn't seen very many movies. When he tried to watch one, they generally disturbed him so much that he resolved to avoid a repeat. He took things too literally and found little room between what was theatrical fiction and what was real. The scene in the farmhouse felt like it should be in a movie, but not any movie he had seen. It didn't even seem connected to the news story, which had only showed an exterior shot of the house.

"How did you get in here?" The man sounded both insistent and confused.

Bobby was thinking he would like to start this over. But he felt a warm reassurance from his Papa.

"*The gun isn't loaded,*" that internal voice said.

This would be one of those times when he could check just how much he trusted what he thought his Papa was saying to him. Because, if that gun wasn't loaded, he could relax quite a bit.

"*Don't worry, my boy,*" said that voice.

Bobby relaxed. "I heard about ya on the news." He gave up on the handshake. "God sends me on all sorts of adventures. I get the feelin' he's gettin' a kick outta this one."

A glimpse of the wide eyes of the woman tied to the chair hinted to Bobby that she might have seen him suddenly appear in the living room while the man with the gun had been turned toward her. Bobby just smiled at her, hoping to infect her with the same peace that had settled on him.

"Are you police?" The man sounded doubtful.

Bobby could understand that doubt. He couldn't imagine the police having anyone so far undercover that they looked like him. "Nope, not the police. The God squad."

The man shook his head and deepened his scowl.

Bobby suspected that if the gun wasn't loaded, the man was wishing it were. Nonetheless, he tried to steer away from provoking the confused man any further. "Sorry, I don't mean to joke. I know yer under a lotta pressure in here. I just gotta think God wouldn't send me in here if there wasn't a way out." He could feel that the house was surrounded by police, though he wasn't getting any specific insights into their disposition. Then he remembered the guy's name from the news. "Ben, is it? I heard that on the news, right? Ben?"

The man nodded. "I know who I am. But I can't figure out where you *come* from or who in hell you *are*."

Bobby was trying to think of a good answer to that when he felt a sudden urge to grab hold of Ben and his gun. It wasn't a violent or heroic urge, more like the sort of thing he felt when he was trying to bring healing or freedom to someone. Hoping the gun was indeed empty, he stepped forward and grabbed one of Ben's arms around the bicep.

The next moment, Bobby was standing on a beach, perhaps along the Gulf of Mexico. He let go of Ben's arm and regretted doing so right away.

Ben dropped onto his behind in the sand, his head swerving in circles. He was trying to say something, but couldn't form any words. Finally, he fell sideways into a dead faint, his upper body making a soft thump in the dry sand.

"Well, that was one way to take care of the situation." Bobby spoke aloud to his Papa. Then he noticed the strong breeze off the water. It was late summer. In Minnesota, it would be considered early autumn. There was no hint of cooler weather along the gulf yet.

Bobby sat in the sand next to Ben and waited for the greyhound-like man to regain the use of his long limbs. Bobby pulled out a cigarette. He rarely smoked alone, generally using his tobacco habit as an excuse to minister to other smokers. But he felt a smoke was deserved, given what his Papa had just put him through. He could still hear hearty laughter whenever he tuned in to what his Papa was saying right then.

Lighting that cigarette reminded Bobby of the last time he had lit up. He had been in Mississippi, working as a day laborer. He and several other guys were pulling junk out of a building that had been taken over by the bank and was supposed to be sold in the coming months.

Two of the guys went outside for a smoke during the late morning. Bobby felt he was supposed to follow them. He patted his baggy pockets to ensure he still had cigarettes and a lighter.

Outside, the conversation quickly turned to the reason one of the guys was wearing a bandage on his left arm. Bobby had noticed earlier, of course, but had found no opportunity to investigate the possibility of a healing.

The dark-eyed man, in his mid-forties, explained how he had dumped his motorcycle and escaped major injury except for losing much of the skin on his forearm. It was not so painful anymore, but itched intensely.

"I think I can take care o' that for ya." Bobby took a drag on his cigarette.

The man recoiled, and his friend snickered. "Yeah, how ya gonna do that?"

"It's already starting to happen," Bobby said.

215

While the other man scowled at that claim, the man with the bandage put his cigarette between his lips and used his free hand to touch the bandage. "What's that?"

Bobby knew he was referring to some new sensation accompanying the healing that had already begun. "God's got under yer bandage and started puttin' new skin on that for ya."

Both his coworkers looked hard at Bobby, but the man with the scraped arm was distracted again by something under his bandage. "It's doing something." He pulled the tape off the end of the tan cloth wrap, which he unwound quickly. Then he dug at the tape holding a swath of gauze in place. At his first glimpse of the skin under the bandage, the man swore loudly. His cigarette fell from his lips to the patchy pavement at his feet. Briefly releasing the bandage to stare at what he was seeing, he finally ripped the gauze entirely from his arm. "I don't believe it." He stopped to swear again.

That had started a conversation that continued through the workday. After work, the three of them had dinner together. And they continued to talk as they worked together the next two days. Bobby connected that guy—Raphael—and several of his friends to the God who could not only heal a severely scraped arm, but who could put brand new skin where there should be a wicked scar.

When Ben awoke with his face in the sand, he struggled to sit up. He rubbed his head and left his shotgun with the muzzle buried a foot deep. "Did God really send you to get me outta there?" He turned his head toward Bobby and leaned back, his arms propping him behind.

"Seems so. Weren't what I expected."

"Ah ... me neither."

Bobby laughed. "I'm guessin' God has some idea that yer worth savin'. He coulda sent me to take care of the hostages and had you shot or jailed by those police."

"I didn't mean to take hostages. I just got scared when the cops chased me from the gas station I robbed. I didn't know what to do. Didn't wanna go back to prison." Ben paused and looked at the whitecaps on the gulf. "I was okay to have 'em just shoot me instead o' goin' back inside. But I got in that house, and it seemed sorta safe to hole up there until I could think o' somethin' better."

"You never had shotgun shells?" Bobby nodded toward the gun.

"No, I never. I know better. And, like I said, I'd ruther have 'em shoot me than catch me and send me back."

Bobby reached in his pocket and pulled out a wad of bills. He handed the whole thing to Ben. "This oughta give ya a start. Find somethin' honest to do. Get somewhere they ain't seen ya before, and just work a job—and stay outta trouble. I think God's gonna make all that possible if ya just agree to cooperate."

Ben held the several hundred dollars between a thumb and forefinger like he was looking at a bone and searching for some bit of edible meat. He examined Bobby for a few seconds. "I reckon I can do what you say. Thanks, mister."

Bobby stood up, patting Ben on the shoulder as he stepped past him. He hoped his Papa would take him back to where he had left his bags beside the diner. He suspected they would still be there waiting for him. "God bless ya, Ben."

And he walked up the beach before making that return trip.

Tying the Ends of the String

Bobby had finally reached his destination in Florida—Terry's place in Naples. At first, for propriety sake, Bobby stayed in the apartment of an old gentleman who lived down the hall from Terry. That neighbor was out of town much of the time visiting various grandchildren. Bobby agreed to water his plants and collect his mail in exchange for the place to stay. That gentleman was old enough to understand why Bobby didn't stay at Terry's place.

"He just thinks we're old fashioned like him," Terry joked about her neighbor.

"Oh, why deny it?" Bobby had enjoyed their relationship just the way it was, uncomplicated by the need for a ring or repentance for doing certain things without that ring in place.

This visit to Terry started Bobby feeling old in a good way. He sat on her back patio under the shade of the neighbor's balcony, a pair of small coconut palms waving for attention nearby. Looking across a retention pond and through a gap in the houses across that pond, Bobby could see a sliver of the ocean. A little ambition and just the start of a sweat would get them down to the beach.

Terry's place felt like retirement, but not in the sense of being set aside and obsolete. Rather in the sense of finding a place of rest after a long life of work. Of course Bobby had no financial retirement plan in place, no IRA or 401k, no stocks or mutual funds. But he had put in plenty of work and was glad for some rest.

He was relaxing in his temporary home when he used a long-distance card to call Anna Conyers. "Jist felt like I was supposed to let you know I made it down to Florida. Terry's place."

"Oh, that's good. I was getting a little concerned. I hadn't heard from you for so long." She was shuffling papers or something in the background.

Bobby checked the clock. "You workin' late?"

"Working from home, catching up on some research." She breathed a laugh. "Working on articles that will actually get published for a change."

"Never got any of that stuff we talked about printed?"

"I stopped trying. I think I could have found a less famous and more faith-oriented magazine, but I didn't feel like I was supposed to pursue it. I'm thinking it was mostly just so I could learn from you. And maybe there will be a book someday."

"Well, it was a blessin' to me. You helped me sort some things about my life and set some priorities straight."

"Is that what you're doing in Florida?"

"Hmm. What makes you say that? I could just be on vacation."

She hummed right back at him. "You know, I think it's just one of those whispers from God." She laughed again. "Or maybe just women's intuition."

"Huh. Whichever it is, it strikes me as somethin' real. Somethin' for me to listen to."

"Good. Glad I could help."

When they ended the call after some catch-up on Willow Pierce and the Dupere family, Bobby felt like calling Tracy. She was in the same time zone as Anna—not too late, probably. He had spoken to Tracy lots more while he was on the road than he had with Anna.

"Tracy? This is ... yer dad." He was still getting used to that title.

"Dad. Good to hear from you. Have you decided on a date for me to come down there? How long are you gonna stay in Florida?"

"Huh. Funny you should say it that way. I been thinkin' about settling in here. Making it my home base, like we talked about when we first met."

"Just a home base, or something more than that? How's Terry?"

Bobby laughed hard. "You hintin' at somethin' there, girl?"

"Would be a pretty heavy hint." She chuckled. "But it's a daughter's prerogative, isn't it? To worry about her dad, to make sure he's taken care of?"

"I'll take yer word for it. And I don't mind if you let me know what you're thinkin' or feelin' about such things. I'm startin' to feel like it's time for me to stop my wandering ways. At least cut back considerably."

"It was a hard trip?"

"Woulda been easier for a younger man, I'm thinkin.'"

"Yeah, but when you were a younger man, you didn't have so much to offer people all across the country."

"I guess that's right." He scratched his beard. "There might be a more grown-up version of what I do that I can look into."

"Ha. That sounds promising."

A Long Line of Walkers and Scooters

It was May, and Bobby stood by the curb in the warm Florida sun where Terry could find him easily at the airport. He slid his cell phone into his pocket and shook his head at the unfamiliar weight of it where his cigarettes used to be. The connection of those two objects provoked a thought about how he had given up one kind of connection—the kind he had found outside a building where the smokers gathered—for another kind where you push a button and another person replies by pushing a button on their own little metal-and-glass device.

Terry and her minivan pulled to the curb, a big grin on her cherubic face.

Bobby noted the feeling of being welcomed somewhere with no questions or reservations. Home was a concept a lot like heaven. He had experienced each briefly during his life, briefly enough that he had come to count on neither for the near future. That was changing, at least where home was concerned.

Climbing into the passenger seat, Bobby leaned over to kiss his fiancée on her blushing cheek. He fully expected his seventy-year-old bride to be blushing. Terry blushed all the time. "Can't hide anything," she would say with only a little chagrin.

As they drove, they discussed Bobby's trip to Arizona, to a big church led by someone he knew from Redwood. And they reviewed plans for Tracy to come and visit them before the wedding, staying in Terry's apartment. Bobby's place, near downtown Naples, was too small for a full-sized guest. Generally he only hosted an occasional palmetto bug or field mouse. It was a temporary arrangement. Bobby had lived in worse places, of course.

Bobby and Terry had announced their pending marriage to friends from all over the country, and a few local ones. Now they waited to see how big a venue they would need for the ceremony and reception. An anonymous donor had committed to paying for everything, according to a phone call from Jack Williams. So it was just a matter of finding out how many wanted to attend.

The generous provision of wedding and reception expenses was not absolutely necessary, but quite welcome. Sixty-five now, Bobby had begun collecting Social Security along with Terry. The government had been keeping track of him even when no one else but God could. He also took the occasional invitation to minister at a conference or church, and accepted an honorarium to help out financially. But they needed little and were easily contented.

Only one spot in their new life had a tinge of trouble in it, and that was their neighborhood.

A few months before, he and Terry had been sitting on the patio. She had glanced at the houses around them. "You know, all of the hips, knees, eyes, and ears that have been artificially re-placed for our retired neighbors are the perfect opportunity for your gifts."

After a dozen remarkable healing miracles since then, Bobby now felt compelled to sneak into Terry's apartment in order to avoid being overwhelmed with requests from the neighbors.

That afternoon, home from the airport, they congratulated themselves for their stealth. Bobby got into Terry's apartment unseen while she parked the van. They prepared a healthy dinner together, and Bobby told stories about the things he experienced at the conference. Over caesar salads and homemade bread, they joked about some of the more unusual miracles.

When they finished, they took iced tea out to the patio to catch the cooling evening breeze. Turning his face toward the wind, Bobby's freshly cut hair and neatly trimmed beard did not flutter like Terry's gray and brown bangs, broken loose from barrettes on both sides of her face. He liked to watch every season of his fiancée's face, treated just then to her squinting smile at the low sun and frisking breeze.

Their smiles disappeared when Bessie Feingold from next door looked over the little stucco wall that framed the patio. "Oh, Terry, how are you?" Then she made a theatrical attempt at pretending surprise. "Oh, Bobby, are you here?"

Both Terry and Bobby revived their smiles in response to the greeting—and to the obvious simulation of surprise.

"Yes, ma'am, I am indeed here."

"I wonder if you wouldn't mind taking a look at my friend, Hazel. She has this bad neck pain from way back when, and doctors can do nothing about it." She gestured theatrically as she explained in her New York accent.

Terry and Bobby expected this from Bessie. She had been an effective evangelist ever since they healed her hearing. It was certainly that healing, in fact, that allowed Bessie to detect Bobby's presence that evening. Before, she wouldn't have been able to hear a thing from next door. Now she heard everything. But Bobby didn't regret the change, only laughed at the irony.

"Would Hazel happen to be nearby just now?" Terry's tone was teasing.

"Well, as a matter of fact, she's right here inside. I'll go get her."

And so the agenda for the evening was set. They knew Bessie would put the word out. The opening through which Bobby and Terry watched the duck pond and just glimpsed the ocean would become a gateway for the lame and the handicapped. Bessie had grasped pretty clearly the strengths of Bobby's particular healing gift, treating him like a medical specialist. Among her Jewish friends, they often referred to him as the miracle doctor, though no one tried to get Bobby to sign any Medicare forms.

As the sun eased into the gulf almost an hour later, Bobby sat in a patio chair, Terry standing next to him. Bobby had settled into that seat as his feet grew tired about five healings ago. It now put Bobby at eye level with a scrunched little woman with a severely curved back who sat on an electric scooter.

While he focused on that one little lady, Terry stepped aside to get a look at the line Bobby knew was stretching all the way to the duck pond. Golf carts, electric scooters, a dozen walkers, and even a couple of bicycles blocked the walking path the last time he looked.

Terry smiled, and it was not the resigned smile of one submitting to her unwelcome fate. She was happy to see her neighbors getting healed, and good at answering the questions those miracles would raise. Answering those questions was most of the preaching and teaching Terry did these days.

When Bobby stepped away from the little old lady who was flailing her arms around to demonstrate her newly healed back, he caught Terry's grinning eyes watching him. He smiled back and raised his eyebrows as if to say, "Well, what do ya think, old girl?"

He knew the answer to that question, the setting sunlight just enough for him to see her blushing in happy satisfaction.

Bobby greeted the next old gentleman, who was pushing a walker and smiling shyly at him. "I want ya' to do somethin' for me," Bobby said.

The old man nodded and awaited instructions.

"Reach back there and take the hand of this pretty lady behind ya. Don't worry, I won't tell yer wife. And, ma'am, would ya take the hand of the woman behind you?" In this way, Bobby linked together nearly a dozen potential miracles.

Terry was watching with her hands on her hips, a spectator along with the dozen or so folks still hanging around after their miracles.

When the waiting group had formed a daisy chain of retirees, Bobby took hold of the first man, and of Terry with his other hand. "In the name o' Jesus, I say, 'Be healed'." He pronounced this with more force and flair than most miracles, but he had more than just one miracle in mind.

As soon as he pronounced that command, the first gentleman stood up straight and grabbed his hip with his free hand. The lady behind him jumped back and grabbed for her ear, releasing the hands of both the person in front of her and the person behind. But the chain reaction wasn't broken. In what looked something like the Mexican wave at a football game, the miracles flowed down the line, hands flying in the air, backs straightening, and exclamations accompanying. It looked a lot like a deck game on a cruise ship, including the animated chatter that followed, intermixed with exclamations, laughter, and gasps.

Terry laughed along.

Bobby smiled at her and just shrugged.

Sign up for our newsletter if you're interested:

Subscribe | jeffreymcclainjones

Thank you!

.

Made in United States
North Haven, CT
09 October 2022

25195240R00136